Separation Anxiety

Books by Michael Lister

(Love Stories)
Carrie's Gift

(John Jordan Novels)
Power in the Blood
Blood of the Lamb
Flesh and Blood
The Body and the Blood
Blood Sacrifice
Rivers to Blood

(Short Story Collections)
North Florida Noir
Florida Heat Wave
Delta Blues
Another Quiet Night in Desparation

(Remington James Novels)
Double Exposure
Separation Anxiety

(Merrick McKnight Novels)
Thunder Beach

(Jimmy "Soldier" Riley Novels)
The Big Goodbye
The Big Beyond
The Long Dark Night

(Sam Michaels and Daniel Davis Novels)
Burnt Offerings
Separation Anxiety

(The Meaning Series)
The Meaning of Jesus
Meaning Every Moment
The Meaning of Life in Movies

Separation Anxiety
Michael Lister

a novel

You buy a book. We plant a tree.

Inquiries should be addressed to:
Pulpwood Press
P.O. Box 35038
Panama City, FL 32412

Lister, Michael.
Separation Anxiety/ Michael
Lister.
-----1st ed.
p. cm.

ISBN: 978-1-888146-35-6   Hardcover

ISBN: 978-1-888146--36-3 Paperback

Library of Congress Control Number:

Book Design by Adam Ake

Printed in the United States

1 3 5 7 9 10 8 6 4 2

First Edition

For Adam Ake

an amazing designer
an even better friend

Thank you

Dawn, Jill, Adam, Amy, Jeff, Micah,
Meleah, Travis, Mike, Judi, Jason, Lynn,
Michael, Emily, Tony, Tim

Author's note

I see this work as a sort of spiritual sequel to *Double Exposure*—the only kind of sequel *Double Exposure* could have. It is also, in a way, the second in the Sam Michaels and Daniel Davis series, following *Burnt Offerings*. While you do not have to read either of those works before this one, I do recommend it. Of course, you could always read them after this one—or not at all. It's just a suggestion. Either way, thanks for reading anything of mine you do. I'm truly thankful.

—*Where is Shelby?*

—*I told you. I don't know.*

—*You're lying.*

—*I'm not. I swear.*

—*What'd you do with her?*

—*Please. God. Please.*

—*Is that what* she *said?*

—What? No. *You've got to believe me. I wouldn't hurt her. I wouldn't—I could never hurt her.*

Missing.

On the day sixteen-year-old Shelby Emma Summers disappears, the late-August air is thick and humid and hard to breathe.

Still.

Stifling.

Beneath the unrelenting sun of the unending North Florida day, the parched planet is unmoving, the withering grass drained, desolate, dying. That which isn't sun-faded and desaturated is overexposed, every squinting element muted, bleached out, achromatic.

Out in the Gulf, Hurricane Christine churns over the warm waters.

Building.

Intensifying.

Expanding.

Soon, the dry, hot stillness will give way to savage winds, flash floods, and the tornadic toppling of trees and buildings and lives, leaving a swath of catastrophic destruction so devastating as to appear apocalyptic.

For now, in the unsuspecting small town of Tupelo, sunlight refracts off the glass-smooth surface of the Apalachicola River, and fall feels far, far away. No hint of autumnal hope, no promise of respite and refreshment, no reprieve from the long, hot Sheol summer.

But every horrific, heartbreaking act committed on this singular, sun-drenched day was brought into being long before it began.

Before daybreak.

Before dawn.

Before Shelby was even born.

False dawn.

In the first faint periwinkle-blue of morning that backlights the black pines against the eastern horizon, Martin Chalmers pads back toward bed, his seventy-seven-year-old bones popping and creaking.

As he passes the large bay window on the second story of his too-big for a single shrinking old man antebellum home, he stops suddenly and studies the water's edge, narrowing his ancient eyes to near closing.

Figure.

Watching.

Shadows.

Dark distance.

Waiting.

Had he seen someone standing among the swollen bases of the cypress trees lining the riverbanks?

He could've sworn . . .

He slowly scans the area again.

Pines and oaks giving way to cypresses. Jagged, scraggy outlines of limbs backdropped by a ghostly gray-blue glow.

Stillness.

Nothing moving beneath the Spanish moss-draped branches.

Grab the binoculars? Call the sheriff? Get back in bed?

You should go back to bed, you silly old man.

What the hell would someone be doing down there?

Looking across the river. That's what.

It's what made him think of hunting for his old beat-up binoculars in the first place. The figure, had there been one at all, was peering across the quiet waters through binoculars at Lithonia Lodge.

Did Taylor Sean have another stalker? Was Shelby's boyfriend as jealous and possessive as everyone said? Or is crazy old Martin Chalmers seeing things again?

The last one. Go back to bed. And hurry. You're gonna be getting up to pee again anytime now.

He looks again. Again sees nothing. Probably all there ever was.

The wolf watches and waits.

Patient. Focused. Deliberate.

Powerful and slender, slope-backed and long-limbed, he is a precise predator intent on his prey.

Many wolves hunt in packs, but single wolves and mated pairs actually have the highest success rates—a statistic this solitary hunter no doubt contributes to. He hunts alone. He never returns to his den empty-handed.

The hunt.

The wolf hunt has five stages.

Locating the prey, stalking the prey, confronting the prey, rushing the prey, chasing the prey.

Typically, wolves search for prey through scent, chance encounter, and tracking. This hunt, this gathering and reaping, is unquestionably the last.

Nothing left to chance.

He's never been more intentional about anything in his entire lupine life.

Tracking her.

Stalking her.

The stalk—wolves attempt to conceal their approach, but as the gap closes, they quicken their pace, getting as close to their quarry as possible without making it flee.

He is close. Very close. And she still has no idea.

There is nothing he won't do. No price he won't pay. He will have his prey. He will work his will. He is the wolf.

The wolf wants. The wolf takes. This is the way of the wolf.

Soon the confronting, rushing, and chasing would begin, but for now the wolf savors the stalk.

It's still a few hours before the horrific ordeal will begin in earnest, but for Taylor the day starts like any other.

Nightmares.

She wakes with a start, heart rattling around her ribcage, a tangle of sweat-soaked sheets entwining her.

So much loss. She lives with it, is unremittingly reminded of it as every tick continues the countdown. It marks her body, haunts her mind, disquiets her dreams, but for all the trauma she's endured, she's about to front fear and loss and terror like never before.

Kicking off the covers, she realizes Marc isn't in bed with her.

Blood.

Wet. Dry. Drips. Pools.

Streaks.

Smears.

Rorschach in red.

What appears to be a particularly gruesome crime scene is actually evidence that starting a heavy period in the middle of the night had not awakened her.

No nightgown. No panties. Nothing to staunch the flow, mitigate the mess.

As she sits up, the hormonal headache begins. Dull grip of an indelicate lover.

No cure, of course, but there is a treatment with unparalleled efficacy.

Must find Marc.

When working on a novel, Marc finally surrenders to sleep when many people are beginning their mornings. When the writing's going well, as it is just now, the world outside the world of his novel becomes dim and desultory, and he works until he loses consciousness each night, often sleeping on the couch in what Taylor calls his scriptorium.

Occasionally, he'll hear Shelby getting ready for school or fixing breakfast and stumble down the hall to see her, unsteady and groggy, having had only a couple hours of rest at best, but most mornings he's oblivious even to his own body and the stimuli it receives from above the underworld he's submerged into.

In many ways, he still feels like a guest here at the lodge—and not just because he so recently arrived, but because his relationship with the lady of the house is so tenuous, so temporary-seeming.

Emotionally erratic as anyone he's ever been involved with, he doesn't know from one moment to the next if she's going to mention marriage or him moving out. And though it's hard to imagine anyone having a more traumatic childhood, he suspects it's her adult experiences with men that most negatively affect their relationship. Of course, it was little Taylor's rejection and abandonment that most likely led to adolescent and adult Taylor's poor choices in friends and lovers.

Regardless of the reason, he's paying a price. Willingly. Gladly. But it's no small toll being exacted from him, and it helps having a place of his own, a scriptorium and study, a womb of silence and solitude, a small sanctuary of serenity, a peaceful port in the storm.

Marc Hayden Faulk.

She loves his name, loves seeing it on the spine of his novels, loves letting her finger drift over it as she passes his shelves.

The small chamber is quiet and candlelit, the reedy, sweet smoky smell of incense and pipe tobacco lingering.

She pauses a moment, taking in the room, the man it is an expression of. She's never loved or been loved like this before. Didn't know it even existed. Never thought she'd experience it. It scares the hell out of her, and she doesn't trust it, doesn't believe it's real much of the time.

Just thinking about the way she feels, the way he loves her, makes her want to flee as fast as she can.

Break things off now before you destroy him. It's not fair to keep torturing him this way. Do it soon before things go any deeper. He's gonna do it if you don't. Eventually. Inevitably. He's gonna grow weary—hell, he already is—and he'll leave you like all the others.

She takes in a deep breath and holds it, trying to still herself, shut off the voice inside her head. None of the thoughts are new, but her period intensifies everything, making the voice meaner, more relentless in its insistence on her misery.

Do things have to be this way?

For her it all comes down to the same thing—from the very beginning, her parents wanting to kill her, the detachment and death of her sister, to the loss of a child, to the emotionally stunted and abusive men she's punished herself with.

Separation.

She's felt it her entire life—like something's missing. Well, like something's present and simultaneously something's missing. It's hard to understand, impossible to describe, but it's something like experiencing both absence and the presence of that absence. As if absence itself is an entity.

She has rare moments when the pain and anxiety of it are nearly bearable, but they are rare.

Life is separateness.

The interval of space that defines separateness is, for her, the vacuous absence of her parents and sister and child and the death of God—the one who might have prevented it all.

He wakes with a start.

Someone in the room. Something wrong.

Jerking up, he spins around.

—What is it? he asks.

Taylor is standing there naked, her scar-slashed body blood-smeared. Beautiful.

—Nothing. Sorry. I just . . .

—Just what?

—Started my period.

—Come here, he says, reaching out for her.

—I'll get blood on your couch, she says, as if it's not her couch.

—I don't care.

—But—

—Come here, he says. We'll get it cleaned.

—I am a rich bitch, she says with a weak smile.

He smiles back, enjoying her calling herself what he does anytime she's hesitant to get herself something she wants or needs.

Standing, he slips out of his shorts and boxers, peels off his shirt, and is as naked as she is by the time she makes it over to him.

Their bodies smell of sleep and sweat, their skin warm and moist, sticking like strips of paste-wet paper as they touch. Between them, his erection presses hard against her tummy and its scars.

She lets out a breathy moan.

—You feel so good, she says. Just what I needed. Actually, you and a steak.

He laughs. She only eats meat when she's on her period—and then the biggest, bloodiest steak she can find.

—In that order?

She nods.

As she showers, he stands in the kitchen cooking her steak, wondering again at how he wound up with one of the most famous artists and infamous twins in the country.

Closed.

Guarded.

Defensive.

Impenetrable.

How had he gotten through? No one else ever had—though countless reporters had tried. And he didn't just get through. He got in. Didn't just get past her outer armor, but down into her deep soul, what she calls her hot lava core.

It still surprises him—and when she retreats into her carefully constructed fortress, he's reminded of just what an unlikely miracle it actually is.

Though returning to the area on assignment with the express purpose of trying to secure an interview with her, he had approached her not as a writer, but as a fan—which he genuinely was and continues to be.

As a novelist with a certain regional notoriety who had written passionately and enthusiastically about her work, he had been hired by Oxford America to attend the event and attempt, most likely futilely, an interview.

He had driven up from Tampa, where he was living at the time, with no real hope or expectation—except seeing the show, the chance to meet her, and the opportunity to drop by Carrabelle, where he had grown up, on his return home.

He had attended an opening of her new show at the Visual Arts Center in downtown Panama City, one at which she made a rare appearance. Breast cancer fundraiser. Favor for a friend.

He was far more moved by the show than he ever imagined he could be.

Everything he said to her was genuine. He ceased being anything but an admirer. Later she would tell him it was his authenticity and openness that had opened her to him.

—I keep trying to think of a way to express what your work means, he had said. What it makes me feel, but everything I come up with sounds so trite. And really lame.

She had nodded and not said anything.

This was when most people in attendance moved on, but not him.

—It's like the most painful experience you can have, and one you wouldn't change for anything.

She had nodded again and given him a hint of what might have been an encouraging smile, were it allowed to continue to grow into what it might have been.

—It mixes loss and longing with a type of cold comfort, he went on, like the perverse pleasure of clawing at an open wound. Reminds me of the complex pleasure in the pain of bondage.

At that there was something—a glint in her guarded eyes, and he knew he'd just glimpsed her saturnine soul.

Instantly, he was in love—not just with the art or the artist, the story or the mystery, but with the woman and the wounded little girl hidden inside her, the lost little twin buried beneath.

Unlike the rest of the world, she had never been an oddity, a carny curiosity to him, but in that moment even his interest in her story faded, as he had seen in her what he'd been aching for for so long.

—Did you hear Shelby this morning?

Taylor, blond hair darker now with water, dripping onto the shoulders of her white terrycloth robe, stands in the doorway.

—No.

—She's not in her room.

He glances down at the clock on the stove. It's still

almost an hour before school starts.

—Is her car here? he asks, picturing the lime-green bug that so fits Shelby's cute, sweet, classic personality parked in the driveway.

She disappears, returning to the room a few moments later shaking her head.

—You worried?

She gives him a wide-eyed "of course" expression as she lets out a harsh, humorless laugh.

Stupid question. She's always worried. Her life has taught her to expect the worst. Like Taylor, Shelby is a single, surviving twin. Taylor has lost a sister and a daughter. In fact, she's lost everything and everyone except for Shelby.

—Trying not to be, she says. Did she mention having to leave early for any reason?

He shakes his head.

At thirty-two, Taylor, who had Shelby and Savannah when she was just sixteen, is often more like a big sister than a mother, and lately her complex relationship with Shelby had been far more difficult for both women than usual. One of the recent strategies they had employed had been to communicate through Marc—something he didn't particularly relish, but never really resisted.

—Call her cell, he says.

She digs her phone out of her purse on the counter and taps it a couple of times.

—Hey baby. It's your overprotective freak of a mom. Where are you? What're you doing? Did you forget to tell me you had to be at school early or did I forget you told me? Either way, it's too bad. Marc's cooking steak for breakfast. Call me back. Soon. Before I send out the National Guard.

—That was good, he says when she clicks off and places

the phone on the counter. You sounded good. Concerned, but not frantic.

—I'm doing better with that, don't you think?

—I do.

—Thanks for that, she says.

—For what?

—Teaching me to trust.

She had trusted one untrustworthy man after another until finally giving up completely. When he came along she wasn't looking, wasn't even open—or so she thought. Somehow, she claims miraculously, he had scaled her fortress wall and captured her.

—Here, he says, handing her a plate with a still-sizzling steak on it. Take your red meat to your studio. I'll call Julian and keep trying Shelby. If I don't find her, I'll come and get you and we'll call the National Guard together.

The deep carmine-like red that is her signature color found in nearly every one of her oils contains her menstrual blood, and he knows just how anxious she is to get to her studio—not only to pour herself into her paints, but because her best work occurs during these few days of hysteria caused by unhinging hormones and womb-ravaged anemia.

What was it he read recently? Something about hysteria originally being believed to be a disturbance of the uterus, the word itself coming from a Greek work meaning uterus.

She takes the plate and gives him a soft smile.

—How the hell'd I get along without you so long? she says.

—Not very well.

—Too true, Mr. Faulk. Too, too true.

Beth Ann Costin dreads Thursdays the way most people do Mondays. It's the day she has to see him.

Recently receiving her masters in counseling psychology, Beth is interning under Douglas Perry, a licensed psychologist, on her way to becoming a licensed mental health counselor.

Blonde. Blue-eyed. Nordic nose. Attractive, if a bit pale and plain, she's twenty-six but looks sixteen—which, she suspects, is why he sees her.

Well this is the day it ends.

No more dread. No more abuse. No more nightmares. No more Davis Allen Grayson, Jr.

Taking a deep breath, she taps on Doug's door and steps inside with Grayson's file.

She finds him making notes in an open folder on his desk, the pen barely visible in the meaty mitt of his canned-ham hand.

Round. Red. Puffy. With his shoulders hunched over his desk, Doug looks rounder than usual, his tangle of curly, graying hair higher on his enormous head. Broken blood vessels and wind-chapped cheeks give the thick, white skin of his face its only color.

—Give me just a minute more, he says.

—Of course.

She takes a seat across the desk from him, and continues to think about how she's going to tell him what she needs to.

Not only is Davis Allen Grayson a rich, powerful man, but he's a friend and former classmate of Doug's. It's part of the reason she's delayed as long as she has in bringing this to him. The situation calls for a certain delicacy she's not sure she has.

The mayor of Tallahassee, Grayson drives over an hour

to Tupelo for anonymity. His dad, Davis Allen Grayson, Sr., was mayor in Tallahassee for decades, and she suspects money and name recognition are the only reasons Junior currently holds the position. But surely it's temporary. Surely not even money and pedigree can continue to keep people from perceiving who he really is.

—What can I do for you? he asks, after tossing the pen onto his desk and closing the folder.

—Need your help.

—What I'm here for.

He remains hunched over, leaning forward, his blue-gray eyes making unwavering contact, and she wonders if it's intensity or intimidation. Hard to imagine him in a therapeutic role.

—I'm feeling very uncomfortable with one of the patients I'm seeing.

—Really. Which one?

—Mr. Grayson.

—Davis? Why's that?

—I'm not sure what's appropriate for me to reveal in this situation.

—You can tell me anything. Your clients know you're doing an internship, that I'm supervising and staffing all your cases. What's making you uncomfortable?

He seems impatient. She swallows hard and clears her throat.

—The things he says in session. He claims to be telling me dreams he's had or fantasies he enjoys, but . . . I don't know. I think they may be things he's done or about to do.

—Based on?

—That's the problem. Only on what he says. How he

says it. The way he treats me.

—What sorts of things? Give me some examples of his dreams and fantasies.

—They're all the same. He's obsessed with young girls.

—You think he's a pedophile? I assure you he's—

—No. Not children. Teenage girls. Fourteen. Fifteen. Sixteen.

How much should she tell him? How much should she clean it up? Is Doug going to be her supervisor or Davis's friend? Ease into it. See how he responds.

—He abducts them, she continues. Rapes them— repeatedly. He doesn't call it rape. Initiating them into the pleasures of their little bodies. That's what he says. Initiating. Teaching them what they don't know they don't know. Giving them what they don't know to ask for.

—I understand why you might find them disturbing or distasteful, but the nature of sexual fantasy is—

—It's not that. I have clients who share much darker fantasies. It's that I don't think these are fantasies.

—But he's not done or said anything to indicate that they are anything but, right?

—Then there's the obvious pleasure he gets out of telling them to me. The way he leers at me, licking his lips, letting his eyes wander all over my body.

She looks away from Doug, letting her eyes drift down to the folder. Opening it, she continues as if she's referring to it.

—When he's telling me about their . . . firm little titties—his words not mine—he stares at my breasts. When he talks about deflowering their soft, tight, sweet, pink little pussies, he stares at my crotch. And the way he does it. So blatant. So haughty. So . . . He knows what he's doing, knows the effect it's having on me.

—Davis is eccentric. He can afford to be. But he's no—what is it you think he is? A rapist? Kidnapper? What?

—I feel like I should call the police.

—And tell them what? There's nothing to tell. Unless a client confesses a crime or threatens to commit a crime—or to hurt themselves or others, you can't breathe a word to anyone. Our concerns are therapeutic. Our clients are our first priority. I thought you understood—

—I do. It's not about that. This is different.

—You're going to treat many clients over the years who you'll find distasteful. People you will disapprove of, or have personality conflicts with.

—I realize that. But that's not what this is. There's a real threat here, something menacing—to me, if not to other young girls. Can I at least terminate care with him and offer him the option of meeting with you?

Doug shakes his head and frowns deeply, and she feels the disappointment as if he's her dad.

—Davis and I went to school together. He sees my interns 'cause I can't see him. Besides, this is a great opportunity for you. What an internship is all about. Learning. Continue to treat all your clients the best way you can—and bring any concerns to me. I'll help you work through them.

Afternoon.

Heat.

Languidity.

Marc wakes disoriented, looks around, hears . . . what? The phone. Not cell, but house. As he rouses to run down the hall, he remembers.

Shelby. Julian. Waiting. What time is it? How long did he sleep?

The ringing stops.

Lifting his cell, he checks for missed calls. Had he slept through them?

None. No calls. No texts. Nothing.

Staggering out of his study and down the hall, he bumps into Taylor.

Pale. Alarm. Eyes wide. Holding the cordless phone.

—What is it? he asks.

—Did you get her? Where is she?

—I left messages—for her and Julian. They never called back.

—You said you'd let me know if you didn't find her.

—I fell back asleep. I'm Sorry.

Something shifts in her eyes. Fear intensifies. Yes, but also . . . beyond it . . . betrayal.

—You've been sleeping?

—I'm sorry. I didn't mean to. Not until I heard back from her. I just . . .

She places her hand over her mouth as if something horrible is dawning on her.

—Oh my God, she says. No. Please no.

—Who was on the phone?

—The school. It was a recorded message from the principal saying she's not at school today. She never showed up. She's missing. My little girl is missing and I've been painting and you've been sleeping and . . .

—She's probably just skipping. Somewhere making out with Julian.

Separation Anxiety

—I'm calling the sheriff.

—Let me go see if I can find them first. Please.

Storm.

Formation.

Expansion.

Intensification.

Six days ago, Christine had formed over the warm waters just north of the Virgin Islands. Four days ago, it reached hurricane strength over Puerto Rico. Yesterday, her ferocious winds and tsunami-like swells clouted Cuba with pitiless impunity. Today, she continues her relentless path over the warm waters of the Gulf of Mexico toward the northwest coast of Florida.

Rural route.

Marc races down the empty road, blacktop shimmering beneath the sun's merciless meridian.

She's okay. She's got to be.

It's normal teenage stuff. She's a good kid, but she's a kid, and needs to act like it from time to time—something he's never seen her do. From what he's gathered, when her twin sister Savannah went missing eight years ago, and her mom became even more paranoid and overprotective, the pre-teen Shelby submitted to it, understanding and forgiving her mom her post-traumatic-stress-syndrome-induced need to possess and imprison. Though lately—perhaps because of her age, but more likely due to her boyfriend—she had been chaffing a bit at her mom's hovering and overbearingness.

31

If something happened to her while you were sleeping, Taylor'll never forgive you.

She's not the only one.

She's fine. Quit thinking about anything but finding her.

Trees line either side of the desolate highway—tall, straight, uniform, produced for pulp, slash pines disappearing down into a lush green underbrush, verdant, varied, naturally occurring, unlike the planted pines towering above it.

Up ahead, near an intersection, a homemade roadside sign, red letters on white background, reads: Tupelo Honey. First House on Left.

Glancing down the side road, he sees people with cane poles fishing the drainage ditch, beer and bait beside them, toddlers in diapers and flip flops playing in the street.

It seems so safe here. Much of the time it feels like he, Taylor, and Shelby are the only people on the planet—an illusion Taylor's particularly partial to. She thrives on solitude and space. And though he'd prefer a little less isolated existence, he must admit this lonely, cloistered-like life is not without reward for his writing.

His cell rings and he snatches it out of his pocket.

—I need you to come home, Taylor says. Now.

—Why? What is it?

He hasn't been gone for very long, hasn't even reached the town of Tupelo yet, much less possible places Shelby and Julian might be hiding.

—I just need you.

For all her desire to hide from the rest of the world, she doesn't like being alone—at least not completely. She wants him or Shelby nearby at all times. Even when she's in her studio, consumed with creating, she wants to know one of them is in the house. And he understands. Knows the reasons, knows the loss she lives with, the constant sense of separation she feels, the acute abandonment issues that are as much a part of her as her name, her face, her art.

—But wouldn't you rather me be looking for—

—I'm calling the sheriff. I need you here.

—Shelby Summers didn't show up for school today, Sheriff Keith McFarland says. Go out to Lithonia Lodge, talk to her mom, find out what's going on. Then go to the school and talk to her friends, her boyfriend. Let me know if she's really missing.

—On it, boss, Will Jeffers says.

—Chances are, kid her age, she's laying out with her boyfriend somewhere, but if you think there's even a chance she might really be missing, I wanna move fast.

—Yes, sir. Understood.

And it really is.

Will's dad had been sheriff when Savannah Summers went missing. Failing to find her cost him a hell of a lot more than just his job. Will had been a deputy then, involved in the case, experienced firsthand everything that happened, witnessed what it did to his dad in a way no one else had, and Keith knew it.

—It's part of the reason I'm sending you.

When Bill Jeffers, Sr. resigned midterm, the governor had appointed Keith to fill the position. Two years later, Will had run against Keith and lost—and was shocked when, instead of firing him, he promoted him to lead detective. The two men, now in their early forties, had been classmates, in competition for everything—quarterback, point guard, girls, homecoming king, and though they'd never been friends exactly, they had always shared a certain admiration and respect.

—What's the other part?

—You're the best investigator I got.

Ordinarily, in a situation like this, a deputy not a detective would be dispatched, but because of what had happened with Savannah, because of Taylor's notoriety, this situation is anything but ordinary.

—I never blamed your dad for not finding Savannah, Taylor says. What happened wasn't his fault.

Eight years ago, on a warm spring day laced with the sweet scent of wild wisteria and confederate jasmine, just two weeks after their eighth birthday, Shelby and Savannah Summers disembarked the Blue Bird All-American school bus at the end of the dirt road leading to their house and the paint-flecked and fawning mother awaiting them there. Somewhere along the quarter-mile walk between the bus stop and the front door, Savannah vanished.

—He did the best he could, Will says. We all did. He's never gotten over it. None of us have, but it's different with him. He feels responsible. More responsible.

—I don't know what happened to her, she says.

—I'm so sorry for that, he says. That's got to be the worst . . . the not knowing.

—I don't know who took her. I don't know why. But I have a connection with my girls. It's like the one I had with my sister. She paused, then said, What?

—Ma'am?

—You're looking at me like I should be in a mental institution.

—No ma'am, I'm not.

—Lots of people have special connections. Marc and me for instance.

She takes Marc's hand at this, an act he's sure she's unconscious of.

From the moment they met, they've felt like twins. Every time they learn something new about the other, they discover yet another similarity, likeness, or preference they have in common.

—But there's a oneness twins have . . . It's . . . Well, I won't try to explain it. I can't. But it's real. I had it with Trevor, my sister. Shelby had it with Savannah. But I have it with both of them too. It's so powerful and profound I can't even tell you. And being a twin and the mother of twins . . . I'm . . . It's like I'm doubly connected.

To lose a sister, to lose parents, to lose a child—any one of them would cause irreparable damage, would cause unimaginable harm, but to have experienced them all, to have lost all . . . Little wonder Taylor is the way she is. To lose Shelby too would be unbearable.

—I understand, ma'am. I do. And I'm gonna—

—There's a reason I'm telling you this, she says. And it's not just that I love my daughters.

—Okay.

—I know Shelby's missing. I mean really missing, not just skipping school or . . . I knew the same thing about Savannah. Knew it long before anyone else did—teachers, cops, anyone.

—But—

—Do you know why I stopped looking for Savannah?

—I didn't know you had.

—You're right. I haven't exactly. But remember how

intense my search was, how much I bugged your dad and the state cop—

—Sam Michaels?

She nods.

—Why'd I stop? she asks. Do you know?

—No, ma'am. I . . .

—You think I got weary? Just wore myself out? Gave up 'cause I was exhausted?

He shakes his head, but something in his look makes Marc wonder if he'd heard she had a breakdown.

—The reason I searched for her the way I did that first year she was missing was because I knew she was still alive. I'm not saying I thought it or believed it. I'm saying I knew it. I stopped looking for her when she died. When I knew she was dead. Not thought it or believed it, but knew it. We're connected, okay? I knew she was still alive long after the search had been called off. I knew she was not being abused, that she never stopped missing me and Shelby, that she never lost her intense instinct to return home, but that she was safe and cared for, and even eventually felt something akin to affection for whoever had her. I knew all this—and . . . knew . . . when she . . . died. Can tell you the exact moment on the exact day. I'm telling you this because I'm connected to Shelby the same way, and she's missing. She's in trouble and needs our help. We've got to find her fast. Do you understand?

—Yes, ma'am, I do.

—Good.

—But her car. She took her car. She left willingly, not forcibly. Had you guys been arguing over anything? She mad about Mr. Faulk living here now? You tell her to stop seeing her boyfriend?

—You haven't heard a goddamn thing I've said.

—I have, but she's a teenager and I know how—

—Yes. All that's true. We're fighting over all those things and more—and they're irrelevant. They have nothing to do with where she is and who has her.

—Okay. Then let me do my job. I need to see her room, take a look around your place, and I need you two to tell me if there's anyone you suspect. Boyfriend? Biological dad?

—Both possibilities, she says.

—About a week ago we had someone out to repair the refrigerator, Marc says.

—That's right, Taylor says.

—Shelby said he was creepy.

—What'd you think? Will asks Marc.

—Seemed pretty harmless to me.

—I should've just bought a new one, Taylor says.

—Then someone would have delivered it, Marc says. We can't keep her away from everyone.

—Anyone else? Neighbor? Housekeeper? Yardman?

—They wouldn't be around if I thought they were a threat.

—We'll make a list, Marc says.

—Anyone else you can think of?

—Taylor has a lot of obsessive fans, but there was one guy who stalked her.

—Yeah, I remember. That was a while back. What was his name? Raymond Wayne . . .

—Hennessey.

—Yeah. You had to get a restraining order, right? You seen or heard anything out of him lately?

—Not a whisper, Taylor says. Which worries me.

37

Relief.

Exhalation.

Release of tension.

When Davis Allen Grayson doesn't show up for his session, Beth Ann's palliative state is palpable. It emanates outward from her and seems to actually lighten the small counseling room.

Wonder where he is. Why he didn't call.

Maybe he was killed in a car accident.

Beth Ann. How can you—

She can't help but smile.

Lets me know just how evil I really think he is. Of course I don't want him dying in a car accident, do I?

You do if he's doing what you think he is.

True. I guess I do. Am I that . . .

You're scared. And you're worried about innocent young girls.

Well, whatever's keeping him . . . I'm glad for it—unless it's an innocent young girl.

High school juniors.

Junior Service League daughters.

Future Daughters of the American Revolution.

Cliquish, of course, but not entirely mean girls, not entirely silly and superfluous. Not entirely.

Blond and brunette ponytails. Fashionable cuts. Trendy

clothes. All the right labels. Just the right body types. Just the right attitude.

—She really doesn't hang with us. Not in our group.

—I was told she did, Will says.

The four girls are circled around him in the gym near the girls locker room. Unlike most of the other students, they are not dressed out, not participating in the volleyball and basketball games being played in the airy, open, largely sunlit enclosure.

—She really doesn't hang with anyone.

—Too busy saving the manatees or some shit.

He remembers reading a profile in the little town paper touting Shelby as a serious environmentalist—conservationist, activist, wounded animal rescuer—and it incenses him that this stupid girl can so easily dismiss and belittle what she does.

—She's kinda stuckup.

—You're being nice. She's a real bitch.

—Thinks she's too good for everyone.

—'Cept Julian.

—Who? Will asks.

—Yeah. 'Cept him.

—Anyone seen him? he says.

—He's not at school today.

—They're probably together.

—Bet she turns up pregnant before we graduate.

—No doubt.

—If they are together somewhere . . . Will says, letting it drift out and linger in the space between them.

As they are talking, he notices another girl—an anti-these-girls girl—in all black, sitting on the bleachers reading a paperback book, leaning in and listening, shaking her head and rolling her eyes occasionally.

—Can't imagine.

—Gross. Don't want to even think about it.

—I feel bad for her.

—Yeah, me too. Freak show for a mom.

—Bad boyfriend.

—The worst.

—I mean, he's hot and all, but Jesus, he's a freak.

—Why do you say that? he asks.

—He just is.

—But why? Tell me about him.

—You know. Some people're just freaks.

—Yeah. You know. You can just tell.

—He totally got Rylee Thompson hooked on pot.

—And he hit her. That's why they broke up.

—He's controlling. You know? Separates younger girls from the pack, then runs their lives.

—Shelby has a pack? Will asks.

—Well, no. Didn't have to separate her like that exactly . . . I guess.

Once he concludes with the prep pack, Will walks up the bleachers and sits next to Tupelo High's closest thing to a Goth.

—I hope you don't believe a single goddamn thing those silly bitches told you.

He smiles.

—They seem like they notice anybody but themselves to

you? she asks.

—So tell me.

The various games being played in the gym are half-hearted and haphazard—no actual competition going on—and it's hard to imagine the skill level involved being any lower. On the far end of the stands, the PE teacher/coach leans back against the bleacher behind him in a pose meant for cool far more than comfort, talking on his cell phone.

—What? she says.

—About Shelby and Julian.

—What's to tell? They're okay.

—Is he possessive and controlling? he asks.

—What guy isn't?

—There are some, he says.

She shrugs like she's unconcerned or unconvinced and continues.

—He's passionate. And he really loves her. I mean really a fuckin' lot. And it's not just him. She's . . . They're all into each other. He sure as shit didn't hit Rylee Thompson—and she was a total pothead before he ever hooked up with her.

—Do you know where they are?

She shakes her head.

—If you did, would you tell me?

She shakes her head again.

He stands.

—I'm not sayin' they're all straightedge and shit. Just that they're not Satan's spawn.

—I knew this was going to happen, Taylor says.

41

Marc gives her a gently incredulous look.

They are alone again, her sitting on a barstool in the
kitchen, him, standing across the counter opposite her. She
is wearing paint-speckled khaki shorts, a white button-down,
the sleeves rolled up, and white sandals. Like her clothes, her
tan skin and blond hair, gathered up in the back, are flecked
with the colors she creates. In one hand she clutches the house
phone. In the other, her cell. Her fingertips clutching both are
so white that no pink remains.

—I did. Been waiting for it. Been trying to prevent it
from happening—even though I strongly suspected it was futile.

Is that where her calm comes from? Belief in the
inevitability of this? Is she experiencing a kind of perverse
release, a relief that the waiting is now over?

A pad of paper and a pen are on the bar top before
him in preparation for the list of recent visitors to Lithonia
Lodge, and though he thinks it's premature, even ultimately
unnecessary, he'll do anything she wants right now. Anything.

—I'm not sure what else I could've done, she says. I'm
sure there's something. I mean, obviously I failed, but right now
I don't know how.

He's seen her like this before—engulfed in futility,
surrendering to the undercurrent of hopelessness that
flows through the center of her life, always present, always
threatening, always overtaking her, pulling her under when her
menses is also flowing.

—You've done everything. Protected her so well. She's
probably somewhere with Julian. Phone dead. Lost track of
time. Typical teenage stuff.

For all the restoration and updating, Lithonia Lodge is
still an old house, and it creaks desultorily as they talk, groaning,
like the old do, about joint aches and pains.

—I can't believe you don't believe me, she says. I'm

telling you. I know. I don't know the specifics, but I know what's happening to her is horrible. I just pray if we don't find her, that it won't last long. Not like Savannah. That went on forever. I can't endure that again.

He nods, attempting to be understanding without agreeing, caring without condescending.

—You think things've been bad before . . .

Between her bouts with depression, her issues with trust, her intense insecurities, fear of abandonment, and her intermittent hormone-induced insanity, this has been by far his most turbulent entanglement—and she knows it. She has repeatedly tried to get him to leave, to break things off, to bring about what she believes to be the inevitability of their end—always with the reassurance that it's not a lack of love for him, but her own feelings of inadequacy and unlovability. But every time she tries and he stays, she seems to trust, to believe, incrementally more. Until, that is, she is again overcome by these demons, and tries to separate in, ironically enough, an attempt to mitigate her own severe separation anxiety.

—You should go now, she continues. Clean break. Don't look back.

He shakes his head.

—I'm not going anywhere. I can't believe you don't know that by now. I wouldn't even leave if you asked me to— not . . . not until we have Shelby home safely.

—Then you'll go?

—No. Let's make the list.

—Fine. Good.

She doesn't release her grip on the phones, but she leans forward and moves her hands a little closer to the pad.

—There's Sabrina, she says. She's been cleaning for me for over ten years. I know she has nothing to do with this, but

43

everybody goes on the list.

He writes Sabrina Raffield.

—Tommy, she says.

He writes Tommy King beneath Sabrina Raffield.

—How long has he done your yards?

—For as long as I've had them. And we went to school together. He'll fuck anything that stands still long enough, but he's not a . . . he has nothing to do with this. Neither of them do. That's why they work for me. And why they're the only ones who do.

—Okay. Who else?

—Refrigerator repair guy.

—You remember his name?

She shakes her head.

—But I could pick 'im out of a lineup.

He writes MP Appliance worker on the list.

—I'll call and get his info. Anyone else?

They both grow quiet, thinking, searching their memories.

—Can't think of any, she says.

—No other deliveries? No phone or cable repair?

—The UPS and FedEx guys have been coming here for years. They're on my Christmas card list for chrissakes. That's it. I don't let anybody in. And this is why.

—What about the politician? What's his name? The one who came to discuss the commission.

—Davis Allen Grayson? He's harmless. Rich and eccentric. Soft and spoiled, but not a . . . I'm pretty sure he's gay.

Will is distractedly driving through the small town of Tupelo when the call from the sheriff comes.

It's midafternoon and Main Street is empty beneath the stroke-inducing heat of the slanting sun. As if drained of all energy, a few brave pedestrians and glare-ridden vehicles creep along, seemingly in slow motion.

—Chief, he says, taking the call.

—Whatta we lookin' at?

—Don't know yet, but it doesn't look like she was kidnapped. Looks like she left on her own, in her own car. Probably with her boyfriend. He's gone too.

Nestled near the Apalachicola River and the Gulf of Mexico, Tupelo is an Old Florida town in limbo—tourism and trade, Southern oligarchy and snowbirds, rich retirees and redneck farmers, fishermen and pulpwooders, all trapped in a briny brackish tidal pool.

Small gift shops selling specialty items for small fortunes and tourist traps selling tasteless trinkets and Florida kitsch stand awkwardly next to faded tin-building dollar stores and auto parts places, like uneasy relatives at a reunion. Beside upscale restaurants with New York names, small-town no-name cafés and trough-like buffets occupy the same block.

—I've talked to her friends—well, her classmates. She's a very private person. Sort of a loner. Haven't found anyone she would confide in. Nobody seems to know much of anything— and I don't think they're lying. The only teacher she's close to is the new biology teacher, but he's out today. Principal's supposed to have him call me in a few.

—I know I'm puttin' you in a tough position, Keith says, but if there's any chance she's been taken—

—If it were anybody else, I'd say no, but I'm being overly cautious. Treating it like she is missing until—

—Even if her boyfriend has her—I want to move fast. And if she's just being stupid, skippin' or somethin' . . . I still want to find her ASAP. If the storm comes where they say it will, in the next day or two we'll need every man dealing with evacuations, looting, road closings, and shelter security. We can't afford to waste a single second.

—I hear you. I honestly think she's with Julian somewhere—everything points to that—but I'm not willing to say that yet. I'm on my way to talk to Julian's mom now. Will know more soon.

—Let me know.

—Will do.

Just as he's about to end the call . . .

—Hey, Will?

—Yeah?

—Can I ask you something?

—Sure, boss. What is it?

—If you'd won the election instead of me . . .

—Uh huh?

—What would you be doing?

—Exactly what we are, chief. Exactly what we are.

East end of town.

Sylvan subdivision.

One-acre lots.

Mostly mobile homes. Occasional brick or vinyl-siding house.

Julia Flax's place. Chain-link fence creating a rectangle around a manicured lawn and aging but clean, well-maintained,

46

and freshly painted single-wide mobile home.

Inside. Immaculate.

How the hell does a single mom with three jobs and a teenage son keep a place looking this good?

—Sorry, Will, Julia says, leading him into the kitchen, but I only have a few minutes. Got to be at the Owl by four.

After working at the Dollar General from seven until three, Julia works from four to midnight at the Night Owl Café. On weekends, she cleans condos at the beach.

Is Julian raising himself?

On the counter, a small television carries coverage of Hurricane Christine, showing the damage and devastation done to Cuba's northern coast. Over 100-mile-per-hour winds. 50 serious injuries. 10 deaths. 360,000 displaced residents.

Lifting the remote next to the set, though pushing the power button on the TV would've been easier, she turns it off.

—What's the latest? he asks.

—Headed this way. Don't know yet where it will make landfall. There's some high pressure that could move in and redirect it—maybe even push it back out into the Gulf, but that's a very long shot.

Without asking, she pours him a cup of coffee, freshens up her own, returns the pot, then sits down across from him. Like Julian, there's something dark and slightly exotic about his mom. Olive skin. Big brown eyes. Auburn-streaked wavy brownish hair.

He finds it interesting a single mom would make a namesake of her only son, but vaguely recalls Julia being named after her dad.

—Thanks.

She stirs some cream and sugar into hers, then slides them toward him.

—Have you heard from Julian?

She shakes her head.

—Did you know he wasn't at school today?

—Not until you told me.

—He often skip?

—Never—at least to my knowledge, but I didn't know he was today.

—Have you tried to call him?

She laughs.

—We can't afford cell phones. He's probably the only teenager in America who doesn't have one—and he lets me know it all the time, but food and shelter first, you know?

He nods, and they are quiet a moment.

This is what a certain type of poverty looks like. Simple. Content. Spartan. Julia and Julian don't have much and nothing they have is nice, but they have everything they need and everything they have is neat and clean and cared for. No clutter. No indulgences. Nothing superfluous. Like her clothes and shoes, Julia's household items appear nearly trendy and costly. Nearly. Their appearance is deceptive and a closer look reveals they are of an inexpensive, almost-nice, made-to-look-fashionable discount-store variety.

—You don't seem very worried, he says.

—Should I be?

He shrugs.

—I'm a single mom. Julian is the man of the house. He's the most mature young man I've ever known. I depend on him—and he's never let me down. If he wants to blow off school for a day . . . Now, if you tell me you think he's in trouble, that's a different matter. But the fact that Shelby's missing too leads me to believe they just wanted a little extra time together.

—I agree. I just . . . with what happened to her sister . . .

—I didn't live here then, but I've heard things—about her mom too. To tell the truth, I was a little worried when he started dating her, but . . . she's a real good girl. They make a great couple.

He nods.

The trailer is uncomfortably warm, and he wonders if it's her preference or an attempt to conserve. He suspects it's the latter—and for financial rather than environmental reasons.

—What does Julian drive?

—He doesn't. You think I can't afford a cell phone, but I can afford a car for him. Shelby chauffeurs him around in her little green bug. Without her, he's grounded.

—Any idea where they'd go?

—Not really. But now that school's over, I'm sure they'll show up soon. Julian rarely misses school, but he never misses work—not ever. If he's not at work this afternoon, then I'll start to worry.

Pulling off Highway 67, Will's tires crunch on the crushed-shell parking lot of TJ's, an automotive repair shop and takeout fast food joint TJ operates out of his house.

Next to a small clapboard house, a two-story, two-car metal garage is surrounded by vehicles in various stages of repair. Inside the garage, a 50s-era souped-up Chevy truck is up on the hydraulic lift, TJ in oil-stained overalls standing under it.

Up near the road, a converted race car trailer advertises hamburgers, hotdogs, and barbecue. Behind it, smoke from a slow cooker drifts up out of the small, wooden screened-in structure that houses it.

Will steps out of his black second-generation Crown Vic police interceptor and walks toward TJ.

A huge commercial fan at the opening of the garage merely stirs the hot air around, providing neither comfort nor relief. From a high built-in shelf a cheap radio is tuned to a country station, blaring tragedy in a minor twang.

—Hide the weed, it's the po-po, TJ shouts.

At a work bench on the far end of the garage, TJ's dad, Buck, the black man who's worked for them for decades, and a customer Will doesn't recognize all laugh.

—Nah, Will's okay. He wouldn't bust a brother for a little grass. Would you?

Will smiles.

—Depends on how little, he says.

—Hell, TJ says, Will and me got fucked up a few times together back in the day.

—It's true.

—Your dad didn't jam us up when we got caught, did he?

—No, he didn't.

—Knew what mattered. Not like today.

Will shrugs.

—Was a different time, Will says wistfully, but not so much has changed. You sure as shit ain't.

—Ain't intendin' to neither.

—Wouldn't have it any other way, brother.

—You lookin' for Julian?

—How'd you know?

—His mom called to see if he had made it in. Said you might be stopping by.

—What time's he supposed to be here?

—No set time, TJ says. We're sorta what you might call casual 'round here.

The other men laugh again.

—But usually by four-thirty. 'Course, he ain't workin' today.

—Why not?

—Told him to take the day off. Boy works too much. I worry about him.

—Do you know what he was gonna do?

TJ shakes his head and shrugs.

—Not my business.

—What can I getcha?

Will recognizes the young brown-eyed, brown-haired girl with the olive complexion from the gym earlier in the afternoon. Whitney something. Anderson maybe. As she leans down to take his order inside TJ's Takeout trailer, her small brown breasts are more exposed than he thinks they should be, and he locks in on her eyes.

—Got it by yourself today? he asks.

—Yes, sir.

—Doesn't Julian usually help you?

—No. I help him. But he took the day off.

—TJ told me he gave him the day off. Made him take it. 'Cause that's the kind of compassionate boss he is.

—Bullshit he did. Julian asked him for it off a while back. Today and tomorrow.

—Any idea what he's doing?

51

—Not exactly . . .

—But?

—I think he's gonna propose to Shelby.

—What makes you say that?

—Just things he's said here and there. Plus, he works all the time and never spends a dime. He's got like a gazillion dollars saved up. About a week ago he had a jewelry catalog in here looking at rings.

—Thanks. That helps. Really does.

—I'm not saying that's what he's doing. He never said anything like that. It's just a guess.

—Keith? It's me. I think I know what they're up to.

—Where are you?

—Just leaving TJ's.

—Meet me at Lanier Landing.

—On my way.

—So tell me.

—I'm pretty sure they're eloping. This was all planned. Julian's been saving money for a long time. They may just be going to buy a ring and get engaged, but I really think it's more than that. He asked for tomorrow off too. They could be running away together, not planning on coming back, or they could be getting married and returning by Monday, but I think that's what they're up to.

—They in his car?

—Doesn't have one. In hers. We need to put out an APB for her lime-green Volkswagen bug.

—No we don't. And we probably need to start the

investigation over from the beginning.

—What? Why's that?

—'Cause, we just found her abandoned car at Lanier Landing.

Transplanted palms.

Oak-canopied park.

Rustic picnic pavilions.

Boat ramp.

Cypress-rimmed river. Apalachicola.

When Marc and Taylor arrive at the landing, there's no sign of Keith or Will, only a parking lot of trucks and empty boat trailers.

Convincing Taylor to wait in the car, Marc gets out in the oppressive heat and rushes toward the river, searching, scanning, scoping.

To his left, a couple of young mothers play with their small children in the park, eyeing him suspiciously as they do.

Beyond the green sign that reads Welcome to Lanier Landing: Discover Old Florida, a truck is parked on the ramp, its trailer down in the water, a couple in cutoff jean shorts and Dixie Outfitter and Mossy Oak T-shirts launching their boat, but there's no sign of Shelby's car or Keith or Will.

On the small floating dock, near the high-water marker, a black man in a Panama hat sits on a brown folding chair, fishing with a cane pole. Next to him stands a large-breasted black woman, life vest hanging from her neck, enormous floppy hat forming an umbrella over her head.

Snatches of conversation come from a group of elderly black people packing up their gear on the right end of the ramp, near the Swim at Your Own Risk sign.

—Willy Charles, you want one or two a these brims?

—Nah. I'm a'ight.

—Is what it is. Hope to do better tomorrow.

—Tomorrow is another day.

—I'm 'bout to go clean these cats. Sure you don't want one or two a these brims?

—Hope to see y'all tomorrow.

—Lord willing and the storm allow, I'a be here.

As he nears the wide green-blue-brown river, he glances to his left, down the small dirt road that runs behind the stilted fishing camps, cabins, and trailers lining the banks of the Apalachicola, and spots them.

In the carport beneath the elevated house of the third place on the left, he sees Shelby's lime-green bug. Keith and Will are standing near it, a deputy by his car at the end of the driveway.

On either side sit old, small single-wide trailers in earth-tone browns and golds, popular in the 70s, atop some four feet of cinderblocks.

Dashing.

He runs so fast toward the car, both Keith and Will step away from it and over to meet him, hands up, attempting to slow and calm him, eyeing him carefully as they do.

—She's not here, Will says. Just her car.

—You sure?

—Yeah, Keith says. Positive.

—You okay? Will asks. Take a minute. Catch your breath.

The tea-colored river flows on by, the subtlest of breezes blowing in off its mostly smooth surface. On the other side, two homemade houseboats are tied to cypress trees—one under construction, its walls built of blue insulation board.

Rustle of leaves.

Distant bird chirps.

Splashing. Yelling. Shrieking. Teenagers swimming around the dock at the landing.

Scrape of dead, brittle palm fronds on hardwood tree base.

Marc, settling down, breath and heart rate slowing, sweat still pouring. Clammy. Sticky.

—You looked—

—We've searched the area, Keith says. And there's no sign of struggle. Looks like she just parked here, locked it, and left.

—Any idea why she'd leave her car here? Will asks.

Marc shakes his head.

—You checked the house?

The two men nod.

Marc glances over at Shelby's car. Both doors are open.

—Thought you said it was locked?

—It was.

—We opened it.

—Anything inside?

—A few things. Nothing out of the ordinary.

—Take a look for us, Keith says, but don't get in and don't touch anything. Looks like she just parked here and went somewhere, but in case it's something else and we have to process the car . . .

Marc steps over to the car, standing close, leaning in, careful not to touch anything.

55

Keith stands beside him, Will, on the opposite side of the car, looking in through the open passenger door.

New-car smell wafts out, and the cream interior is still spotless. Shelby is the one thing Taylor spares no expense on—especially when it comes to her safety and happiness.

Right away, he notices a few irregularities.

—Anything? Keith asks.

—What is it? Will asks, almost at the same moment.

—Her iPod is gone. It's always there on the console, plugged into the auxiliary jack.

—She could've taken it with her.

—She has three. One in her car, one in the house, one in her purse.

The two men look at him with raised eyebrows.

—I know how it sounds. Her mom indulges the hell out of her, but she's not spoiled. She's not. She's a good kid.

—What else? Will says.

—Cover for her sunroof is closed. Never seen that before. For a while, I'd remind her, but gave up because she told me she planned on leaving it open the entire time she owned the car.

—Okay.

—And her flower is missing.

—Her what?

—Julian—her boyfriend—gave her a flower for the little vase. See. On the dashboard just behind the wheel. It's empty. The day she got the car, Julian gave her this elaborate paper rose he made. She's never taken it out.

—Think they broke up? Keith asks.

—If they're together, Will says, especially if they're

eloping, she may have taken it with her.

—Eloping? Marc says, his voice spiking.

Keith winces.

—It's just one possible working theory, Will says.

—Less likely now that we found her car.

Out on the river, an aluminum bateau races by, its outboard motor whining. All three men turn toward it to see a young boy in the back, hand on the throttle arm, older man in front, capped head ducked down into the wind, hand on bill.

—Where is she?

The three men turn again, this time in the opposite direction, to the road behind them, as Taylor comes running up.

—Where is she? she says again.

—She's not here, Marc says. Just her car.

—You sure?

—Yes, ma'am, Will says.

—Where's Steve?

—Who?

—Steve. Where is he?

—Steve? Marc says.

—Is he here?

—Who's Steve?

—Shelby and Savannah's dad. This is his fish camp. Is he here? Is she with him?

The surface of the river swirls with bits of debris—leaves, blossoms, bugs, the occasional limb or log, the last, sometimes, with turtles hitching a ride.

Across the way, some two-hundred yards to the opposite side, rising out of the riverbank, an impenetrable thicket of trees lean toward the water, their tall, tilting bodies appearing wind-rocked and storm-ravaged—though that was yet to come.

With Taylor trying to get Steve on her cell, Keith and Will walk into the backyard, near the water's edge.

—Should we call in Crime Scene? Keith asks. Process the car?

Will realizes just how lost and unsure Keith is. And why wouldn't he be? He's just an elected official, a small-town boy with a little education and training, a deputy who won a popularity contest.

He's never thought it before, but surely his dad must have felt the same way. His hero, his idol, the man he's spent his life trying to please, impress, emulate, is just a man, had been just a public servant in over his head with the Savannah Summers case.

The way you and Keith are now.

—We wouldn't if it were anybody else, Will says.

—True.

—But it's not, is it?

—No, Keith says, it's not. I'm just not sure what to do.

Will is so appreciative of Keith treating him as an equal, as a confidant, he continues to like and respect him more than he ever imagined possible. Hell, had I known he'd be like this, I'd've voted for him myself.

The longer he works with Keith, the more he's around the man, the more he thinks the competition he feels—or has felt all these years going back to high school—is one-sided.

I've always been a step behind, a little slower, slightly, perhaps imperceptibly to others—even to Keith. I'm aware of it. He's not. I make comparisons. He doesn't seem to feel the need to.

—Guess there's no harm in doing it, is there? Keith says.

—Just the embarrassment of overreacting. And it might violate her constitutional rights.

—Did that when we jimmied the door.

—Did, didn't we? Will says.

—So you think I should?

—I'm sayin' I would. Hell, you can say I did it. Rather overreact than under.

Keith nods.

—I agree, we should, but it's on me. I'll take the heat if there is any.

Will nods, and they are silent a moment.

—Can I ask you something? Will says.

—Shoot, Keith says.

—I appreciate you always gettin' my input.

—Yeah?

—But it surprises me. Not sure it'd be the same if the situation was reversed.

Will recalls the things he said behind Keith's back when they were both running for homecoming king or lobbying for quarterback or competing for the rural electrification Washington, DC trip.

—That your question?

Will laughs.

—I'm asking why.

—Only reason you're not in this position is a few votes.

Will smiles and shakes his head. It's like homecoming all over again.

—It was more than a few.

—Would he take her?

With that question, Marc is reminded again of how little he knows about Taylor, her family, her past. After their first date, when she had drunkenly told him so much, she has since remained reticent, often remote.

Though the cell phone is to her ear, she's yet to reach her ex-husband, but she still doesn't respond to his question.

I didn't even know he had a camp here, he thinks.

What else don't you know?

At certain moments, he's seen into her soul, visited the secret garden of her heart, and she feels like his twin, like he knows her as well as he knows himself. At others, she's the stranger lying next to him, as opaque, as inaccessible, as unavailable as a member of the same species can be.

He finds himself immensely curious about Steve. What's he like? What's his side of the story? Would he tell me to run? Did he? Or did Taylor banish him? Is he unstable? Troubled? Deranged?

Are you saying you have to be in order to be with Taylor?

Am I?

Taylor had asked him during one of their many discussions about her trust and abandonment issues what it said about him that he was with her.

What does it?

Am I fucked up? Or just fucked because I found my twin, my soul mate, and she's so damaged?

When she is off the phone, he waits a moment, but she doesn't say anything.

—Would he take her? he asks again, dragging it out, emphasizing each word impatiently.

—He's never shown any interest in her. Barely remembers her birthday.

—Would he help her if she were running away?

—Running away? She's not— I told you, someone took her. Oh my God, my baby.

She looks over at the car, and begins to move toward it, as Keith and Will walk back up.

—You get him? Keith asks.

She doesn't respond, just stares at the car.

—Ms. Sean, Keith says with more force, did you reach your ex-husband?

She shakes her head.

—Left messages. Home. Work. Cell.

—We'll find him, Will says.

Attention affixed to the car, Taylor continues to edge toward it, and it appears she's about to climb inside.

—Please don't touch the car, Will says. We honestly believe your daughter is fine, gone somewhere on her own, but we're going to go ahead and have the vehicle processed to see if it turns up anything.

Eyes glistening, she blinks several times as she steps back.

—Why don't y'all go on home—in case she shows up there. We'll call you the moment we find out anything.

Marc gently places his arm around Taylor and begins to lead her away, then stops, withdraws a folded piece of paper from his pocket, and turns toward Will.

—Here's a list of people who've been at the lodge the last few weeks.

61

—We'll follow up on everyone, Keith says. We're gonna find her. I swear it.

Clear.

Calm.

Equanimity.

The serene day is so sunny, so Florida picture-postcard perfect, that the approaching storm seems something from an alternate reality, a darker dimension incompatible with this one.

Having rolled off Cuba's coast, Christine steadily strengthens, her northmost fringes felt in the Keys and Miami. Sustained winds at 60 miles per hour, gusts 105.

Downed power lines.

Flash flooding.

Uprooted trees.

Overturned trailers.

Southeastern Gulf of Mexico. Warm waters. Incubator of intensity.

Reconnaissance reports: barometric pressure plummeting—1 millibar per hour.

Tracking toward Tupelo.

Stalking.

Slow, steady approach.

Relentless.

Inevitable.

Canis lupus.

Separation Anxiety

The wolf is as relentless as the storm. And as beautiful. More so.

The wolf is as destructive as the storm. More so. More devastating. More demanding. More deadly.

The great wolf god created order out of chaos, but on occasion the chaos shows through. The storm is that chaos. So is the wolf.

The storm is a rip in the fabric of the cosmos, a tear where the chaos on the other side shows through the façade of order on this one.

The wolf is a storm unleashed on the unsuspecting. A reminder. A reckoning. The wolf says you think you're safe, but you're not. You think the little existence you've constructed makes you immune from injury and pain and death, from the wolf, but it does not.

Chaos lupus.

Cheryl Rouse never thought she'd wish the previous two hurricane seasons hadn't been so mild, but here she is, if not exactly wishing it, at least wondering if things would be different if just one storm would've approached the Panhandle in that time.

As a probation officer with the Florida Department of Corrections, Cheryl's caseload contains a number of sex offenders, who are required to either have an emergency residence to evacuate to or check in to the local jail during a hurricane. Obviously, they can't go to a shelter, and with so many conditions and ordinances requiring them to stay at least a thousand feet away from children and schools, daycare centers, bus stops, etc., having a legit emergency address is a challenge.

With the approach of Christine, Cheryl has been verifying the emergency addresses provided to her by inmates on probation or conditional release when they were first assigned to her, ensuring the addresses are valid and no minors will be present.

After two days, she has verification of emergency addresses or has gone over the instruction forms for temporary incarceration with all the offenders on her caseload but one.

Raymond Wayne Hennessey.

Of all the sex offenders assigned to her, he's the one she least wants in the wind.

Had there been more hurricane activity in the Gulf over the past two years, she would've found out the emergency address he'd given her was bad long before now. Perhaps it was good when he first turned it in. Probably was. Hell, she probably verified it. But since it's been so long, it's no longer valid, and she can't find him.

Where the fuck are you, Raymond?

—Will you talk to me? Marc asks.

They are winding around the serpentine river road, heading home from the landing, a thick verdant forest extending out from each shoulder, its infinite variety of species far more indigenous than the rows of pines planted for pulpwood found on most highways around here.

—What's there to say?

—How you're feeling. What you're thinking. What I can do.

She doesn't respond, just continues to sit still, rigid, staring straight ahead.

When she's like this, he's filled with an intense longing, as if his twin, the person he's one with, is dead, the connection severed, and it makes him desperate, the desire to close the distance, to reestablish their rare union nearly overwhelming.

—Is there any way for you not to get so distraught until we know more?

Nothing.

—Would you at least not shut me out? Let us deal with it together?

He understands how she feels, doesn't blame her for the need to turn in, to close out, but she does it way too often, and too often it's over nonexistent issues, trifles magnified by her moods.

This is something real, a valid concern with the potential to be devastating, yet it feels like all her other inexplicable withdrawals.

—Why go through this alone? Why not let me help you? I can.

—Nothing you can do, she says, her voice flat, futile, resigned. Nothing anyone can.

He shakes his head and sighs.

His frustration flares and he wants to confront her, provoke her, do or say something to force a reaction, but he reminds himself how counterproductive that would be, how vulnerable she is at the moment. And he realizes he's not angry about how she's acting now. It's all the shit that has come before. Don't bring anything else into this. Now's not the time. For now, everything's got to be put on hold.

—Can you tell me about Steve? he says.

—Just a mistake I made as a kid. I was acting out. He was an available bad boy. We fucked. I got pregnant. We tried to be a couple, then a family. We failed miserably at both. Since then, he's continued to fail at being a father.

—Is he in Shelby's life at all?

—When Savannah was taken, he came around and . . . I

don't know. Tried, a little, I guess. Didn't last long. She probably talks to him about once a month. She usually visits him when he's at his camp.

—Don't you think that's what's happening now? They're together. Maybe they rode into town to eat or something.

She shakes her head and lets out a harsh, humorless laugh.

—Goddamn it, Marc. She's not somewhere getting a fuckin' hamburger. She's in real trouble. You know how we're connected?

—Me and you?

—Yeah. You know how intimate and intense it is, how you call me your twin, how spooky alike we are?

—Yeah?

He's so happy for her to refer to their connection in this way, to acknowledge him as a twin, that he can't help but grin.

At first, during their early heady days of constant companionship and continuous discovery, when they were fronted with commonality after commonality, thing after thing they had experienced the same way, believed the same about, he had floated the idea that he felt like her long-lost twin finally being reunited with his match. Since she was literally a lost twin, the sole survivor of the infamous Taylor and Trevor twin case, he wasn't sure how she'd feel about the concept, but it seemed to really resonate with her, and she responded in kind.

All that seems so far away now—nearly a lifetime ago— as lately it seems nearly all they do is deal with depression, hormones, and issues of trust and abandonment.

It's been so long since she's even mentioned the idea of them being twins, he thought she had abandoned the notion, abandoned, in a way, him, her twin, allowing temporal conditions, chemicals, and trauma from the past to eclipse that which is eternal and inexplicable.

—Multiply that by . . . a lot, she says. That's what I have with my girls.

He chastises himself for being bothered that her connection with Shelby is a multiple of theirs. She's her daughter for fuck sake. Her own flesh and blood. From her body.

Yeah, but she said what we have is unlike anything she's ever had with anybody.

—Don't look like that, she says.

—What?

—Like I hurt your feelings. It's not better or more, it's just different. I can feel if they're happy or in danger or—I'm sure I can with you too. It's just I've been doing it a lot longer with them.

—I understand, he says. I really didn't mean to look any way.

—Just don't. I can't deal with us right now.

—I'm not asking you to.

—Good. Tell me we're fine. You love me, aren't going anywhere, and will do whatever it takes to get Shelby back.

—We are. I do. I'm not. I will.

Stepping out of the August heat into the cool lobby is refreshing, and Will stands a moment letting his eyes adjust, feeling the sheen of sweat begin to dry and turn frigid.

The singular smell of movie theater popcorn wafts over him in a hot buttery haze, the airy poof poof and dat dat dat of its transformation from the kernel the most dominant sound in the hushed, palatial movie palace.

Located on Panama City Beach, Shangri-La dwarfs every

other movie theater Will's ever seen. Though nearly brand new, the Cineplex is made to look like a restored old, opulent, opera house-style theater.

Dark.

Gilded.

Plush.

Patterned carpet. Plaster ornamentation.

Passing beneath an enormous chandelier, Will walks around cardboard cutouts of fall films with Oscar potential, jolting and out of place here—made all the more kitschy by their surroundings as he makes his way over to the concession counter.

To the too-small teenager in the too-big tuxedo, he flips open his badge and ID and hands him a business card.

—Take me to the manager.

—Huh?

—I need to see the manager. Now.

Will rarely plays bad cop—or even comes on very strong, but he has little time or patience, and he can tell this approach will probably work best with a kid like this one.

—I'll radio him and—

—No. Take me to him.

—Yes, sir.

Leaving his coworker behind the counter without a word, the kid leads Will through the lobby, up carpeted stairs, past ornamental columns and rich tapestries, all beneath vaulted ceilings, chandeliers, and accent lighting.

Before they reach the manager's office, they encounter him in the hallway.

—Steve, cop here to see you, the kid says, jerking his head and thumb back toward Will.

Separation Anxiety

The long carpeted hallway is dotted with double doors every twenty feet or so, all of which are closed. From beyond them come the muted sounds of movies—low rumblings, dull, barely audible and indistinguishable conversations, muffled and distorted.

—What can I do for you? the manager asks, smiling warmly, friendly, eager to help.

—You Steve Summers?

—Yeah. What's up?

The diminutive man, who looks to be in his early thirties like his ex-wife, is thin and boyish, and wears a tux even more ill-fitting than the kid's.

—That's all, Will says to the lingering teenager.

—Yes, sir. Thanks.

The kid glances at Summers, who nods, then takes off back down the hallway.

Steve Summers's pale, acne-scarred skin, thinning sandy hair, and spotty blond stubble give him the look of a hayseed—something the cheap tux only accentuates. He has the uncomfortable look of a hick having to dress up for prom or his cousin's wedding.

—What's this about? Steve asks.

—Your daughter.

—Are you serious?

—Why do you say that? Do you know where she is?

—Yeah. You the school resource officer? This seems a little overly—

—Where is she?

—Here. She's taking one day off school. One little day. She's a great student. Deserves a day off with Dad occasionally. I have the right to do this, you know. I haven't done anything

69

wrong.

Relief washes over Will so forcefully, he takes a step back.

—Get her for me. I need to see her. Talk to her. Confirm she's okay.

—She's watching a movie. She's not just okay. She's great. Can't this wait?

—Afraid it can't. Won't take but a minute.

—Okay. I'll get her.

When he leaves, Will pulls out his phone. His first call is to Taylor. His second is to the sheriff. He says the same thing to both of them.

—She's okay. She's in Panama City with her dad, watching a movie.

When Taylor clicks off the call, she says two words to Marc.

—Must paint.

—Who was that? Did they find her?

He follows as she makes her way to her studio.

—What'd they say? Is she okay?

—She's with Steve. At Shangri-La. Seeing a movie. That's all I know. And I've got all these questions and feelings . . . and I need to paint.

She marches to the back of the house, up the stairs, and into her studio.

Creaking wood floors.

Canvases.

Easels.

Separation Anxiety

Pungent odor of paint.

Dust particles drifting in shafts of perfect light.

Located on the second story and taking up the entire back half of the floor, Taylor's studio is the best room in the lodge. The large, open space is filled with the soft, warm diffused light of late afternoon. Enormous windows on the three exterior walls along with the glass skylights overhead ensure the naturally lit loft provides the artist with the best illumination possible for the longest possible time.

Though there's a vast openness to the room, there's clutter too. Every corner is filled with tables, tubes, pallets, and brushes of every size, every wall supports large, leaning canvases of her recent work—even the center is an obstacle course of paint-speckled easels, chairs, drop cloths, and wooden crates.

Within seconds of being in her space, she is removing her clothes, dropping them in a heap on the hardwood floor. Positioning herself in front of the enormous mirror and easel, she places her cell phone on the high chair beside her. It's the first time she's released it since the call from the school came.

Though all her works are self-portraits of a type, only recently has she embarked on a series of actual, literal paintings of her own figure.

For weeks now, she has spent hours standing in the small forty-five-degree angle at the intersection of mirror and canvas, fully nude, fully engaged with her body once again.

Her body is a work of art, her flesh the medium for expression over the years. Building on the brutal zipper-like scar running nearly the full length of her torso, she has burned and carved a stunning, disquieting mixed-media masterpiece into her own exquisite body.

He recalls his utter amazement when she disrobed before him the first time.

71

The intricate and infinitely fascinating sculpture and painting the canvas of her flesh holds is unlike anything he's ever seen. Peerless. Matchless. Secreted away from the world until now.

Both artist and art object, Taylor transformed her scar-torn and traumatized body, through scarification and tattooing, into something ancient and sacred.

The body modification involved in scarification is so severe, requires so much time, involves so much pain, it's virtually unheard of that someone would do it to themselves—especially when the work is as ambitious and abstruse as that adorning Taylor's torso.

On each side of the puffy pink protuberant line down the center of her and reaching unseen to her core, the cut that forever marks the before and after of togetherness and separateness, oneness and aloneness, life and death, are twin girls—Trevor and Taylor—arms extended, reaching for one another, nearly but not quite able to cross the seemingly narrow but actually infinite gulf of scar dividing them.

The little girl on the left, who he assumes is Trevor but has never asked, is being yanked away by vines wrapped around her feet and extending over to and up Taylor's left side where they become a series of twin-like concentric objects and symbols being ripped apart, pried away from one another. Bending. Breaking. Bursting.

Watching her work, he realizes he's seeing an artist paint a self-portrait of a self-portrait she already painted and carved into her own skin.

She is brilliant and disturbed, gifted and gorgeous, shy and traumatized, vulnerable and volatile.

What the fuck am I doing with her? How did this ever happen?

Their first date had been the night of their first meeting.

Separation Anxiety

Leaving the Visual Arts Center in downtown Panama City, they stumbled over to the Place, finding each other far more intoxicating than the reception wine.

Drinks at the Place.

Music.

Quick smoke out back.

More drinks.

Admissions.

Confessions.

Her: I don't believe in love.

Him: I believe in love more than anything else.

More drinks.

Leaving the crowd.

Staggering down Harrison to the Fiesta, her more drunk than him.

Alone.

More drinks at a booth in the lounge.

Him: I'll be your lover or your friend.

Her: How about both?

Him: Friends make the best lovers.

Her: You sure you're not gay?

Him: I seem gay?

Her: You seem too good to be true. We're in a gay bar.

Him: It's the best bar in town. Always has been.

Her: No judgment. I'm bisexual.

Him: I'm not gay.

Courtyard kiss.

Red brick enclosed. Swaying palms lit from beneath by

pink and green spots. New Orleans-style patio. Wrought iron gate, a peek out at abandoned downtown, empty Harrison Avenue. Fountain. Dance music drifting out from inside. Other lovers exploring each other in the sexy darkness. Small wire mesh table.

Her: I think you should kiss me.

Him: Really?

Her: I think you should.

He leans in and kisses her, the cold, refreshing mix of booze and lime on her lips and tongue.

He pulls back and looks at her.

Opening her eyes slowly, breathlessly, she smiles.

Taking her face in his hands, he kisses her again. Deeper. Harder. Longer.

Wobbling down Grace Avenue, her trashed, him steadying her, them halting often.

Laughing.

Kissing.

Laughing.

Hugging.

Laughing.

Holding.

Laughing.

He loves making her laugh, loves that she gets and appreciates his wit, his humor, his intelligence.

Fully out of her fortress, she tells him story after story, experience after experience, revealing herself to him. There's no mention of childhood, of death, of trauma, of court battles and custody cases, but she appears to be telling him everything else.

You stupid son of a bitch.

Will realizes his mistake the moment he sees Steve Summers at the far end of the hallway, a little girl at his side.

How could he make such a rookie blunder?

He should've asked if he had more than one daughter, should have inquired about Shelby by name.

Always verify. Confirm. Don't get in too big a hurry.

How could I have—

It's not the dumbest thing you've ever done.

No, that would be calling her mom and telling her.

—Who's this? Will asks when he reaches Steve and the little girl.

The movie manger looks confused.

—My daughter. Santana. What's going on?

—I'm looking for Shelby. Have you seen or spoken with Shelby?

—No. Why? What's going on?

Without seeming conscious of it, he reaches down and takes his daughter—the one present—by the hand. She is small and her tiny hand vanishes into his.

—What's wrong, Daddy? Santana asks, gazing up at him, her small, roundish face scrunched up.

She looks to be about seven or eight, which means she was probably conceived not long after Savannah disappeared. Cute outfit, curled hair in a matching bow, Santana appears to be a very cared-for little girl.

An elderly man emerges from theater seven, the movie's soundtrack spilling out of the open door behind him, and spotting Steve, walks over.

—You work here?

—Yes, sir. What can I do for you?

—It's freezing in there. My wife's very cold. And someone brought a retarded child who keeps blurting out at the screen.

—I'll see what I can do.

—Please hurry. It's ruining the movie for her.

—Yes, sir.

The man turns and shuffles back into the theater.

—You have no idea where she is? Will asks.

—None. What's this about? Tell me what's—

—How long's it been since you talked to her?

He shrugs.

—I'm not sure, he says. A while.

—Why would her car be at your house?

—Is it? It wasn't when I left for work. I'll call my wife. Maybe—

—Your camp. On the river.

—I didn't know it was. I haven't been there in at least a month—probably more. Tell me what's going on?

—I fucked up, boss, Will says to Keith.

He's on his cell, making his way out of Shangri-La.

—Oh yeah? How's that?

—Wasn't her. Taylor's ex-husband has a new family and a new daughter. The little girl is skipping school—here with him today to watch a movie and hang out with Dad.

—What's he say about Shelby?

—Says he hasn't seen her in a month or more. Has no idea where she is or why she'd leave her car at his camp. Says he wouldn't be surprised if she was on the river with friends. Drinking beer. Sharing a joint. Skinny dipping.

—I've still got Cleve riding up and down the river looking for her—checking houseboats, hangouts, Sand Mountain. Crime Scene's almost finished processing the car. Should know something soon.

—I haven't gotten to my biggest fuckup yet, Will says.

—No?

—No. I called Taylor and told her Shelby was here with her dad right after I called you.

The truth is, he had called her first, but he couldn't bring himself to admit that.

—She thinks Shelby is safe and sound, he continues, that we have her back and—

—Okay.

—I'm sorry, Sheriff. I truly am.

—You just wanted to give her the good news.

—I did. It's true, but I also wanted to be the one to do it.

—Understandable. It's your case.

—Still?

—I know, but—

—No, Will says. I'm asking if it's still my case.

—Oh. Yeah. It is. For a little while longer at least.

—Oh.

—No, I just mean it's about time for CART. Don't you think?

—Reckon I do.

—Head on back over here. I'll call Taylor and let her know.

—No, I'm the one who—

—I got it, he says. It should come from me.

When Taylor ends the call with Keith, she is visibly upset, but only in the most subtle of ways—ways only someone like Marc, who observes and studies the nuance of her every twitch and tick, every expression and eye movement, could detect.

As volatile as anyone he's ever known, and far more so than anyone he's ever been in a relationship with, Taylor often retreats, withdraws, withholds—usually following times of intense intimacy, but this is different.

What concerns him most is her utter and complete calm.

Stepping over to the door, she carefully places her phone on the floor of the entryway, then walks back into the room, grabs a length of galvanized pipe from the far corner, and begins to smash both her supplies and the art she has made with them.

Broken boards.

Splintered and snapped antique easels that had belonged to her grandfather.

Ripped canvases.

Scattered brushes.

Splattered paints.

Shattered glass.

As Marc grabs her, attempting to subdue her without getting knocked unconscious, her final reckless, violent act is to sling the pipe at the large, full-length mirror she's been using to paint herself.

The angry image of the nude, scared artist, paint-smeared and bleeding, cracked, fractured, and fragmented. Shelby's disturbed mom revealed in splintered shards, as the last of the rolling and collapsing objects come to rest amidst dripping paint thinner and the utter silence bursts of unexpected violence bring.

As Keith pulls away from the landing, leaving behind Shelby's now processed car, he gets a call from Paige Hill, Tupelo High's SRO.

—We are still looking for Julian Flax, aren't we?

—Yeah. Why?

—Thought his whereabouts was some big mystery. Whole department's looking for him.

It had been Keith who appointed Paige to the position of school resource officer, and he's been pleased with her work, but she's a bit dramatic—one reason he thought she'd fit in with the teens and tweens.

—Something like that. Why?

—'Cause, he's right here. Plain as day.

—Where is here?

—The Courts. Playin' a pickup game.

—On my way. Shelby Summers with him?

—Don't see her.

—Keep an eye out.

—You want me to grab him?

—Nah. Just watch him 'til I get there. Unless he tries to leave.

—And then?

—Detain him.

—You got it, boss.

The Courts is a chain-link-enclosed asphalt lot with eight basketball goals—two on each side—a few random aluminum bleachers, a couple of ill-placed streetlamps, and a perpetual pickup game.

Julian and one other white kid are involved in a three-on-three half-court game with four much taller black guys—one of three games being played.

Keith walks onto the court in the middle of the game.

The action stops.

—Sorry to interrupt guys, he says. Just need to talk to Julian. It's important.

—Yes, sir, one of the boys says.

—Sure thing, Sheriff.

Julian doesn't say anything.

The tallest kid, and the one who appears to be the most alpha of all the males, looks over at the nearest set of bleachers where other guys are waiting a turn—occupying themselves with talking to girls, listening to iPods, fiddling with their phones, playing their handhelds.

—Ryan, he yells. Come in for Jules.

—This can't wait? Julian says. I really gotta stop in the middle of my game?

—Afraid so.

—I'm back in next game, he says to the alpha who picked his replacement.

—Shee-it, a small kid with a do-rag says. Next time yo ass be playin' it be in jail.

—What's going on? Keith asks.

—Whatcha mean?

They are standing against the fence away from everyone else, Keith looking at Julian, Julian watching the games.

—We've been looking for you.

—Why?

—Where have you been?

—Here.

—How long?

He shrugs.

—Where were you before you came here? Keith asks.

—Just around. Why?

—Why didn't you go to school?

—Just took a personal day.

Keith smiles and nods appreciatively.

—A personal day?

—Yeah. You know. Had the day off work, so . . .

—You hang out with Shelby?

He shakes his head.

—Just me.

—What's she up to today? Keith asks, trying to sound nonchalant.

Julian shrugs.

—No idea.

—Where is she?

He shrugs again.

—I know everybody's different, Keith says, but I tend to keep up with my girlfriends.

Julian doesn't respond.

—She is your girlfriend, isn't she?

—Was.

—Not anymore? What happened?

—We broke up.

—When?

He shrugs again.

—Had to be recently.

—Guess.

—This before or after you bought her an engagement ring?

Julian spins around toward Keith, then catches himself.

—How'd you know?

—My job to know shit.

—After.

—Where is she?

—Told you. Have no idea.

—It's real important that we find her. You need to tell me what you know—no matter what it is.

—Don't know anything. Haven't seen her.

—If something happened, if you did something, I can help, but you've got to tell me now.

—Give me a lie detector test. I have no idea where she is.

—The fuck do we do now? Keith asks.

Will shrugs.

They're leaning against the front of Keith's car at the Courts, watching Julian, who has rejoined the game.

—We got nothing, he continues. Car's clean. No sign of foul play. Boyfriend's back. She's obviously not with him.

—Doesn't mean she wasn't, Will says.

—No it doesn't. Says we can hook him up to the machine. Seems like he's telling the truth, but . . .

—What?

—Not sure. Don't think it's the whole truth.

—We gonna have another go at him? Will asks.

—Think we have to. Gotta be careful. Juvenile and all. Hasn't done anything but skip school.

—We can bring in his mom.

Keith nods.

They are quiet a moment, looking at the games before them, but not watching them.

—What do we do? Keith asks. We got nothing.

—We've eliminated a few possibilities maybe.

—Maybe, Keith says. And maybe all we've done is waste some precious time.

—Maybe.

—Time to call in CART, you think?

—Be dark soon.

—Fuck, Keith says. I should've moved faster.

—Think you've done everything just right. Now we take

the next step. Ramp it up. Begin a search. Call in CART.

—And if she's dead because we didn't do it sooner? Keith asks.

—Then we still did the best we could. And that's the job.

Keith nods contemplatively.

—And that's the job, he says. That's the job.

People say life goes on, but it doesn't.

Sure, the world keeps revolving, people keep rushing around, but not Marc. Not Taylor.

For them, full stop.

Ordinarily, he'd be writing right now, Taylor, painting, but there's nothing ordinary about this.

Life isn't going on. Not for them.

They breathe. Their hearts beat. But is this life? There is no normalcy. No mundane. No routine.

Beside him on the floor, beneath his arm, in the destruction and chaos of the studio, Taylor is calmer now, though continuing to catch her breath and sniffle from the hysterical cry following the ravaging of her art and creative environment.

How closely creation and destruction are sometimes, he thinks. As if some of the same impulses power both, one the shadow of the other. Destruction is so easy compared to creation, so blunt, so benighted, but there's a connection, a symbiosis he'd have to dig into another time.

Everything has to wait for another time—a time, if one can ever again exist for them, when life goes on.

—We'll have to take care of her animals, Taylor says.

—Huh?

—Shelby's little hospital. We'll have to take—

—She'll be back to care for them herself.

In the backyard, in cages down by the river, wild, wounded animals Shelby has rescued rest and recuperate, mend and recover. Part of Shelby's environmental activism, one of many things she does, and because of her growing reputation, she routinely receives calls from up to fifty miles away from people who've encountered the hurt and helpless, the dying and endangered.

—I mean because of the storm. We'll have to move them inside.

—I'll take care of it, he says, thinking in some ways life does go on—even for them.

—Tonight?

—In the morning. Storm won't hit for a while— probably tomorrow afternoon.

—I don't want anything to happen to them. She's worked so hard to heal them.

—I won't let anything happen to them, he says. When she gets back, she'll be so impressed she'll probably put me in permanent charge of them.

—You are good at it, she says. I've often thought you captured me the way you do a wounded wild thing.

—Really? How's that?

—Grab it and hold it firmly, but loosely. Carefully. Let it feel your heart beat. Breathe together. Be still, be patient, gain trust.

He smiles. It may be the nicest thing she's ever said to him.

—You find me irresistible?

—Of course, you idiot. Isn't it obvious?

—What're you doing? Daniel asks.

He has just walked into what will be the guestroom to find Sam searching through the boxes.

—Looking for my box of broken hearts, she says.

—Old love letters?

Sam smiles, the corners of her eyes crinkling.

—Unsolved cases.

—Oh. Sorry.

Having recently moved back to Tallahassee, their new-to-them home, an old two-story red brick and hardwood floor Southern classic atop a hill on Briarcliff, is a work in progress, but most of the remaining boxes are confined to this upstairs back bedroom with a window overlooking the oak-canopied backyard.

—What? she says, continuing to be preoccupied with looking through the boxes. No, it's fine. I have broken a lot of hearts in my day.

He smiles.

The unlikely couple—him a professor of religion and philosophy, her an agent with the Florida Department of Law Enforcement—recently reunited by, of all things, a serial killer, are far more in love and happier than either thought they could ever be.

They had first met when he was consulting with FDLE on a series of ritual murders in Miami, but were both originally from North Florida and found each other again after returning home.

Nearly all the boxes left have Daniel Davis written on

them and contain books from his excessive, according to Sam, library, but there are a handful that read Samantha Michaels on them, and at least one of those contains the files she's searching for.

Daniel joins Sam in lifting boxes and looking around.

—If I had the chance to do one case over again, what would it be? she asks.

—That's easy. Savannah Summers. Why?

—I get to.

—Huh?

—I'm on the Child Abduction Response Team being called in to investigate the disappearance of her sister.

—Her sister?

—Yeah. Shelby. Eight years after Savannah was taken, her twin sister Shelby is missing.

In the short time Daniel and Sam have been together, he's seen her open and study the Savannah Summers file at least three times.

—I can't believe it, he says.

—I know.

—Their poor mother.

He shakes his head and shudders as he continues to look.

—I haven't told you about her, have I? she asks.

—Don't think so.

—The artist, Taylor Sean. You familiar with her work?

—Vaguely.

—What about her story?

—Not as far as I know, he says.

—It's very famous—though most people don't know it's
her because she changed her last name. She was part of a set of
conjoined twins.

—Taylor and Trevor Young? he says, the excitement in
his voice apparent.

—Yeah. How'd you—

—You kidding? Their story is in one of the philosophy
textbooks I use. The author uses it as an example of
utilitarianism.

The children of Ron and Rebecca Young, Taylor
and Trevor were conjoined twin girls connected at the
lower abdomen. Medical experts said that if the two weren't
separated, they'd both die, but if they underwent the difficult
and dangerous operation, Taylor would live and Trevor would
die. What to do? Perform the operation to save Taylor and kill
Trevor or take no action and allow both girls to die? Devout
Catholics, Ron and Rebecca opted not to have the surgery,
stating they couldn't go against God's law and kill their daughter,
Trevor. Instead, they put their girls in God's hands, trusting his
perfect will.

But this isn't the end of the story.

Dr. D. Kelly David, a noted expert on conjoined twins
separation, petitioned the court and in a case that went all the
way to the Florida Supreme Court, won the right to override the
parents' wishes and separate the girls.

Taylor Sean, who grew up as Taylor Young, did so with
enormous guilt over surviving when her sister didn't and with
the certain knowledge that her parents had wanted her dead.

—Utilitarianism? Sam asks.

—The philosophical position that posits when faced
with a moral decision, the right thing to do is maximize
happiness.

—As in it's better for one twin to die than both.

—Exactly.

—Isn't it obvious? she asks.

He shrugs.

—If both twins are recognizably human, then both have the same fundamental rights—namely to life and justice, then Taylor doesn't have more rights than Trevor. They have equal rights under the law. The separation denied Trevor both of these rights. If your sister were dying and needed a new heart, should anyone be able to tell you that you had to give her yours?

—No, but that's different.

—Sure, but it makes the point.

—How could parents wish both their children to die instead of saving one?

—They're radical pro-lifers. They believed it was murder. They said there are no exceptions to thou shalt not kill, that the operation transgressed not only God's law, but that of our society. That it is never permissible to kill—even to save an innocent life. It's why they're against abortion even if the life of the mother is in jeopardy.

—Here it is, she says, lifting a box from the back corner.

—All that wasn't enough—she had a daughter get abducted too?

Sam nods.

—Eight years ago. She had twins of her own—not conjoined—and walking from the bus to their house on a short dirt road somehow Savannah was taken with Shelby right there.

—And now eight years later, Shelby's been taken?

—Not sure, but she is missing, which gives me the chance to revisit Savannah's disappearance as I look for Shelby. Who knows? They may be connected.

—Things're about to get real—real fast, Will says.

Julian doesn't respond.

—Do you know what CART is? Keith asks.

When Julian still doesn't say anything, his mom turns to him. She is seated beside him across the small table from the sheriff and deputy.

—Son, the sheriff asked you a question.

—No, sir. I don't.

Sullen. Hunched. Sulking. Seething. The small interview room at the sheriff's department is filled with the negative energy emanating off Julian.

He feeling guilty? Will wonders. Know he's in trouble? Or just mad he's missing the game? With teenage boys you never know.

—Well, it's kind of a big deal, Keith says.

—Stands for Child Abduction Response Team, Will says.

—If Shelby's really missing, I'll do whatever it takes to find her, Keith says. You should know that.

—The team is made up of members from several different agencies, Will says. We'll have cops of all kinds— FDLE, police, correctional and probation officers, deputies. They've all been specially trained, and will come from all over to help in the search. It exists because most departments don't have the manpower to have a specially trained team of their own.

—I make the call and they're here, Keith says. This all gets real—real fast.

Will smiles. Did he pick up the expression from Keith or was it the other way around? He can't remember. How many other words, sayings, mannerisms, and traits had they unwittingly taken from one another?

—It becomes public, Keith is saying. There'll be a lot of attention. It's a whole other level. That's not something I want to do if I can avoid it. And we think you can help us keep from having to do it.

—Help us, Will says. Tell us where she is.

—Do you know? Julia Flax asks her son.

He shakes his head.

—We think you do.

—Why? Julia asks, turning back to face Keith. Why do you think that?

—Will, he says.

Will tells her.

—You two ran off together? she asks. Eloped?

—No, ma'am. We broke up. I haven't seen her today. I swear to God.

—Did she change her mind? Will asks. Is that it? Maybe she made you mad and . . . Anyone would understand that. You didn't mean to hurt her, but . . . it happens all the time. We've all lost our tempers. Made mistakes.

—Takes a man to stand up and own them, Keith adds.

—Julian, his mom says. Look at me. Did something happen? What are you not telling us?

—Mama, I swear on your life I haven't even seen her today.

—That's good enough for me, she says. He wouldn't swear on my life if he were lying. Call your CART.

—I already have, Keith says, but I just feel like there's some things you're not telling us. It's not too late to tell us the truth.

—If she's in trouble and you didn't do all you could to help us find her, Will says, to help her . . . You could get in a lot of trouble. Maybe even go to jail.

—Do you know where she is? Keith asks. We'll help you—no matter what's happened. We'll take care of you. We've just got to find her and take care of her too.

—I swear I haven't seen her. I swear I don't know where she is. I'll take a lie detector test. I'm telling the truth.

—Test him, Julia says. He's telling the truth. No doubt in my mind.

White.

Plush.

Large.

Lacey.

Immaculate.

Shelby's bedroom is a spotless, colorless, seemingly soulless fortress of solitude and whiteness.

White carpet. White drapes. White linen, atop of which are white polar bears and poodles. White dresser and vanity. White laptop on a white desk.

—Any idea what her password is?

Taylor sits in a white chair, Shelby's laptop open on the desk in front of her.

Marc shakes his head.

—No idea. What're you doing?

—Gonna check her computer.

He nods, realizing it's a violation that wouldn't even occur to her under any other circumstance.

Separation Anxiety

Standing in the white room, Marc is struck again by just how pathologically white it really is. Is this Taylor's doing or Shelby's? If Shelby's, is she making a statement about her overly pristine, overprotected, hermetically sealed existence?

But perhaps he's being too harsh. It's not as if she has no color in her life. She has both a rec room and an art studio of her own, full of color and life and vibrancy. Still, her bedroom is always so perfect, so something from a Hollywood set or out of an interior design catalog. It means something.

No wonder she ran.

Or if she didn't, why didn't she?

Savannah. Has to be. She submits to her mother's insanity and won't let herself really live because of what happened to Savannah, because of what it would do to Taylor if something happened to her.

—What have you tried? he asks.

—Our zip code, her birthday, variations of pet names over the years. It's five characters.

He thinks about it.

What's she into?

He can't come up with much, and it hurts his heart that this sweet, smart, sad, artistic kid he's been getting to know is still such a mystery to him.

Is she not into much or do I really not know her that well?

—Favorite book? Character? TV show? Movie? Band? he offers.

She tries a few. Comes up empty.

Don't just think about Shelby, he tells himself. What are teenage girls into?

One word. Boys.

—Try Jules, he says.

She does. And she's in.

—I am right to try this? she asks. I've got do something—besides destroy another room.

He nods and gives her a small smile.

—She'll understand, he says.

She nods, and begins her search in earnest.

Regardless of its ultimate fruitfulness, he's grateful she has something to occupy her.

As she clicks and scrolls and navigates, he thinks about how responsible he feels for her. And not just now, not just during a serious crisis like a missing child, but all the time. At differing times, when it looked like their relatively new relationship was going to be stillborn or die in infancy, she had been devastated, utterly and completely shattered, unable to function, feeling the full futility of what she was convinced was going to be her future—a life lived alone. Marc was her best last hope of making it work with a man, and she knew it. This often led to serious contemplations of suicide.

How can he not feel responsible for her? How can a novelist, an empathetic man whose life is spent channeling the emotions and experiences of others, not be distraught when she's distraught, hopeless when she's hopeless? How can he not feel as if he would die if anything he did in any way led her to kill herself?

—Anything? he asks.

She shakes her head.

—Oh my God.

—What is it?

—She's deleted everything.

—Everything?

—Everything. All documents, all communications—email, IMs, webmail—even her journal.

He steps over and looks for himself—and confirms that all Shelby's data is missing.

—Why would she erase everything? she asks.

—To hide something, he says.

—What?

He shrugs.

—No idea.

—From me?

He doesn't answer, and they fall silent.

And then, out of the vacuousness, a truly terrifying thought surfaces— What if it wasn't Shelby at all, but her abductor?

Lanier Landing.

Late afternoon.

Sinking sun.

Keith and Will stand not far from Shelby's car, watching as Keisha Bowers pulls up in the white DOC truck and parks at the end of the short driveway.

From inside the truck comes the squawk of amplified ten-code transmissions from Potter Correctional Institution, while on the back, bloodhounds in dog boxes pace and turn and whimper in anticipation.

—Can't help but think we should've done this a lot sooner, Keith says.

—We haven't wasted a single second, Will says. We've done everything we could as fast as we could.

Leaving the truck running, Keisha climbs out and marches toward the two men.

In black boots, fatigues, and a short sleeve prison polo, the thick, square, flat-chested woman looks more like a man than most of the male correctional officers at PCI, her corrections ball cap and large dark shades adding to the effect.

Her caramel and cinnamon skin, visible only on her face, neck, and arms, glistens beneath a thick sheen of sweat, and she wipes her face often, steepling her fingers over her nose, sliding down and over, then drying them on her sleeves.

—Sheriff, she says. Will.

They nod at her.

—Thanks for coming, Keith says.

—This the little Summers girl's car?

—Uh huh, Will says.

—She the last one to drive it?

—Not sure. No way to know for sure.

—Best guess? she says.

—We really have no idea, Keisha, Keith says. Why?

—Gotta obtain her scent. Took a couple a scent articles from her house—pillowcase and a shirt she wore yesterday, but if she was the last one to drive the car, I'd swab the steering wheel and seat for the freshest trace.

—Can you use both? Will asks. What happens if it's two different scents?

—If I had the one here that I don't want them following for a scent discretion that'd be fine, but since I don't they wouldn't know which one to follow.

Ten years the junior of the two men, Keisha had worked with them at the sheriff's department before becoming the K-9 lieutenant at PCI. Tough, with no tolerance for foolishness,

Keisha, who had practically raised herself, had the respect and good regard of everyone who knew her—and their appreciation for leading Tupelo High's softball team to a state championship.

She scans the area, taking in the surroundings, the terrain.

—If she got in a boat, I can't help you, she says, but if she went in the water, I can probably figure where she came out—if she came out. Problem is, moving water carries the scent away, so I'll have to work to keep 'em on the real one. If she's in the swamps, we'll find her, but my dogs can only go about two miles before I switch 'em out—something I usually do on dirt roads or loggin' trails. Have someone drive my truck ahead and switch 'em when we reach it. But ain't no roads out there.

They follow her gaze across the wide river to the thick, green swamp on the other side.

—Goddamn, I hope she's not in there, Keith says.

—Amen to that, Will says, shaking his head.

—I'ma find her wherever she is, Keisha says. Bet on that.

As Taylor continues to search futilely through Shelby's empty computer, Marc slips into Shelby's studio, her real room, and looks around.

Opposite the white room in every way, Shelby's den is a chaotic explosion of color, an expression of an idiosyncratic soul. Intelligent. Interesting. Irreverent.

If she's left any message behind, this is where it will be.

The smallish room has a leather loveseat on one wall, a home theater system with a huge wall-mounted TV on another, and built-in bookshelves on the remaining two with far more books than they were designed to hold. Stacked. Packed.

Crammed. Stuffed.

In between and around and on top of everything are exquisite environmental and wildlife posters, printouts, and framed photographs. Among them, the slogans she's now known for—some on bumper stickers and T-shirts, others actually angrily scrawled by hand.

Spill Cum, Not Blood.

No Drill, No Spill.

Every time history repeats itself, the price goes up.

WWND? What Would Nature Do?

Ignore it and it WILL all go away.

Can you hear that Eco?

Love Your Mother!

Where do you think the environment is?

This is the real Shelby. Passionate hippie-chick environmentalist. Fire-breathing. Fuck the man and mouth-breathing fundamentalists.

Sinking into the soft, cool leather sofa, he studies the room, taking her in through it.

The sweet smell of candles and incense lingers in the air, every single fragrance, object, experience in the room an expression of who she is.

Mixed in among it all is *Last Night in the Woods* by Remington James, a stunning collection of North Florida photography. Each incredible image carefully and loving matted and framed and affixed to the walls.

Incandescent.

Luminous.

Radiant rain.

Arcing sparks.

Separation Anxiety

Falling drops of fire.

Field of fireflies.

Black and white.

High contrast.

Palmettos, hanging vines, fallen trees, untouched undergrowth, unspoiled woodlands.

Bounding. Loping. Barreling.

Black as nothingness.

Buckskin muzzle bursting out of a forest of fur, chest ablaze.

Shy eyes.

Florida black bears.

Looking up from a small slough, rivulets of water around large, sharp teeth, dripping, suspended in midair.

Sleek.

Dark, tawny coat.

Flattened forehead, prominent nose.

Spotted cub.

Crouching.

Red tongue lapping dark water.

Playful cub pouncing about.

The elusive and endangered Florida panther.

The collection is extraordinary and he can see why Shelby so reveres Remington James—both for his photography and what he did in the woods to save lives and stop a pack of psychopaths that fateful night a while back.

Glancing toward the shelf to his right, he spots *Last Child in the Woods* by Richard Louv, and retrieves it, then returns to his seat. Flipping through the well-worn paperback, he smiles at the many dog-eared pages and underlined passages. When he reads the subtitle, Saving Our Children from Nature-Deficit Disorder, he realizes that's something she's mostly done herself.

She's been saving herself in so many ways for so long. Not that Taylor's been a bad mom, but her own not inconsiderable deficits, not to mention the absence of a dad, have forced Shelby to at times parent herself.

Unbidden, unwelcome, he thinks he may never see her again, and it's unbearable.

Standing quickly to return the book to the shelf, getting lightheaded and blinking back tears as he does, he notices, through the gap of the missing volume, something on the shelf behind the row of books.

It turns out to be instructions for cleaning oil off pelicans printed from an environmental Web site, and most likely unintentionally slipped behind the books, but it gives him an idea, and he begins to search the shelves.

Within a few minutes, his violation of Shelby's privacy nets an assortment of pictures, mementos, date memorabilia—movie ticket stubs, photo booth strips, a couple of concert tickets and programs—her vibrator, which made him regret even more having to do what he is doing, and two items that actually hold promise of helping. A small blue netbook computer and a New English Dictionary book safe.

He starts with the netbook.

Unlike her laptop, it has no password protection, so he's inside looking around in moments, but it appears to be relatively new and has only the beginnings of a poem about the Apalachicola River and an impassioned essay on protecting North Florida in general and the Gulf and Apalachicola Bay in particular.

As ever, he is challenged and convicted by her dedication and tirelessness, and feels a mixture of admiration and guilt.

I've got to do more. Hell, just help her more. I will. As soon as she's back, I'll help her. It'd give me a chance to make a difference and us more time together. Please come home, angel. Please.

Inside the book safe, which he is able to open because he searched all the shelves—the safe itself was beside real dictionaries and writing books, while the key was hidden behind a teenage vampire series—he finds condoms, cash, two joints in a pill bottle, and a jump drive in the shape of an oak leaf.

Inserting the drive into the computer, he finds a file titled Journal.

Rejoining Taylor in Shelby's room, he shows it to her.

—What is it? she asks. Her journal?

—Not just. Everything she wiped off her laptop, she pasted in this one file. She must've done it fast too. It's a mess. Out of sequence. Out of context. But it looks to be everything—all her communications. Email, IMs, webmail, texts. I think her journal entries are still there too.

—You haven't read it? she asks.

—No.

—I can't. You'll have to.

—Me?

—I can't violate her privacy like that.

—And I can?

—It's different if it's you. She'll understand. It's what you said.

He wonders if she wants him to read it because he's expendable, because his days in their lives are numbered anyway.

—At least skim it, she says. See if anything in it might tell us where she is and who has her. Sit here. I need to pace.

She stands and he sits, and as he begins to examine the

secret confessions of the teenage girl increasingly feeling like his daughter, she starts to pace around the room behind him as promised.

If you're reading this, you're a fucking creep. I mean it. This is private. Okay, sure, if it was truly private I wouldn't be writing it down, and who knows, I might publish this one day, but that's different, and you know it. Put my journal down and back away slowly you mental rapist motherfucker!!!!!!!!

Could my mom be any more ridiculous? I mean, god to the damn. I know she's got serious childhood trauma, but why does she keep trying to make mine so traumatic too? I am so sick and tired of living in Taylor Sean Penitentiary. Will I EVER get paroled? I feel like the biggest douche on the little blue dot for even thinking it, but was Savannah's early release a blessing? Is she the lucky one? Shit. Now I do feel like a fist full of douches. Makes me wonder again. How did it happen with me right there? Who took her and why? Why her and not me? Why not both of us? What's wrong with me? Did I really just ask that—why wasn't I abducted? Really? REALLY? What the fuck is wrong with me? Of course I'm the lucky one. I'm sorry. Help me be better and more grateful and not such a lamo loser. Who was that directed to? Whoever's listening!

Real. Random. Raw.

He's glad Taylor's not reading it.

As he scrolls through Shelby's rants, he gains an even greater appreciation for and admiration of her. She's pouring out, processing, feeling, experiencing, really working through things. It reminds him of why he writes, of just how therapeutic it really is.

There are no dates, no way to tell context or relation to anything else, and he's truly trying to skim, to do as little violation as possible—all of which makes it all the more difficult to decipher.

He stops at some email exchanges with Julian she's pasted into her journal. Having just inserted the text from the bodies of the messages, there's no way to know when they were sent, but they seem old—going all the way back to when they first started dating, even though they appear late in the relative order of entries.

What're you doing messing around with me? You lose a bet? Seriously, I want to know your intentions young man! :-) If you're just fucking around, do it with someone else. Okay? No harm. No foul. Stop now. Let's not go down this path if you're not sure (and I mean certain) you want it. What's the point? You know? Why start something we're not going to finish? Why put ourselves through the hassle? I think we could be great friends. Let's not fuck that up. Cool? Agree? Good.

WTF? I'm not messing with you. You know my intentions. I'm very serious about this, want to see where it goes. I thought you did too. I'm certain. Have you changed your mind? Where's this coming from? Tell me. I don't understand.

McKenzie told Santana you were still hung up on Rylee. Just using me since you couldn't have her. That I'm either rebound girl or worse that you're just trying to see if you can get me to give it up. I can answer that. No. You can't. I won't be rebound bitch. And I won't be just some fuck holes.

Whoa. Wait just a second. Simmer down there, sister girl. I'm gonna call you so we can talk. This is crazy. Why won't you answer my calls? This would be a lot easier to talk about in person.

I'm too mad to talk.

McKenzie asked me out. I said no. That's why she said that shit. I broke up with Rylee. She didn't break up with me. I could have her back if I wanted, but I don't. I want you. You're not a rebound or just someone to fuck. And I've never given you any reason to think I thought you were. Are you dooming us before we really begin? How about a little trust? You keep telling me you're not like other girls. Well, guess what? I'm not like other guys. Get over yourself and stop listening to jealous skanks.

Did you get Rylee hooked on pot?

No, it was crack.

I'm being serious.

No you're not. No, I didn't get her hooked on anything. We went out nearly a year and in all that time, we smoked two joints that SHE got from her brother. NOT me. And before you ask, no, I never hit her. I've never hit anyone. And I'd never hit a girl. NOT EVER. Not even fucking lying loser McKenzie Woodrell.

WhoDey is playing at the Moon. Wanna go?

Hells yeah. Not sure I can manage a jailbreak. Warden Taylor is tightening down even more (I know, I know. I didn't think it was possible either), but I'll try. Love them. Want to hear them with you. They rock out with their cocks out.

Know how much you like that! :-)

Once and for all. I'M READY!!!!!!!!!!!!!!!

You sure?

If you ask me again (and I mean this), my first time will be with someone else.

Separation Anxiety

I love you.

Love you more.

Not possible.

You calling me a liar?

My computer's acting funny. I'm gonna get a new one. I'm so scared of losing our chats and messages that I'm pasting everything into my diary. Texts too. Then making a backup.

Cool.

It is. And it's random too.

Why random?

I'm cutting and pasting as I open them. It's like if you took all the words we've ever said, put them in a bag, shook them up, then dumped them out.

Any patterns emerge?

Yes. We're crazy about each other.

We are?

Yeah! You know how reliable random word patterns are.

You're the cutest most adorable thing EVER!

I wrote a song for you.

You did? You're the best most sweetest boyfriend EVER!

It's true.

How?

With a guitar, a pen, and paper.

I wasn't finished. How did you find the time? You work ALL the

105

time (when you're not in school) and I know I'm cutting into your music time. And I hate it. I feel so guilty. I want to see you all the time, but I know I'm pulling you away from what you need to be doing.

Need? And no you don't.

You do need to! And not just because it's like this amazing pure awesome talent the goddess gave you, but because it makes you happy. I can always tell when you've been playing.

You know what I like playing more than my guitar?

I can guess.

Your amazing body. I love the way you feel in my hands.

I love your hands. And the way you play me.

It's like you were made for me.

I was.

You really believe that?

With all my precious little heart.

:-)

Can't wait for the next concert. I need to be played right now!!!!!!!!!!!!!!! For fuck sake. You're like a drub.

A drub?

Sorry. Drug.

What is a drub? Spell check didn't give a red squiggly. Must be a word.

A blow made by a club. Which works too. Same result. I've lost my mind. You're all I think about, the only person I want to be with—ALL the time. I love you so so so so so so much!

You've given me the best drubbings of my life.

Thought I was your ONLY drubber!

You take shit too literally!

My mom's new boyfriend is pretty cool. Seems like a really nice guy. So what the fuck is he doing with her? I want to tell him to RUN! Leave while you still can! But she's so happy (for her). I haven't seen her like this since—well, ever. I hope it lasts. It's nice to have someone to share the crazy with. He's a pretty good writer too. Haven't told him I want to be a writer. Not sure why exactly. Know he'd be nothing but supportive and encouraging. Is that a show for mum? Seems legit, like he's all authentic and shit.

Are you mad at me?

Why?

You are, aren't you? About what? What'd I do? Listen to me. I take it back. I haven't done anything. What is it? What's going on?

Nothing.

No. Don't do that. Tell me.

I'm not mad at you.

Okay. Then what? Why are you acting all funky.

Don't want to talk about it.

Not giving you a choice.

Just sick of being so goddamn broke all the goddamn time.

I've got money. How much do you need?

I don't want your goddamn money!!!!!!!!!!!

Don't be a dick. The phrase you were searching for is, Thank you for your generous offer, but I couldn't possibly.

That's the fuckin' point. I want to take you places and buy you things and I can't. I don't even have a car. I don't take you out. You take me! It's embarrassing. I'm sick of it.

You want out?

NO! That's not what I'm saying. I'm just pissed off about it.
Sorry. Didn't mean to be a dick.

Don't let it happen again! :-)

Yes, ma'am.

Knife.

Bottle.

Blood.

Taylor sits alone on the floor of the shower stall, the spray of water raining down on her bare back.

Tears trickling.

Glass bottle of vodka just out of the water.

Straight.

Swigs. Then some more.

Scarred body. Moist. Blood and water.

More pulls from the bottle.

Small, sharp knife.

Pressure. Building.

Cuts.

Reliving.

Slide of knife over skin. Tiny, sliver-like slices. Fresh wounds next to old ones.

Release.

Relief.

Recalibration.

As traces of blood crimson-tinge the water sluicing down her body and swirling around the drain.

After swabbing the steering wheel and dashboard of Shelby's car with a sterile gauze pad, Keisha drops it into a large plastic bag and slides the bag up over the bloodhound's snout. Breathing it in, the animal reacts immediately, its entire body responding, alerting, pulling against the lead.

Sealing up the bag, she stows it in one of the large pockets of her fatigues, zips it, and they're off.

—Find, Champ, she says. Find.

From near the car, Champ darts straight for the stairs of the house.

Though on a twenty-foot lead, Keisha has about half of it wrapped around her arm.

—No way she's in that house, Will says. I searched it myself.

Keith nods.

Built on stilts to a level exceeding the historic high-water mark from previous floods, the small wooden house can only be accessed by a set of weak and weathered wooden steps on the side. With no hesitation, Champ climbs them, straining against the lead, pulling Keisha along with him.

Keith and Will remain outside so Champ and Keisha can work, but they don't have to wait long.

Within minutes, Champ is descending the steps two at a time.

—She's not in there, Keisha says. But she has been.

Will and Keith look at each other, quizzical expressions on their faces.

—I'll get Crime Scene back out here to process the house, Keith says, pulling the cell phone from his belt.

When Champ hits the ground, he cuts to the right. Runs about thirty feet. Stops. Turns. Heads back to the left, passing the house and continuing toward the landing some fifty feet.

Will watches from the house, Keith beside him on the phone with the FDLE.

Stopping abruptly, Champ turns and heads back in the direction of the house, Keisha, giving him more lead now, about fifteen feet behind, then suddenly dashes to his left and darts toward the river.

Will steps under the house and into the backyard to watch, Keith joining him when he finishes his call.

Champ runs all the way to the water's edge, stops, sniffs, then takes off again, following the bank downriver.

—That mean she went into the water and her scent was carried downstream? Will asks.

—Not sure what any of this means yet, she says. Never seen anything like it.

—Anything? Taylor asks.

—Nothing direct so far, but I'm just getting started. There's a lot here. Sounds like to me her relationship with Julian is pretty solid. They seem good together.

—Well, look closer. We have a way of attracting assholes.

—Thanks.

—Don't be so sensitive. You know I didn't mean . . . You're the exception that proves the rule.

—I didn't know. I never know with you.

—Now's not the time, Marc. Okay? Save your hostility for when we're not in a crisis.

There are no such times, he thinks, but has the wisdom

and restraint not to say.

—Sorry, she says. I'm just upset. Do you want me to take over?

—No. I got it. You were right to let me do it. And I'm trying not to read too much. It's just hard to know what might be useful.

—Better to read it all than miss something that could help us find her.

He nods.

—Diving back in now.

—That your sweet way of telling me to shut the fuck up? she asks.

—'Tis, he says with a smile.

The wolf waits. The wolf watches.

Some wolves are solitary, sure, but most are not.

He had thought he was, but knows now he is not.

The basic social structure is of course the wolf pack. But the pack is actually, usually, made up of a mated pair and their adult offspring.

That's what the wolf wants. That's what the wolf will have again. A family.

So for now the wolf waits and watches.

I feel like somebody's watching me. It's creeping the fuck out of me. I'm sure it's just my imagination. I'm told I have an overactive one. Is that even possible? Can you be too imaginative? If it is my imagination, why? What's making me make it up? If it's not, who's stalking me? Is it even me? Could be Mom? More likely her. Should tell her. I will if I keep sensing it.

I miss Mother Earth so bad!!!!!!!!!

She taught me so much. Did so much. Did more for the river and swamp than all other environmentalists, government agencies, and groups combined. I'll never be able to do even a fraction of what she did, but if I don't do more, who will? Nobody seems to give much of a damn about anything but themselves and money. Sure as hell don't care about protecting the environment.

I can't do it. Can't do what she did. Not even close.

As much as she taught me, I've got so much to learn. So much I don't know. So much I can't do.

I know. I know. I can hear her voice saying, Just do what you can, honey. All any of us can do. It'll be fine. I promise. You just trust Mother, okay?

I will. I promise. But, God, I miss you so much!

Why does everything have to be so hard? I mean really. I know how lame this sounds, but why can't we do the Rodney and all just get along? Life would be so much better if we'd all just chill the fuck out. And don't get me started on people who are supposed to be in love. How can we be so cruel? How can we let ourselves be treated that way? Why is love so hard to find? So hard to hold? It's like we can be alone and miserable or with someone and a little less miserable. Maybe. Sometimes it's far more miserable. I love Julian. I'm IN love with him (whatever that means) and I've never been so happy and so miserable in my whole life.

Reading this entry by Shelby reminds Marc of a

conversation they had a while back, and he wonders if it was around the same time as when she wrote this.

—You mind if I ask you something? Shelby had said.

—Not at all.

Taylor had just had one of her episodes and stormed out of the room, leaving the two of them sitting in the psychic turbulence of her wake.

—How do you do it?

He knows she means his relationship with her mom, but doesn't assume.

—Do what?

—Deal with that? I mean, for fuck sake. She's my mom and I love her, but . . . how can you stay with her? Did you like roller coasters as a kid?

—Still do.

—Obviously.

—Your mom is not without challenge.

She laughs.

—That same understatement is in your writing, she says. I love it.

—Thanks. She's had an extremely traumatic life. Her scars are part of who she is. And I love who she is—all of her. Every aspect. Don't get me wrong. I'm sensitive and too often get my heart clobbered, but most of the time I'm able to see it for what it is. She's hurt, angry, traumatized. She's acting out. What she's been through is unimaginable.

—But . . . Seeing it for what it is is truly amazing, but it doesn't explain why you put up with it. How you can.

—There're no easy answers there, he says. I think who we're attracted to and why, who we're willing to invest in, give ourselves to, are mysteries beyond our comprehension.

—But—

—When things are good between us they are really, really good. Best I've ever experienced.

She nods.

—That said, he continues, I wouldn't stay in an abusive relationship. And you shouldn't. Nobody should. A lot of people mistake drama for passion, insanity for intensity. I'm a grown-ass man who's pretty together and I know what I want, what I can handle, and it's still not easy. I hope you'll be very, very careful, and not let anyone treat you badly in any way.

—Thanks. I won't.

—How does Julian treat you?

—Good. Really, she says. He's one of the good ones.

—It's not my place to and even if it were I wouldn't tell you what you should do, but I will say if you want a rewarding, fulfilling, and healthy relationship, you're gonna have to work at it, gonna have to address some of the, ah, challenges your mom and circumstances have passed on to you.

—It is your place, she says. Thank you. Thanks for giving a damn. I'd really like for Julian to spend some time with you. I think it'd help him. Like me, he really doesn't have a dad, but unlike me, he doesn't have a you.

Marc's eyes sting and he blinks several times.

—I'd be happy to hang out with him some. Maybe we could play basketball together or something. Bring him over more.

—You know how Mom is. Don't want to subject him to that.

—I'll help with that. How serious are you two?

—As serious as I know how to be, she says. I'd die for him.

—Whatta you think? Will asks.

Keisha is following Champ back to the truck, now parked on the far side of the house in the shade, having just returned from running a few hundred yards down the riverbank before losing the scent.

—Not sure yet. She was here for a while. Went into the house, around the yard, down to the water—maybe in.

Keith having returned to the station, it's just the two of them now.

Dropping the tailgate, she grabs a stainless steel bowl and a plastic jug of water. Placing the bowl on the ground, she pours the water in, the panting Champ sitting nearby watching.

—Champ. Drink.

He does.

—Good boy.

She pats him as he drinks, continuing to praise him in the kind of sweet, high-pitched, singsong voice people use for small children, animals, and the mentally challenged, and Will is surprised at the genuine affection and softness the tough, take-no-prisoners Keisha is capable of.

—'Course it may not even be her scent. If somebody else drove it here—or even got in and touched the wheel after she got out—I could be tracking them all over the place.

—So whatta you—

—I'ma start over.

She removes the lead from Champ's collar, then opens the door to his cage.

—Champ. Load.

He does.

She then places the water bowl inside the cage with him and closes the door.

—Start over? Will says.

—Do it all over again with Duke.

She opens another cage door.

—Duke. Out.

A bloodhound that looks nearly identical to the first one leaps out and onto the ground.

—Duke. Sit. Stay.

Duke does as he is told, and she attaches the lead to his collar. She then steps up to the cab, withdraws a large plastic Ziploc bag with a white silk pillowcase in it.

—I'ma use a scent article from her house this time. Compare. If Duke tracks the same trail as Champ, we know it's her. If not . . .

Will nods.

With the lead wrapped around her arm, she opens the plastic bag and places it over Duke's nose. He reacts immediately and she removes the bag, zips it back up, and tucks it into one of her pockets.

—Duke. Find.

Over the next few minutes, Duke follows nearly the identical route Champ did. As he does, Will steps back and takes in the late afternoon sky.

Beyond the tops of pines and cypress trees, the pale blue sky is dappled with pink-streaked clouds, the vivid pastel vista breathtakingly beautiful.

How the hell can Shelby be missing beneath such a sky?

—Think we can say for sure it's her scent we're tracking, Keisha says when she returns with Duke.

Her breaths are fast gasps, and her face and shirt looks

as if she's just been in the light mist of an afternoon shower.

—But it stops a few hundred yards downriver? he says.

—Means she probably went into the water at some point and the current carried her scent downstream.

Will shakes his head.

—You sayin' we've got to drag the river?

—I'm sayin' I need a boat.

—For what?

—See where she came out.

—If she came out.

—If she came out we should be able to pick up her scent. If we can't, then we call in the divers.

—Goddamn I hope you find her scent.

—Be dark soon. Best hurry.

Are we really going to do this?

Do you not want to?

No. I do. I'm just scared.

If you're not ready, we can wait.

I'm ready. Are you?

Yes.

We really leaving everything behind? Even my critters?

It's the only way. We'll have our own nature center one day with all kinds of critters to care for.

You think anyone suspects?

Don't think so. Not sure. Your mom is who we have to worry about. She's got the money to track us down unless we're very very careful.

I can't wait to be Mrs. Julian Flax. You make me so happy.

That's what I'm going to spend the rest of my life doing.

Me too. For you. Do I make you happy?

You know you do! I tell you all the time. The happiest.

I'm about to copy this over then erase everything. See you in the morning love. Can't wait. Can't wait to continue writing our story. I'm so excited. No way I'll be able to sleep tonight.

—I think they were running away together.

Taylor stops pacing and steps over to him.

—Who?

—Shelby and Julian. To get married.

She lets out an exasperated sigh and shakes her head.

—Silly little girl. They're just children.

—I'd be wrong to dismiss their relationship or—

—Relationship? Are you serious? They're children.

—Actually, they're not. You were having Shelby when you were her age.

—And look how well that turned out. We've got to let the sheriff know she's with him.

—He's gonna want this, he says, nodding toward the screen. Don't think we should give it to him.

—But what if it'll help them find—

—I'll keep going through it. If I find anything else, I'll let him know.

—Okay. So how do I tell him I know?

—It's probably just a matter of time 'til they come and search her room. I'm gonna put the file on my computer. That okay?

—I guess. Just don't lose it.

—I won't. That'll give us a backup. I'll print out this exchange between them and you can give it to Keith. It's not dated and there's no way to know when it was written. Could be from way back and for whatever reason they decided not to.

—Keep reading. I'm gonna call Keith.

She starts to leave, then stops.

—And, Marc.

—Yeah.

—Thank you so much. You're the most amazing, sweetest, best boy ever. I love you.

—I love you.

—And I owe you.

—When she's back safe and sound, you know how you can repay me.

She smiles.

—I already owe you so much. I'll be making pussy payments for the rest of my life.

—There are far worse debtors' prisons, he says.

—Oh, with you, baby, it's strictly briar patch. It's like I'm the one being paid.

—Sweet.

—True.

She begins to leave again.

—If she's running away with Julian, she probably packed, he says. Why don't you check to see if her suitcase is missing and what all she took?

She nods.

—I will. But if they're eloping, why leave her car? And why at Steve's?

—We know, Keith says.

Julian doesn't respond.

—Know what? Julia asks. What is there to know?

When Keith doesn't respond, just continues to keep his glare locked on Julian, she turns to her son.

—What is there to know? she asks again. Julian.

—Obstruction of justice is a very serious crime, Keith says. Maybe you didn't know, but if you lie to a law enforcement officer you can go to jail.

—Lie about what? Julia says. Julian. Julian. Did you lie about something?

—We wouldn't be back in here if he didn't, Keith says.

They are seated in the small interview room again—just like before, only without Will.

—How about the truth this time—the whole truth. Once and for all. Get it out. Don't carry it around anymore. It's gonna come out anyway. All of it. Be so much better to tell us now. Let me hear your side. I know we'll understand. We will. Things happen. Things you don't plan. Things you don't even mean to happen. We've all been there. All had that happen. You want to take it back—everybody knows that—but you can't. Can't undo it, but you can make it right by helping us, by telling us where Shelby is and what happened. Let us hear your side. You can explain it better than anyone. If you wait, if you don't tell us, then forensic investigators and reporters are going to do the telling, and they will make you out to be a monster. You're no monster. I know that. Your mom knows it. Talk to me so we can let everyone know.

120

—Keith, Julia says. Look at me.

For the first time, Keith shifts his gaze off of Julian.

—Stop being sheriff for ten seconds and answer me as a friend, as a parent. Do we need a lawyer?

In a gray-green 16-foot aluminum bateau with a 30hp Evinrude motor, Will, Keisha, and Duke leave the landing.

Before them, the eastern horizon grows darker by the moment, its bleak bruisedness hinting at the approaching storm. Behind them, rising up from beneath the rim of earth along the western horizon, the vertical, tubular clouds resemble the Eagle Nebula, bright salmon at the bottom from the unseen sun becoming plum, fading into blue, elongating into white tips in the aura of backlit sky.

Will is in the back, his hand on the throttle, Keisha in the center, the lead wrapped around her arm, Duke, in the bow of the slow-moving boat, sniffing, seeking, searching for scent.

As they venture downriver, the boat bounces on the wake of other crafts returning to the landing, driven in by descending dark.

—Where to? Will asks.

She points across the river to the side opposite the landing.

—Let's start across from the house where her car is.

He nods and eases the boat across the wide water to a spot on the bank where the soil has washed away from the root systems of cypress trees.

On either side, the bank is a solid green blanket of verdant vegetation. Intimidating. Impenetrable.

—You get in there? he asks. Not a lot of options.

She smiles.

—Get in anywhere, she says. Can't we Duke?

When the bow of the boat glides into the twisted thicket of gnarled roots, Duke lurches out and clambers up the bank, trying to find traction in the wet sand, Keisha right behind him.

Soon, the two disappear, and Will is left to wait.

—You encouraged her to lawyer up? Sam asks.

—No, Keith says. Not exactly.

—Sounds like you—

—What would you have done?

—Wasn't in the room, Sam says, her voice softening a bit. Don't know the context or circumstances, but if finding Shelby matters more than anything else, stall, delay, hedge, lie your ass off if you have to.

The two of them are standing in the brightly lit courthouse hallway near the vending machines waiting for Julian Flax's attorney to arrive. Sam Michaels, FDLE's contribution to CART, having just arrived herself.

—Keith, Sam continues after a beat, we've got a young girl missing and a big bastard of a hurricane gettin' ready to beat the fuck out of us.

—I'd forgotten, Keith says with a smile. You're kinda pushy.

Keith speaks in a certain, deliberate drawl—the rhythm and pace of which she has to acclimate to again.

—Well, thank you, Sheriff, she says, her words coming out more slowly than before. I try. Not easy being a girl in this world.

He's a good guy, she reminds herself. Good enough cop.

Don't push so hard you piss 'im off.

—Is it in any world? he says.

—None I've found so far.

—Poor little special agent with a gun and a badge.

Sam smiles.

—And an attitude, he adds.

—Those things do make it a little easier. Help mitigate all the macho horse shit.

—Oh, he says, and I know there's a young girl missin' and a storm on the way. Know it like a son of a bitch.

—I know you do, she says, then adds with a smile, I's just bein' pushy.

They are quiet for a brief moment.

The tile floor is blindingly bright beneath the fluorescent lamps, its gold-flecked white tiles polished to glossy perfection by inmate trusties from the jail in back with too much time and not enough work. From around the corner and down the hall, Sam can hear the click of heels—one of which has a worn-down tip.

—So, Sam says, you're working on the theory that boy and girl are running away together? Girl changes her mind or says or does something boy doesn't like. Boy hurts or kills girl?

—More or less, he says.

—Based on what?

He tells her.

—Taylor and . . . what's his—who's the man in her life at the moment?

—Marc.

—Found a diary or something in which Shelby says that's what they're doing?

—Yeah, he says. And her suitcase and clothes and stuff are missing.

—But they won't give it to you?

—Right. Printed some pages out.

—And you didn't make them? she says.

—We can't just— Keith begins, then stops himself. We figured you could do that.

—Because I don't have to run for re-election here?

—Because you're kinda pushy.

—A trait that makes me good at interviewing suspects, she says. Sure you don't want me to take a turn at the kid?

Twilight.

Gray gloom.

Cacophony.

Chirp of crickets.

Cluck of frogs.

Bellow of bull gators.

Will alone in the boat. Waiting. Water lapping at bank and bateau.

Somewhere in the sultry swamp before him, Keisha and Duke are searching for Shelby's scent, but the only proof he has of that is an occasional yelp or random yell.

Behind him, the dark river is empty and quiet, making its way toward the Apalachicola Bay.

In the distance, he hears the whine of a small boat motor, and he turns toward the sound. As the day grew darker and darker, the returning boats grew fewer and fewer, and it has been nearly half an hour since what he had thought was the final remaining straggler passing by. The lateness of this one is a bit surprising, but also, because of the circumstance and darkness, disquieting.

His eyes drift over in the direction of the throttled engine's whir, but he sees nothing, and grows even more disturbed by the disembodied noise.

Jumping up and rummaging around beneath the center seat, he withdraws the Nitehawk Patrol Light. Holding the battery pack in one hand and the light in the other, he pulls the trigger and shines 140,000 candlepower out into the dim distance.

The beam is powerful, but narrow, overexposing pinpoint spots. Bark. Bank. Water. Leaf. Moss. Log.

He kills it and waits.

The sound of the stressed motor grows.

Closer.

Closer.

Almost.

Now.

He hits the light and begins to sweep the vicinity of the sound.

Still surface.

Hanging vine.

Cypress branches.

And then . . .

There it is.

Boat.

Baseball cap.

Blur.

Blond.

Michael Lister

His beam first finds the hull of the passing boat, then a man in a red baseball cap, then Shelby—or was it?

So fast. Too fast.

Would any blonde girl out here look like Shelby right now?

It had been just a streak, but . . .

The man in the cap had been driving, the girl peeking up from the bottom of the boat, her fingers, face, and hair barely visible above the small craft's top edge.

Seconds.

The boat is through the narrow shaft of illumination within a moment, and Will spins around, training the beam, trying to find it again. As he does, a light every bit as bright as his strikes him in the face, and he's blinded.

Covering his eyes with one arm, he grabs his badge off his belt with the other and holds it up, yelling for the boat to stop.

In another moment, the light is no longer on him, the boat, flying by the landing, continuing to race upriver.

Untying the line from the cypress roots it's wrapped around, Will kicks off, shoving his own craft out into the water, rushes to the back, sits, starts the engine, and takes off after the boat, his partial vision dotted with star-like spots as he does.

—There's not a day that goes by that I don't think about Savannah, Sam says.

Just words, she thinks. No less inadequate because they're true.

Taylor nods.

—I appreciate that, she says. And all you did.

126

—I'm so sorry it wasn't enough. That I failed her. Failed you. I won't do it again.

Sam isn't quite sure what Taylor's next expression is intended to communicate, but figures it's some form of futility wrapped in the restraint of courtesy.

The two women consider each other a moment. Sam wonders what she sees. Have I changed as much as she has? A beautiful, slightly exotic-looking woman, Taylor is aging gracefully—much of her insecurity and unsteadiness from years ago now gone. Is it time, the settledness years can bring? Is it Marc?

Does he do for her what Daniel does for me?

When Sam glances over at Marc, he gives her a quick, small smile. In it, she senses genuine warmth and kindness. From the moment she arrived, he's been courteous, but so attentive to Taylor, he's barely looked at Sam. Had Taylor, like Sam herself, finally found a good man? Seems so, but how often are things what they seem? She's unfamiliar with his books, but bets Daniel isn't. She'd have to remember to ask him. It's interesting. Marc reminds her of Daniel. She has no higher compliment to offer a man.

The two of them make such a striking couple, look as though they were created to fit together, but Sam can't go on how things appear. Either one of them or both could be responsible for what's happened to Shelby—and she can't forget that. Not for a second.

They are seated in the Florida room of Lithonia Lodge—a large rectangular room on the back of the house that looks to have been a screened-in porch at one time—now enclosed in glass.

—Have you thought of anything else since you spoke with the sheriff or Will?

—You know . . . Taylor says. This seems so farfetched

it's ridiculous, but I keep coming back to it, so thought I should mention it.

—Nothing's ridiculous. Nothing's too farfetched.

—Well, Shelby's my little hippie chick—nature girl, animal rescuer, and hardcore environmentalist.

—That's cool. I didn't know.

—It is. She's a bit . . . extreme at times. I think it comes with being a teenager, you know, but . . . But yeah, she's very committed and does a lot of good. As you can imagine, she's made a lot of enemies. Just last week at a tri-state water management meeting, she stood up and embarrassed a general in the Corps of Engineers.

—How?

—He was saying how he had to weigh the concerns, wants, and needs of all the people sharing the same river system in Georgia, Florida, and Alabama. And she stood up and was like, you can't think that someone who built a house on Lake Lanier and is concerned about their fuckin' property values can compare to the Apalachicola River system and Bay, which is one of the most diverse and important estuaries in the world.

—Wow.

—Yeah.

—Caused quite a stir, Marc says. We were very proud of her. Made a lot of people mad.

—But not enough to kidnap her, Taylor says.

—You'd be surprised what motivates people—especially someone who'd do something like this. It's often shocking how small and seemingly inconsequential their motives are.

They nod.

Beyond the glass enclosure, night falls fast, and Sam tries not to think about how long Shelby's been missing, how much time has been wasted, how remote the possibility for a safe return is now.

Security lights illuminate the fortress-like backyard all the way down past the pens and cages of Shelby's critters to the river's edge. Sometimes you can take every precaution and still be unable to keep them safe.

—That was just one example, Taylor says. The person I was really thinking of is Brock Connelly.

—Who?

—A developer. She fought him—and so far has won— to stop a development worth millions because of wetlands, endangered species, and storm water runoff issues. I'm not saying he'd do this—or it'd even help his cause if he did—but he's used to getting his way. No one else is even fighting it. And it's worth the kind of money that makes people do crazy things.

—I'll look into it. I'm glad you told me. That's just the kind of thing we need to know. Okay? Everything. Just tell me everything. You never know what pieces of information come together to solve a case, so we need to know everything. It's why I need to see her journal or whatever it is.

They both start shaking their heads before she is finished.

—I know it's difficult to think of a stranger pouring over her most intimate thoughts and confessions, but it really is the best chance we have of finding her.

—Marc's reading it, Taylor says. He'll give you anything relevant.

—That's just what I mean. Only someone involved in the investigation, someone with access to all the information, will be able to make connections. There's no way for you to know what's relevant.

—If there's anything that could even be remotely relevant, Marc says, I'll turn it in. In fact, I've got something for you now.

He crosses the room and retrieves a couple of printer paper pages.

—We can get a court order, Sam says, but I know you want her found more than anyone. You wouldn't want to do anything that you'll regret later because you could've helped us find her sooner.

Marc returns with the pages and hands them to Sam. She reads.

You're jealous of Kerry?

No.

You're acting like it.

Well, I'm not. But he's got a thing for you.

We just share a similar goal. We're like the only two green people in the area.

Are you attracted to him?

He's got a girlfriend.

That's not an answer.

He's a lot older.

That's not either.

What do you want me to say?

I wanted you to answer the question, and you did.

I find him attractive, yeah.

And he wants you, so what are you waiting for?

What? You're being silly. Nothing's going on between us.

But you want there to be.

No.

And he does.

No.

If you want to be with him, be with him, but tell me.

I'm with you. I want to be with you.

But if you could be with him . . .

You're saying I could have him if I want. And I'm still with you. Still want to be with you. Or I did until you became such a jealous spaz.

—Who's Kerry?

—Science teacher, Marc says. Environmentalist. He's helped Shelby with several of her causes.

—We're not saying we suspect him, Taylor says. But they do spend a lot of time together and he's still relatively young. And he's single. And he stays in town alone during the school week.

—Taylor's very protective of Shelby, Marc says. If she had any reservations about Kerry, Shelby wouldn't've been within a million miles of him.

—But, I've been wrong about people before. And it's not like I know where Shelby is every second of every day.

—Well, yeah, you pretty much do.

—Or that she really is where she's supposed to be—doing what she's supposed to be doing.

—Actually, Marc says, I was thinking this might be most relevant as it relates to Julian's jealousy.

Racing upriver.

Full throttle.

Heart pounding.

131

Bow bouncing.

One hand steering, the other scanning the black body of water with the Nitehawk Patrol Light.

No sign of the boat.

No cell signal.

He feels bad for leaving Keisha, but knows she'll understand—hell, she'd do the same thing.

She'll be fine. She can handle herself out here far better than I can.

Slow down.

He knows he should, knows how dangerous what he's doing is, but just can't quite make himself do it.

How many people have been killed out here doing this very thing? So many things to hit, to crash into, so many ways to get thrown from the boat, knocked unconscious, swallowed up by this giant, twisting snake, like so many, never to be seen again.

Every time the river takes another one, every time someone goes in and doesn't come out, those who remain return to the same old theories. Gator got him—no body left. She's beneath a log on the bottom. A pocket of sand created by all the dredging the corps has done sucked him under, buried him below the river bed.

Don't want people theorizing about you, do you? Now, slow down.

The rise and fall of the boat's bow on the surface of the water decreases in frequency as he throttles down a bit.

After getting around the next bend, the river straightens out for a stretch, and he is able to sweep the beam across the entire section. He can see that the boat he was chasing has disappeared.

No way he outran me.

Must've stopped and hid somewhere back along the way.

As he throttles back, the bow of the boat drops and the entire craft sinks down into the water. Slowly turning around, he continues to shine his light in all directions, scanning the wide river and its sloping sandy banks.

Downriver.

Deliberately.

His eyes dart about, following the narrow beam, darkness enveloping, encroaching, extinguishing it at a certain point in the distance.

Where the hell could they have gone?

Had he imagined the whole thing?

Just as he's about to abandon his search to head back and retrieve Keisha, then return to the landing to call in additional help, something—movement, sound, reflection, or perhaps some combination of all three—in the periphery catches his attention.

—We know you and Shelby were going to elope, Keith says.

—You know this how? John Lee George, Julian's attorney, asks.

Keith is surprised the man didn't air quote the word.

John Lee George, Tupelo's sole lawyer, is an aging hippie with longish, graying curly hair that starts at about the halfway point of the top of his head. He's honest, poor, does mostly pro bono and environmental work, and has, at one time or another, represented nearly everyone involved in litigation in the town—including Keith.

They are back in the small interview room, Keith on one

side of the table, Julia, Julian, and John Lee on the other—the teenager in the center, flanked on either side by a protective adult.

—We have Shelby's journal.

Julia Flax's eyes widen.

—And it says she and my client were running away to get married today?

—It does.

—May I see it?

—It's being processed right now. As soon as it's—

—So I should just take your word for it?

—We don't have much time. Please. It's dark. Shelby could need medical attention. If Julian ever cared for her he should help us locate her. And no matter what happened, I'll make sure everyone knows how helpful he was. I just want to know where she is, what happened to her. I know you bought her a ring.

—I didn't.

—Son, let me do the talking.

—You were going to, Keith says. Why didn't you? What happened? Did she break up with you? That it?

—I didn't buy no damn ring, Julian says.

—I think you did. Did she go with you or stand you up?

—Keith, John Lee says, his voice scolding in an almost fatherly way, if you keep trying to provoke my client, I'll be forced to end the interview.

Silence descends upon the inhabitants of the small room.

Eventually, John Lee clears his throat.

—As I told you before we began, he says, Julian is

innocent. It's true. He knows it. His mom knows it. I know it. And because he's innocent, because he's concerned about Shelby—even though she is no longer his girlfriend—we're here to help. Do you want information or not? Then quit trying to provoke him and let Julian help you.

Keith nods.

—Why'd you and Shelby break up? he says. Let's start there. Why and when?

John Lee pats Julian on the hand.

—Their relationship ended, John Lee says, because they were going in two different directions. Wanted different things. It was only recently that Julian realized just how different.

—Meaning what? What happened?

—We're not going to sit here and talk poorly about Shelby. Nor or we going to rehash painful and personal details that have nothing to do with where she is or what she's doing.

—Is she involved with someone else now?

Julian's angry expression lets Keith know she is and he's not happy about it.

—My client has no knowledge of that. Do you know who your ex-girlfriends are seeing?

—The recent ones. Yeah. Who's she seeing, Julian? What if he's done something to her? What if she needs help?

Julian looks like he wants to say something, but doesn't.

—There is no one new, is there? Keith says.

—Not his business whether there is or not, John Lee responds.

—Julian, just tell me who she dumped you for.

—She didn't—

—Keith, I told you not to do that, John Lee says.

—Do what? If Julian's not involved with Shelby, I've got to know who is. This isn't adding up. You're not giving me much here, John Lee. And you know it.

—My client's not involved in any of this. Doesn't have much to give. Doesn't know much.

—He knows more than he's saying, more than you're letting him say.

—We're answering your questions—the ones we can. Ask us something we actually have an answer for.

—Okay. Why weren't you at school today?

—Just didn't feel like it.

—Gotta do better than that, Keith says. You never skip school—and the day you do, Shelby does too, and she goes missing.

—That's not a question, John Lee says.

—You're really being this unhelpful when Shelby's missing? Here's a question for you. What did you do today?

—Just hung out.

—No. I mean exactly. Take me through it moment by moment.

John Lee nods to Julian.

—Slept in. Hung out. Walked around. Went to the Courts. Talked to some girls. Played some ball.

Something in Julia's reaction lets Keith know her son is lying. It was brief and subtle, and she recovered well, but it had been there, and he had seen it.

—What is it, Ms. Flax?

—Huh?

—What's he lying about?

—What? Nothing.

—John Lee, you need to explain to your client and his mother how serious this is, how they can be arrested right now.

—You don't have to answer anything you don't want to, John Lee says, but don't lie.

—I'm not lying, Julian says. I swear. I did all those things.

—Then you're leaving a lot out.

Julian doesn't respond.

Keith shakes his head and looks over at Julia.

—What'd he lie about or leave out?

—It's nothing. No big deal. I'm sure I just—

—What is it? Keith says, his voice flaring.

Julia looks at her son.

—I'm not lying, Mama.

—But Julian, you didn't sleep in. You were gone before I got up. You never get up that early.

Julian has the look of a kid caught in a lie.

—What were you really doing? Keith asks.

—I . . . I wanted her to think I was going to school. I waited 'til she left, then came back home and got in bed.

—More lies. What will your friends say? Your neighbors? Everything will come out. It always does. What will they think when they find out you wasted our time instead of helping us find Shelby? You either know where she is—whether she's dead or alive—or you know something that would help us find out who does, and you're just jerking us around.

—Keith, John Lee says, we all need to take a—

—I swear to God I don't know where she is, Julian says. Swear to God. But I'll tell you who might. And he wasn't at school today either.

—We've already talked to everybody who didn't go to

school today. You're just trying to—

—Oh you did, huh? Including Mr. Ake?

—Who?

—Mr. Ake. Our biology teacher.

—Kerry Ake? Julia says. What does he have to do with—

—He's the reason we broke up. He's been fuckin' her.

NOAA data buoy.

East-central Gulf.

Sustained winds 111 miles per hour, gusts up to 143, sea heights 35 feet.

Christine. Category 3.

Consuming. Growing.

Coming faster now.

Maintaining course.

Projected landfall. Panhandle of Florida at or near Tupelo.

Warnings issued.

Evacuations ordered for low-lying areas.

Bracing.

Boarding up.

Preparing.

Riverview.

Roadside motor court.

Small.

Stripped down.

Cinderblock buildings.

Oyster-shell parking lot.

Pulling up to Fishermen's Paradise, the motel where Kerry Ake lives during the school week, Sam feels like she has traveled not so much across town but back in time.

On River Road, just a couple of miles from Lanier Landing and Shelby's dad's camp where her car was found, the all-white compound looks as if she's seeing it on a 50s black–and-white TV show, the dark night surrounding it adding to the illusion.

At one time, a popular spend-the-night spot for men coming to fish the Apalachicola and Chipola Rivers and the Dead Lakes, the small block buildings of the mostly empty establishment look more like military barracks than civilian recreational lodging.

As Sam steps out of her big, boxy state-issued car, a fine white mist of oyster shell dust swirls about her, eerie and fog-like in the streetlamps and security lights.

Unsnapping the strap on her holster, she lets her right hand linger near her firearm, while knocking on the door with her left.

—Florida Department of Law Enforcement, she says. Mr. Ake?

A young, handsome in a not too obvious way man with blondish hair and tanned skin opens the door wearing khaki shorts and a light blue button-down shirt with the sleeves rolled up.

—Kerry Ake?

—Yeah?

—I'm Special Agent Samantha Michaels with the Florida Department of Law Enforcement. I need to ask you a few questions. Mind stepping out onto the porch?

—No. Not at all. What's going on?

As he steps out, she moves forward and scans the room. It's small and outdated and plain—and no one else is inside, which she can be certain of because the bathroom door is open. For a bachelor pad, the room is tidy—most of the clothes confined to an open suitcase on the floor, most of the books piled on the nightstand, most of the cans and food containers on the small round table in the corner.

—You live here?

—During the week. My girlfriend and I have a place in Thomasville, but this was the only school I could find a job at this year, so I crash here during the week.

Science teachers are in big demand. Why is this the only place he can get a job?

—Has something happened to Joann?

—Who?

—My girlfriend.

—No. I'm here on another matter.

—What is it? What's wrong?

—Why'd you miss school today?

He shrugs.

—Officially, I was a little under the weather. Unofficially, I was working on an article I hope to publish.

—For the paper?

He smiles.

—Scientific journal.

She nods, noting that he's ambitious.

—So what's this about?

—Just some questions. I'll get to them. How do you like

it here?

He shrugs again.

—It's one of the most beautiful and diverse places in Florida. Heaven for an environmentalist. Getting a lot of research and writing done.

—But it's gotta be tough, she says. Living like this.

—It is. And I miss Joann, but it's temporary. And I'm taking advantage of the opportunities here.

—Do you like teaching?

He frowns and shakes his head.

—Find it very frustrating. Small town. Small school. Kids are only interested in each other, sports, drinking, smokin' weed.

—No bright spots?

—No. Yeah. There's a few, but it's tough. I'm trying to make a difference but feel frustrated by how little impact I'm having.

—What about the Summers girl? I hear she's quite the activist.

—She is. She's a bright spot for the community, but— Is she okay? Did something happen? Are you here about her?

—When's the last time you saw her?

—Yesterday at school. No, wait. She passed by here pretty early this morning.

—You saw her?

—Pass by? Yeah.

—Who was with her?

—Didn't see anybody, but she passed by pretty fast.

—She didn't stop?

—No. I wouldn't've seen her except I was getting

something out of my truck. Is she okay?

—Which way was she heading?

—Toward the landing.

—What time did she pass back by?

—No idea. After I got the book I needed, I went back inside and didn't come out until around one to get some lunch. Did something happen to Shelby? Please. What's all this about?

—Describe your relationship for me.

—With Shelby? Fuck. Did somebody say something? Is that what this is about? It's strictly teacher and student and fellow environmentalists. That's it. I've never said or done anything inappropriate. Not ever.

—Why would you jump to that conclusion?

—It's always a threat—just sitting there like a coiled snake waiting to strike. It's why I'm always so careful. That's not it?

—Anybody confirm you were here all day? Except for going to lunch?

He shakes his head.

—Not that I know of. I mean, my truck was here right in front of the room all day. I got my food to go and I'd think the waitress who rung me up at the Frog Pad would remember me. Please tell me what this is about.

—Shelby's missing. Any idea where she might be?

Blackness.

Backwater branch.

Tree-covered tributary.

As Will steers the boat into the small slough, he feels

particularly vulnerable. No cover. Nothing to crouch behind. The canopied water trail is closed off, cavelike. He could be pulling into an ambush. Probably is.

—River County Sheriff's Department, he yells. Anyone in here?

No response.

The sawing of crickets continues. Maddeningly loud.

Back and forth of water. Slapping at tree base and bank.

The hum and whir of his motor.

Nothing else.

Eventually the slough will grow too narrow for his bateau, too shallow for his Evinrude, and he'll know if what had caught his attention back in here was the boat he's after or a figment of his imagination.

Some of the tree bodies and branches hang so low over the water, he has to lift them by hand or, if the area is wide enough, navigate around them.

Attempting not to overexpose himself, he only turns on his Nitehawk occasionally, and he continually changes his position, leaning to one side, then the other, then nearly prostrate.

—River County Sheriff's Department, he yells again. Identify yourself.

No response.

Anxious.

Nervous.

Clenched.

Tight.

He's holding so much tension in his body, it aches, his neck and shoulders so tense they feel injured.

143

Breathe, he reminds himself.

This small vein of the river is longer than he thought, and as he ventures deeper in, his sense of dread expands until it envelopes him.

So dark.

So isolated.

So vulnerable.

From up ahead, just a short distance away, he—what? Hears something? Senses something?

Squeezing the trigger on his patrol light, he brings up the beam to illuminate the man in the red baseball cap standing on the bow of his boat some seven feet away, a shotgun aimed directly at him.

Sometimes I think you care more about your animals than you do me.

Are you for real?

You spend more time with them.

Only because of Warden Taylor's lockdown. I wish I could be with you more.

You do?

Duh! I want to be with you all the time.

You'd give up the animals for me?

You could help me take care of them.

Oh.

You wouldn't?

I would.

But only to get in my pants?

That is the way, isn't it?

Wow. You're right. And it'd totally get you to go green. What a great idea!

What is?

Totally the way to win.

Huh?

Nature girls. Use the power of pussy to affect policy.

Needing coffee, to stretch his legs, and to check on Taylor, Marc carries his laptop into the kitchen and places it on the counter. Stiff and a bit stupefied, he's been reading Shelby's journal so long and so intently, he's lost all track of time, and is just now becoming aware of the world around him again.

Filter.

Coffee.

Water.

On.

Off to find Taylor.

Clos du Bois.

Empty, overturned bottle.

Sign.

Warning.

Portent.

He finds Taylor passed out on the couch in the living room, empty glass on the floor, empty bottle on its side on the coffee table beside snapshots of Shelby.

Some of his best and worst memories of her involve the crisp, delicate, fruity taste of wine in her mouth. She's never as amorous, never as wanton, as when knocking back glasses of her favorite sauvignon blanc—and never more vile and vitriolic. The latter affect causing her to swear off drinking—how many times in the course of their short relationship? Ten?

Seeing the drained bottle as a form of communication reminds him how he's often thought of her drinking as the Chinese symbol that means both danger and opportunity. Adding alcohol, particularly wine, to her fragile system and volatile nature always leads to an extreme—you just never know which one.

How can she still be such a mystery to me?

The last time she drank, about a week ago, when Shelby was at the one friend's house Taylor actually let her stay the night at, they had gone to dinner, and three glasses later had skipped the movie because she had to have him, couldn't wait.

Beginning her sexual aggression in the car as he attempted to drive, she barely waited until they were inside the house before the full-on assault began.

—Fuck me, she had said, beginning to disrobe.

They are in the large entryway of the house, the front door not even closed yet.

Continuing to paw at his clothes with one hand, she licks the fingers of her other and begins to touch herself.

—Hurry, she says. I want you in me right now.

Her aggressiveness is alluring, for even in the midst of it, there's a vulnerability about her, a shy-child quality, and he loves her even more because of it.

As he removes the last of his clothes, he wonders if she really means for them to fuck on the floor. To the right, the dining room has a rug and chairs to offer, to the left, the formal living room has a couch and a loveseat.

Separation Anxiety

By the time he is naked, he has his answer.

He finds her on all fours on the stairs, hands and knees on different steps, her wiggling ass in the air.

Part of what makes them twins, part of what gives such intensity and intimacy to their relationship is their mutual, nearly equal love of sex. Making love some of the time but mostly fucking often suits him just fine—except when it feels compulsive or like a shortcut or as a way of actually avoiding true intimacy.

—Are you okay? You're not too—

—Don't start that shit, she says. I'm great. Everything's . . . it couldn't be better. I love you. Okay? So shut up and fuck me.

As he moves over toward her and steps up on the stairs, she turns, grabs him, and brings him to her mouth.

Her twisting and contorted torso causes the scars on her stomach and side to transform into new patterns. Ripply. Scaly. Zippery.

She seems edgy, irritated, shaky, and he wonders if it's just the wine or if she failed to take her meds this morning.

Taylor takes a low dose of Zoloft daily—when she remembers—and ups it during times of hormonal battles or stress. She certainly needs an extra dose or two on a day like today, and Marc wonders if she's had any.

You can't ask her. You know what that does.

Carefully.

Gently.

One.

He slides inside her, and for the moment, all is right with the world.

They fit and feel so good, as if they truly are long-lost twins reunited at last, but his pleasure is twinged with the pain of knowing how very temporary the feeling of complete connection really is.

For the moment, they are lost in the oblivion of sex, in the simultaneous hyperconsciousness and unconsciousness of rejoining, yet even in the midst of the ecstatic experience, he is aware of its fragility and finitude.

Reaching up, he gathers her hair in his fist and pulls her head back. Giving in to it, she rolls her neck in obvious enjoyment and lets out something that can only be described as a purr. Releasing her hair, he begins to caress her body, knowing just what she likes, just what makes her dizzy and drunker, working from her neck to her breasts, down her ticklish torso, the rippling concave and protuberant scars on the left and front a reminder of the far deeper unseen psychic wounds inside.

Caressing.

Kneading.

Tracing.

He loves her body like no other. Can't imagine it without this vicious, violent mosaic of pain and beauty, of sensuality and survival.

Who would she be without her scars? Without her experiences? Would he take away her wounds if he could? Not if it would change who she is. And how could it not?

We are our wounds. We are our scars as surely as we are our secrets. She is hers. I am mine.

Still, he wishes she didn't have so much scar tissue around her heart, wishes she would let him in and leave him there, not continue cutting him out of her the way her sister had been.

Glancing to his right, he sees the highly erotic image of their conjoined bodies through the wrought iron spindles of the banister in the large hanging mirror on the opposite wall, and it sends him.

Looking down at her now, he sees the wounded little girl who's lost so much, and his heart aches for her.

She can't lose Shelby too. She just can't. It's too much. She'll never survive it.

As he's trying to decide whether to cover her with a blanket here or help her to bed, she opens her eyes.

—Hey, she says, dragging it out. Sweetly. Sexily. Drunkenly.

—Hey.

—Hey, she says again. Hey, baby. How's my handsome man?

She reaches up for him and he bends down to meet her.

Wrapping her hands around the back of his neck, she pulls him into an open, sleepy, sloppy wet kiss that tastes of sweet fruit.

Stopping suddenly, she pulls back, and looks toward the pictures on the table.

—How the fuck could I forget? Even for a second? Fuck. What's wrong with me? Oh God. What's wrong with you? Why didn't you tell me?

—Tell you what?

—Do you even care about her? About me?

The dam holding his anger gives and it bursts out.

—Are you kidding? Who's in there pouring over her journal for any clue about where she might be, who might have her?

—Don't be such a goddamn martyr.

—What? Are you . . . You can't be that . . . Drunkenness is no excuse for—

—I want you out, she says. Out of my house. Now. Tonight. Out.

He's stunned, but not shocked. This is always a possibility. It doesn't happen often, but just often enough to always be a threat coiled unseen beneath the surface.

She's irrational, crazed. Soon, she'll be hysterical. There's nothing to do when she gets like this—no argument he can make, no overture, no way to get through, to get in, to get past the emotional electrical storm swirling around her right now.

But, as is so often the case, it sneaks up on him before he realizes what's happening, and his anger propels him forward.

—Here we go again.

—Don't be such—

—You really want me out?

—Don't act like it's not what you really want.

—You're gonna regret this in the morning, he says. Please just stop now. Instead of saying you're sorry in the morning, you could just not do anything to be sorry for.

She doesn't respond.

—Two days ago, we're talking about forever, about being twins, how you've never loved anyone like me before, and now you want me out.

She shrugs.

—Things change.

—Yeah, he says. Rather quickly around here.

—Right. So I don't know why you'd want to be here anyway. It's got to be a relief.

—Do you remember telling me how good I was for

you—and Shelby? How you'd never loved anyone the way you do me, how happy I make you?

She doesn't say anything.

—Are those things suddenly not true?

She shrugs.

—How do you feel about me right now?

—I don't feel any way toward you.

It hurts and it's hard to hear, but he suspects it's liquor, hormones, and the unimaginable nightmare of Shelby being missing.

He starts to say something but sees that she has fallen back asleep.

Am I a martyr? A masochist? What am I not seeing, not getting?

He loves her like he's never loved anyone. Finds her attractive and fun and funny, intelligent and wise and witty, but she's damaged, and he pays a high price for remaining so close to the feral thing inside her.

He's never had quite this dynamic before, but he does have a history of caretaking, maybe even a bit of a savior complex. Is that what this is? Or just the challenge? Is there something in him that's causing this?

Why can't I walk away? Just let go and move on. That's what I'd advise anyone else to do. But God I love her so much. I so want this to work. What am I doing wrong? Why can't I help her any better than I am?

As he covers her with a blanket, she opens her eyes and looks up at him so lovingly, she seems like a different person.

—I love you so much, she says, her voice small, sweet, childlike.

—I love you too, precious.

Shotgun.

Full stop.

Freeze.

Think.

No. Don't think. React.

Will keeps the light trained on the man, holding steady, the narrow, bright beam overexposing the barrel and casting an elongated shadow across his face and hat.

—Think about what you're doin', partner, he says, his voice low, his words slow. Put the gun down before you twitch and accidentally kill a cop.

As he talks, he attempts to see into the boat, but it's too dark, too far away.

—Ain't goin' back to prison, the man says, his voice dry, his words shaky.

The chirping crickets and other nocturnal noises are impossibly, irritatingly, infuriatingly loud, making even the motor difficult to hear.

—Who said anything about prison?

—You can back outta here and let me go or I can shoot you where you sit. Up to you.

—I'm not here to jam you up. Just trying to find a missing girl. That something you can help me with?

—Don't talk to me like I'm your goddamn buddy.

The middle-aged man has likely used up far more than half a life, the weathered leather hide covering his malnourished and whiskey-brittle bones just the most obvious sign.

A plan.

Separation Anxiety

Will realizes that the moment he cuts the light, the man, who's been staring into it, will be night-blind and befuddled.

A shotgun at this range? Won't matter.

—Okay, Will says. I'll back out of here nice and slow and then—

Killing the light, dropping down and leaning to the left, he throttles up the motor, gunning toward the armed man and his boat.

Shotgun blast.

Thunder-like boom.

Reverberation.

Silence.

Nocturnal noises cease.

Ping of pellets.

Moving.

Racing.

Crashing.

Will rams his boat into the other one.

Drops the light.

Hears the man fall.

Kills the engine.

Up.

Drawing weapon.

Step. Step. Leap.

Landing on top of the man, Will blindly swings with his fist and the butt of his gun. At first, the man fights back, but is soon only defending himself from the barrage of blows.

Cuffs.

Wrists.

153

Struggle.

Subdued.

—Shelby?

No response.

He can hear someone else in the boat.

—Who's there? Identify yourself now or I shoot.

—Don't shoot.

The small, disembodied voice is weak and frightened, but unmistakably male.

—Identify yourself. Now.

—It's my boy, the man beneath him says. Don't shoot.

—You got a light? Will asks.

—Yes, sir.

—Turn it on—but don't point it toward me.

The boy does as he's told.

Within minutes, Will has seen everything—the twelve-year-old boy with long blond hair, the father training him to be a ridge runner, and the plastic and Styrofoam coolers full of recently harvested pot leaves.

Going over the phone dump from Shelby's cell reminds Sam she should call Daniel, and she calls him while pouring over the records in a random vacant office at the sheriff's department.

—Hey, she says.

—Hey.

—Whatta you doin'?

He laughs.

154

—Let's see how well you know me. What do you think I'm doing?

—Trying to solve my case for me?

—Don't know about that, but I am reading the old case file. That okay?

Now she laughs.

—Why you think I left it out? she asks, her voice still warm with laughter.

A religion and philosophy professor, Daniel is routinely used by FDLE and other agencies when a case has religious or ritualistic elements, but he's good at profiling, making connections, and seeing things others miss, and often helps Sam unofficially.

—It's fascinating, he says.

—I won't get mad if you solve it, she says. I promise.

She looks up from Shelby's cell phone records, pausing a moment to appreciate how good things are, how comfortable they are with each other. She'd given up on ever having a relationship like this, of ever finding a man like Daniel Davis, a long time ago.

—You sure? Don't want to risk you making me sleep on the couch.

—I've never made you sleep on the couch.

—Meant that more metaphorical than literal.

—Oh. You're scared I'm gonna withhold your favorite thing.

—Not saying you would, just that it's not worth the risk. Of course, you could be so happy and grateful, you smother me with . . . ah, my favorite thing.

—I know I've been a competitive bitch in the past, but this time there are two cases. One for each of us. You solve the old one. I'll solve the new one.

—Brilliant, he says. But if I do happen to solve both . . .

—I'd be so happy I'd forget to be competitive.

He lets out an incredulous laugh.

—While I've got you, he says, can I ask you a few questions about the old case?

—Sure. I'm just— Oh my God.

—What is it?

—I'm gonna have to call you back.

—The fuck you been?

After delivering the grower and his son to a deputy at the landing, and giving a game warden directions to the slough holding their boat, Will finds Keisha waiting for him where he dropped her off, irritated and impatient, she and Duke both so wet with sweat they look like they've been running in a rainstorm.

—Sorry. Was stupid. Went on a wild goose chase.

He helps her into the boat.

—Get a goose?

He smiles.

—Did, as a matter of fact, he says.

She nods.

—Sorry I left you so long, he says.

She shrugs and sits down, this time Duke lying on the floor of the boat at her feet.

He puts the motor in reverse, the engine clicking and locking into gear, then backs up, turns, shifts into forward, and heads back toward the landing in the darkness.

—Anything? he asks.

She shakes her head.

—Covered a lot of ground—even more than I planned 'cause I had some extra time 'cause somebody left my ass—but she didn't come out over here.

He nods.

—So . . . whatta you think happened?

—She was here. She moved around some. She may've gone into the river, but if she did, she either came out close to where she went in or didn't come out at all—either drowning or gettin' in a boat and leaving that way. That's about all me and ol' Duke here can tell you.

—Play time's over, Sam says. You understand?

She is seated next to Keith and across the table from Julian, John Lee, and Julia.

It's her interview now.

A few minutes before, she had called the sheriff out into the hall, shown him her discovery, and asked to have a go at Julian. Weary and at wit's end, he relented.

—Keith, I'm not gonna sit here and let my client be subjected to abuse.

—You got something to say, say it to me, Sam says, her voice as hard and frosty as her face.

—We're outta here, John Lee says, standing.

—You got two choices, Sam says. Sit down and advise your client to answer my goddamn questions, or I arrest him for murder right now.

—Murder?

—Two, actually.

John Lee drops back into his chair.

She looks at Julian, locking her green eyes onto his brown ones until he looks away.

—I meant what I said, so don't try me. You've been jerkin' us around all afternoon. That ends now.

He doesn't respond.

—Understand?

He still doesn't respond.

—Grunt if you hear me.

He nods.

—You said you and Shelby broke up, right?

—Yeah.

—When?

—I don't know. A while ago.

—That vague bullshit's not gonna work anymore. Tell me exactly when.

—Tell her, son, Julia says.

—We've got her phone records, Sam says.

He still doesn't say anything.

—It shows a certain pattern. You guys are together, all in love, and you call a lot. Just what you'd expect. Right? But then you break up. The calls stop, right? Or, let's say she dumps you. So maybe you keep calling for a while. Maybe she even talks to you some, but the calls would be less frequent, shorter—a different pattern. Actually, I guess I really don't need you to tell me when you broke up. I can tell from her phone records.

Sam pauses, but no one says anything.

Picking up the printouts again, she pretends to peruse them.

—Okay . . . let's see . . . according to your calling pattern . . . you guys . . . haven't broken up.

Julia and John Lee turn and look at Julian.

—What? he says. We're broken up. I swear.

—Not only have you not been calling less, Sam says, you've been calling more. You guys have talked more this week than any other time. These are the records of a couple still together, still in love, still in nearly constant contact. Where is Shelby?

—I don't know. I swear.

—For fuck sake, you spoke with her this morning.

—I didn't.

—You called her as recently as one o'clock.

He looks at his mom, who's looking at him a little differently now.

—Mama, you've got to believe me. I'm—

Sam slams her hand down on the table.

—Where is Shelby?

—I told you. I don't know.

—You're lying.

—I'm not. I swear.

—What'd you do with her?

—Please. God. Please.

—Is that what she said?

—What? No. You've got to believe me. I wouldn't hurt her. I wouldn't. What about Mr. Ake? He called her all the fuckin' time.

—Julian, his mom nearly shouts.

—They talked, sure. And we're talking to him, but I'm more interested in some other calls she made right now.

—It's getting late, John Lee says. I think we should—

—Planned Parenthood, Sam says. Not just once, but a few times—and not that long ago. About the time you started looking at rings and talking about running away together.

—Julian, look at me, Julia says. Is Shelby pregnant?

Sitting in a chair in the living room, feet on the coffee table, computer in his lap, sipping coffee, listening to Taylor sleep, Marc scrolls through the pages of Shelby's life. He's finding this young lady he shares a house with interesting, intelligent, insightful. Her charm, humor, and compassion pour forth from every page, but he's finding nothing that he needs to report—at least not until the next page comes up and he sees this:

FUCK!!!!!!!!!!!!!

But we've been so careful.

We've been sort of careful.

How late are you?

Late. And I never am. I've never been a day late and now it's weeks.

What are we going to do?

I bought a test. I'm about to take it.

Keep texting me as you do. I'm here.

Do we wanna talk about what we're going to do if it's positive, or wait to see if it is?

What do you want to do?

Separation Anxiety

I don't want to have a baby right now, but I don't want to have an abortion either.

We could get married. I could get a job. You could finish school.

Really? You would want to?

You kidding? I love you.

You're so sweet. There's no way we can but it's so sweet of you to say.

Why can't we?

I'm taking the test.

Right now?

Peeing on th litle thingy rihgt now. Texing with one hand.

How long does it take?

Five minutes.

Want to have phone sex while we wait?

:-)

I'm serious. Sext me.

Sext yourself.

Did you really just tell me to go sext myself?

Can we really handle this?

Yes. We'll be totally awesome fucking parents. We can handle anything together.

You think?

Don't you?

I'm scared. Understatement. I'm freakin' right now.

Settle down. It's going to be okay no matter what it is. I promise. I'm with you.

But you're not. You're there and I'm here.

You want me to come over?

And sneak in? See? We can't have a baby.

We can do anything. I swear it. We'll figure it out. We will.

I hope so, because it's positive.

Marc wants to wake Taylor, but he knows she's in no condition. He needs to call the sheriff or the FDLE agent, but can't tell them before he tells Taylor, can he? Got to. No choice. Shelby matters more than anything right now.

—Yes, Julian says, his eyes falling with his demeanor. She is.

—How long have you known? Julia says. Why didn't you tell me?

—Not long.

—You should've told me, she says. I would've helped you.

—Sorry.

—So you two didn't break up, Sam says. And she's pregnant.

—Were you running away together? Keith asks.

Julian nods.

—What happened? Sam asks.

—She didn't show up. Stood me up. Went to have the abortion instead.

—Where? Keith asks.

—No idea. She didn't include me.

—So she decided not to have the baby, Sam says.

He nods.

—Not to run off with you, not to marry you, not to be a

family?

—Right.

—That'd make anybody mad. Would me. I understand. You just lost it for one minute. Just—

—What? No.

—She's killing your baby, your chance at keeping her, at making her yours forever.

—No. It's not like—

—Tell us what happened. We'll understand. You know we will. Where is she? You didn't mean to hurt her. It was an accident. No one's fault.

—I haven't even seen her today. I told you. She didn't show up. I swear. I don't know where she is. Check the clinic, check with Mr. Ake—it's probably his baby anyway.

—Son, Julia says, you've been telling us all day that you and Shelby broke up.

—We did, he says. The moment she didn't show up this morning. Whether she's having an abortion or it was never mine to begin with, we broke up when she left me standing there waiting like a fuckin' fool.

—Julian, his mother scolds again.

—You stupid son of a bitch, Keith says.

Julian jerks his head around at Keith and glares at him.

—What'd you call—

—Think about it, Sam says. Maybe she didn't stand you up at all, but was abducted on her way to meet you.

Running.

Stumbling.

Falling.

Rolling.

Leaping.

Running again.

The swamp she's running through is thick and green and humid. Hands and face stinging. Flesh cut, ripped, torn. Branches. Limbs. Vines. Twigs. Thorns.

This morning, she had been so hopeful, so happy, so excited about her future. Now, she wonders if she even has one.

Frantic.

Running for her life—and the potential one inside her—on what was supposed to be her wedding day.

Who's doing this to me? And why? Why me? Why today? Why?

Cant . . . go . . . any . . . further.

Whatta I do? Whatta I do? Whatta I do?

When she can run no more, she slows and searches for a place to hide. To her left is a pine flat filled with palmettos. Tight. Compact. Full fans. Perfect.

Entering the flat, she scans the area. Sees no one. Carefully, she wades into the thicket, picks out a spot, and lies down flat on the ground, disappearing beneath the blanket of branches.

Aware the clumps of little palms are a favorite nesting spot for rattlesnakes and wasps, their fruits a favorite food of black bears and feral hogs, she knows hiding here is not without risks, but they are relative. She's got to stop. Got to hide. Would rather take her chances with the dangerous creatures down here than the one chasing her.

So tired.

So thirsty.

So distraught.

I'm gonna die. I'm gonna die out here all alone. I'm never gonna see my mommy again.

As her heart rate and breathing decelerate, she begins to cry.

She should be more prepared. Mother Earth had trained her better than this.

Nearly everything she knows about the river and swamp and environmental activism, she learned from Marshelle Mayhann, a local legend everyone referred to as Mother Earth. Radical tree hugger, river swamp savior, leathery lady of the land, Mother Earth had been one of the few people Taylor had allowed Shelby to hang out with. For years, she had ridden up and down the river and traipsed through the swamps with Mother, listening carefully, learning all she could, so she too could fight the good fight to save her native soil from the greedy motherfuckers who were so set on raping it.

A few moments later, glistening, as if seen through a rain-streaked windshield, her tear-filled eyes behold a red-banded hairstreak butterfly float down and flutter around, a delicate, dancing dot of blue-gray. Rust-colored streaks. Small black smudges.

Its beauty and fragility simultaneously buoy and break her heart.

She had awakened so in love with Julian, so thrilled to be heading out on an adventure with him. Now, she's hurt and hungry, terrified and lonely, and in serious doubt she'll ever see him again.

What's he doing right now? Is he looking for me? Is Mom? Marc? Sheriff Keith? Anyone?

Marc jumps when the doorbell rings.

So focused on Shelby's journal, he's forgotten the world around him. The noise is startling in the quiet house, but Taylor, still passed out on the couch, doesn't stir.

Hopping up and placing the laptop where he has just been, he rushes to the door before a second chime could rouse Taylor.

In the few moments it takes him to cross the house, he realizes he could be running to receive bad news about Shelby.

Please, God, no.

In the open doorway, Julian looks diminutive and depleted. Is it fear? Guilt? Worry? Or what the cops put him through?

He hesitates to come in even after Marc invites him, then glances around nervously when inside.

Marc realizes how little he's visited the lodge, how scared he must be.

—Ms. Sean here? he asks tentatively, as if he hopes the answer is no.

—She's asleep.

—Oh. Okay.

Marc finds it difficult to believe the boy before him could have hurt or killed Shelby—an opinion the sheriff just called and told him he shares.

—Anything I can do for you? Give her a message?

—Nah. I's just . . .

The house is night quiet and has an aura of emptiness—absence of something more than light and movement.

—How are you, Julian?

He shrugs.

—Me and Shelby were gonna . . .

—I know.

—You do?

—You guys were gonna marry. Start a family, right?

He looks wide-eyed and surprised at first, but then slowly nods.

—I've spent all day thinkin' she just didn't show, he says.

Marc nods, but doesn't say anything.

—Thought all kinda bad stuff about her.

Marc continues to nod and they are quiet a moment.

—But she wouldn't do that, would she? Just not show up, not say anything.

—No, she wouldn't.

—I've been so fuckin' mad at her. So stupid.

Insecurities make monsters of us all, Marc thinks. He's learning a valuable lesson about perception and projection, but at what price?

—She's the best person I've ever known. Who would take her?

—I'm not sure. We're all trying to figure that out.

—If something happens to her . . .

Something already has, Marc thinks. The only question is what.

—Do I disturb you? Sam asks, a sweet, playful lilt in her voice.

—Greatly, Daniel says, completing the favorite and oft quoted movie line.

—I'm on my way to track down and interview a few possible suspects, she says.

He knows she'll work through the night and the following day—as long as it takes, as long as she can. She's the most relentless person he's ever known. She'll go until she drops, then rest just enough until she can go again. No matter what's going on, she's the best hope Shelby Summers has.

—Have a few minutes in the car, she is saying. Thought we could talk. You got questions for me?

—Yes, I do.

—You still reading the case file?

—I am. How's it going there?

—Not good, she says. Every minute that passes . . . you know? And they're passin' by in a hurry.

He doesn't say anything, and they are quiet a moment.

—So I'm really counting on you, she says.

He laughs.

—Seriously, thanks for what you're doing.

—Just doing it hoping to get in your pants, he says.

—So I have two vested interests, she says. Win win. How can I help?

—Looks like from the file, you didn't have a lead suspect.

—Really didn't have any suspects. Really was like she just vanished.

—What I gather. You looked at both parents hard?

—I did. Dad especially, but Taylor too. There was nothing.

—Shelby?

—Yeah. I mean, she was only eight. She couldn't've

moved Savannah, so if she'd done anything to her, we'd've found her right there in the woods. But she wasn't even late getting home.

—So her mom says.

—Yeah?

—What if Shelby killed Savannah and instead of losing both girls, Taylor helps her hide the body?

—Damn that's dark, she says. Wow. That honestly never even occurred to me. Are you darker than me, Professor?

He laughs.

A gentle-souled philosopher and religious scholar, the only thing truly dark about Daniel is his imagination. Not without certain traumatic experiences—as a child and as an adult—but they seem to have only helped him be more humble, empathic, and insightful. Whatever the damage, it hasn't resulted in a heart of darkness.

—You have no idea, he says.

—But what does that—

—I'm just trying to think of everything. Not saying we should—

—It's a good thought. Keep thinking.

—The woods? he says.

—They're not that big. Just five acres or so adjacent to the lane leading to Lithonia Lodge. We searched every inch. No way she's in there.

—The parents?

—I told you. We—

—Taylor's parents.

—Ah.

—They wanted her dead, he says.

—After the surgery, the doctor who did it, a twin expert and researcher—

—D. Kelly David.

Daniel glances at the online entry he found about Dr. D. Kelly David.

A conjoined twin who survived separation surgery from his brother Karl, who did not, D. Kelly David grew up to become one of the world's foremost experts on twins in general, conjoined twins in particular, and in surgical separation. He is credited with more successful separations than any surgeon in history. In midlife, he founded the River Park Inn Center for the Twin in North Florida, a treatment and research facility specializing in separated and sole surviving twins, but after nearly a decade of operation the center was closed amidst allegations of insurance fraud and accusations of unethical experimentation. Eventually, David would lose his license. He is best known for his role in the Taylor and Trevor Young case, winning a suit against the girls' parents, Ron and Rebecca Young, in which he performed a court-ordered separation to save Taylor's life that cost Trevor hers.

—Yeah, Sam says. He sued for custody of Taylor, claiming Ron and Rebecca were unfit, but he lost. They raised Taylor, but from what I gather it was not a warm environment. When she turned sixteen, she got pregnant and ran away. As far as I know she hasn't had any contact with them. Hard to blame her.

—You interview them?

—No. They still live in Citrus. Creek County sheriff's investigator did. Why?

—They seem like obvious choices. Replace the daughter they lost—or the daughter that was lost to them.

—Oh my God. What a fuckin' idiot I am. I should turn in my shield right now. But why take just one?

—Who knows? Maybe they saw Taylor and Trevor as one—unable to live apart. Maybe they thought they were being kind. Leave Taylor one.

—Why take the other now?

—I don't know. Maybe they decided they have to have both. Maybe they saw or read something about Taylor recently that made the thought of her having Shelby intolerable.

—She does have a new live-in boyfriend.

—There you go.

—The novelist Marc Hayden Faulk. You read him?

—Yeah. That's interesting. Very interesting.

—We've got to interview them. How about we do it together first thing in the morning?

—I'm so sorry, Taylor says. I feel like shit.

She is awake now, sitting awkwardly on the couch, sobering up, but still hung over.

—Always do when I'm mean to you, she adds.

Marc just listens, nodding, not saying anything. He's stopped reading, placing the papers on the coffee table.

—What is that? she asks.

—What?

—All those papers?

—Shelby's journal.

—You printed it?

—In case the power goes out from the storm.

She nods slowly, appreciatively, then they are quiet a beat.

—I don't even know what I said, just remember it was

171

mean. Felt mean. You don't deserve this. I'm a monster. Get as far away from me as you can.

—That's what it was, he says. Always comes back to that.

—Huh?

—You sending me away. When you're hormonal, hurt, or drunk you want me out. Want me away from you, out of your house, out of your life. When you're sober, sad, or remorseful, you say I don't deserve this, that I should leave. Comes down to the same thing. You wanting to end this. Us.

—But only because I don't deserve you and you don't deserve this. That's all it ever is. When I'm feeling monstrous, I want you away so you don't see me and so I don't hurt you.

—You really expect me to believe that?

—It's true. I mean it. I know I don't deserve someone as good and kind as you. And I know you're sick of me, my moods, my goddamn post traumatic stress disorder. I'm sick of it too, but I can't leave me. You can.

—Like everyone else has? he asks.

—Well, they have.

He shakes his head.

—I know. I'm sorry. But I'm also sick of having to be sorry. To be the one who's always wrong. I don't think you get it.

—What? he asks. What don't I get?

—Can you imagine what it's like to have your parents want you dead? To have your sister cut out of you—for her to die so you could live? To have a mangled body to remind you every single day? To grow up in a loveless, laughless, lifeless home with strangers who couldn't be colder? Who're unhappy because you lived, because you killed their other daughter? To be the town freak of a small town where everybody whispers and shuns? To have the whole fuckin' world know you for one thing? Every man I've ever had has let me down—or worse.

—I'm so sorry.

She doesn't respond.

—Things are different now. You know that. I'm different. You can count—

—I'm sorry, she says, but we don't have time for this right now. I can't even think straight. All I can think about is Shelby.

He nods.

—My two girls are all I've ever had, she says. I barely survived losing one—and that was because of the other. Now, I've lost her. I'm damaged beyond repair. But that doesn't matter right now. It doesn't matter that I'm sorry or that I warned you from the very beginning.

You did, he thinks. You told me you didn't believe in love, weren't capable of having a relationship, but I thought I had changed all that.

—All that matters right now is Shelby.

Cypress swamp.

Soft, soggy soil.

Wetlands.

Black willow, broadleaf cattail, pitcherplants, sweetbay, elephantgrass.

Occasional pond pine.

No longer running. No longer able to. Shelby stumbles through the swamp, mosquitoes humming around her head, dive bombing her arms and legs, draining blood from her dehydrated body.

Exposed.

Sandals.

Shorts.

Spaghetti-strap shirt.

Her sore, cut, and torn feet sink into the muddy bog, her inadequate shoes getting sucked down deeper with every step, slowing and tripping her. The only thing worse than the barely there sandals she's wearing would be no shoes at all. These at least help protect the bottoms of her feet.

When she had left the lodge this morning, she had been pretending to be headed to THS, dressed in the casual, requisite attire for North Florida public school in August—next-to-nothing shirt, shorts, and sandals.

Her wedding and honeymoon and new life clothes are in her backpack and shoulder bag, which he must have taken while she was unconscious, because she saw them in the boat.

Now, her chalk-colored, ruffled crochet cami that hits at her hips and the rip-and-repair double-roll denim shorties hugging them are sweat-stained and mud-soiled, ripped and torn for real. Irreparable rags.

Why'd he take my things? Hell, why'd he take me? Murder? Rape? Ransom?

She thinks about it.

Got to be rape or ransom. Why else abduct her? Why not just kill her on the spot?

Doesn't mean he's not gonna kill me.

No it doesn't.

Walk faster.

Where am I?

She fears she may be far more lost than she realizes, wandering around in circles—something easy to do in the swamp.

Picking up her pace, she's only taken a few strides when she trips over a cypress knee and falls to the ground hard.

Lying flat on the wet earth, her face is just inches away from a crayfish chimney—the pale adobe-looking stack of wet soil from the crayfish burrowing into the ground.

She's so spent, so sad, so in pain, she just lies there a moment looking at the crayfish chimney, spotting others in the short distance—and a few moments later when he passes by, his boots sloshing near her head, she reckons it saves her life. Or at least prolongs it.

After stepping near her head, the barrel of his rifle just inches away, he takes a few more steps, then stops.

The wolf waits and watches.

She's near. He knows it.

The wolf's sense of smell is relatively weak, undeveloped compared to that of many hunting dogs.

He can't smell her. But he knows she's here.

He likes her running. Wishes she still was.

The third step of the hunt—confronting.

Confronting the prey—once the prey detects the wolf, it can either approach, stand its ground, or flee. Large prey usually stand their ground. When this occurs, wolves hold back, as they require the stimulus of a running animal to proceed with an attack.

There had been no standing her ground. Only fleeing.

Shelby had run. She didn't know not to. She had run and the wolf found it intensely stimulating.

The fourth stage of the hunt—rushing.

175

Rushing the prey—when the prey attempts to flee, wolves immediately pursue. This is the most crucial and critical stage of the hunt, as wolves may never catch up with prey running at top speed.

The wolf had rushed. Shelby had run.

The fifth and final stage of the hunt—chasing.

Chasing the prey—actually, a continuation of the rush, the wolf attempts to catch up with his prey. When chasing small prey, the wolf attempts to catch up with it as soon as possible, while with larger prey, the wolf prolongs the chase, wearing out the animal.

Shelby is small prey.

He will have her. He will end this soon. It is inevitable.

Stop breathing, she tells herself.

Be still.

Everything in her is screaming get up and run.

Don't move.

She wants to cry.

Don't cry.

Her empty stomach churns and she feels like she's going to vomit.

Stop it. Now.

Psychobilly freakout.

Her mind hurls so much at her—so many questions, so many thoughts, so many feelings, so much hopelessness, loss, and despair—that she can't process it and she freaks the fuck out.

What do I do? What do I do? What do I do? Should

Separation Anxiety

I run? Should I run? Roll? Try to hide better? Just wait? Is he about to shoot me? That what he's doing? Getting his rifle ready? I'm gonna die. Right here. Right now. Alone. My goddamn face in the mud. I can't just lie here waiting for my head to explode.

Stop. Just stop. Don't think.

A mosquito lands on her cheek.

She wants to slap the shit out of it and her face.

It begins to bite her, to suck her irritable, mad blood.

Don't do anything.

But—

Nothing. Don't do a thing. Do you hear me? Listen to what I'm telling you. Be still. Be quiet. Just don't move.

Part of her just wants to stand, to get this over with. She's tired of running. Sick of being lost in the swamp, thirsty, hungry, hurting. End it right now. It'd be sweet relief.

Unbidden, her mind fills with photographs of the river swamp and the wildlife it's home to. The incredible images were taken by Remington James, a local man who's famous not just for the rare wildlife his camera captured, but because it also made a frame-by-frame chronicle of a crime committed out here where there's not suppose to be any witnesses.

His images, the story behind them, and the way they connect to Mother Earth, had always haunted her.

There are no cameras on her now, nothing recording her or the man after her.

I don't want to die alone out here in the swamp.

—You're not alone, a kind male voice says.

That startles her. It seemed to come from within her as much as without.

She looks around. Slowly. Carefully. Quietly.

No one is there.

Who was that? Where'd it come from? It's not her abductor. She can tell that much, but beyond that she has no idea.

Well, she does have one idea. Just not one she relishes.

I'm losing it. Cracking up. It's not bad enough that I have to be raped and murdered by a fuckin' psychopath, not horrible enough that Mom has to go through losing another child. No, I have to lose my goddamn mind in the process.

—I hope that little girl's not really in trouble, Gary Dobbs says. I'd hate to think you're wasting your time asking silly questions of someone like me if her life's in jeopardy.

Gary Dobbs is a general with the Army Corps of Engineers and the man Shelby humiliated at a meeting sponsored by the Apalachicola Riverkeeper recently.

Sam would prefer to talk to him in person, but he resides in Mobile and can't afford the eight-hour round trip it'd take to make that possible, so she's called his home phone from her car in between interviewing other suspects. She figures if he answers his house phone chances are he's not involved. Doesn't mean he can't be—or might not be behind it, but she calculates that a very long-shot anyway.

—I appreciate that, Sam says. But I follow all possible leads. Never know which one will be the one.

—Well, I sure as hell ain't the one.

—From what I hear she really embarrassed you in a big public way.

—Don't believe everything you hear, missy. I can't be embarrassed by a little girl. No matter how bright or passionate or misguided.

Separation Anxiety

Though Gary Dobbs talks like an alpha military man, his voice is soft and somewhat high-pitched, undermining his authority—or would, but it's as if he can't hear how sweet he sounds.

—You think she's misguided? From what I hear she made some extremely salient points.

—She expressed some valid concerns and did so eloquently—especially for a child—but, as usual with people like her, she can't see the bigger picture.

—Which is?

—Balance.

—Balance?

—Everybody wants the same water. Everybody thinks their little sliver of the pie is the most important.

—You think they're all equally important?

—I didn't say that.

—'Cause property values on Lake Lanier or greedy overdevelopment in Atlanta can't compare to the rare estuary of the Apalachicola River flood plain and the Bay. We're talking about species dying off, never coming back. That can't compare with making money.

—Are you a cop or a radical?

—Those aren't radical notions, sir. I can see why Shelby said your head was shoved so far up your pompous ass your policies were shit.

—The problem with people like you and that misguided little girl is you've got passion but not the right information. I don't make policy. I enforce it. I'm a soldier. You want to change policies, talk to congress. And I'm not stupid. Not a little girl you can trick. I know you're trying to provoke me, but I'm not taking the bait.

—You sound pretty angry to me, Sam says.

179

—Actually, that's my sweet voice.

Sam laughs.

—What? he asks.

—Your sweet voice. That's so cute.

—I'm hanging up now, he says.

—One more thing before you do, she says. It's patronizing, sexist, and dismissive to keep referring to Shelby Summers as a little girl. Or to say you can't be tricked like a little girl. From where I sit, that little girl is making the world a hell of a lot better than you and me.

Lying still in the sodden soil, her clothes soaked, her skin sweat-moist and mosquito bitten, Shelby is motionless, wondering if these few moments will be her last.

What's he doing?

She wants so badly to look at him, to at least see if she's about to be shot.

The not knowing is nearly unbearable.

—You're doing just fine, the kind voice says again. Just hang in there a little longer. Don't move. Don't look. Just breathe. Try to relax.

Who the hell are you? And what the hell are you doing in my head? Are you in my head? It sounds like you're sort of outside and inside at the same time.

No response.

Really, Shelby? she asks herself. Sort of inside and outside at the same time?

Hey, this is uncharted territory. All of it. Cut me some slack.

Separation Anxiety

Think of Julian, she tells herself. If these are your final thoughts, don't let them be dark and fearful, but good and loving.

Her mind rushes back to the morning and the happiness and hope she felt.

The plan had been to meet at the landing, leave, romantically, by boat for their new lives together, get married in Apalach, and honeymoon in Julian's grandfather's old camp on the Brothers River—which can only be reached by boat. Because they are minors, they're required to have parental consent and a license has to be issued by a county judge, but because she is pregnant, parental consent is not required, and they found a sympathetic and discrete judge in Apalach willing to do it.

She had arrived early. So excited to meet her man. Make their escape. Parking her car beneath her dad's camp, she had started unloading and preparing.

Seemingly out of nowhere, her attacker, her abductor, appeared and apprehended her from behind. Somehow she had gotten away.

Running.

Screaming.

Falling.

Standing.

Running.

All she had seen of him was from a quick glance over her shoulder, a jarring, disjointed view as she attempted to elude him.

She has only the vaguest image of the man who wishes her ill.

Long. Lanky. Lupine.

Yes, that's it. Lupine. There's something decidedly

181

wolfish about him. Something deranged and deformed about him too. Monstrous. Simian creature beneath the basement of her subconscious. But mostly wolfish.

She had been able to avoid him for a little while, but no one had responded to her cries for help, and soon he was on her, tackling her from behind, pulling her down like a small prey animal separated from the herd. Then something on her face—a cloth. Force. Acrid smell. Panicked breathing. Then nothing.

Regaining consciousness in the bottom of his boat, her things piled before her, she pretended to still be asleep. A bend in the river. A turn. Slowing. Bow dropping. Near land.

Another boat. Old man. Friendly.

—Hey neighbor, you're out awful early.

No response.

—Best part of the day, the old man continues. Don't know why more folk aren't out here of a mornin', but don't mind havin' the river to myself. How 'bout you?

Again, no response.

—Not much a one for shootin' the breeze, are you? Is that a— Is she okay?

Gunshot.

And another.

Old man falling over in his boat.

As her abductor had edged over to ensure the man was dead, she had made her move.

Standing.

Lunging.

Landing.

Swimming.

Bank.

Climb.

Run.

Ducking. Bending. Tripping. Stumbling. Falling. Pushing. Running.

Running.

She'd spent the day running from an unknown, nearly unseen abductor.

Running in circles.

Running in place.

She has no idea where she is, no idea how long she was unconscious, how long they had motored—and if it was upriver or down. All she knows is he's now just a few feet away from her with a rifle and most likely more chloroform.

That thought leads her to another.

For all she knows he could've raped her already. No telling what he did to her while she was out. She does a quick inventory of her wet, tired, hot, aching, hurt, hungry body. She can't be sure whether or not she's been violated, but she can tell she hasn't been brutalized.

—He didn't rape you, the unfamiliar but not unfriendly voice says.

Who are you? How do you know?

Again, no response.

She's so nervous, so much tension inside her ready to burst out, she wants to scream, to face her fate, fuck hiding and running and—

And then he's gone. Stepping away from her in his heavy boots the way he had stepped toward her.

She waits a long, long time, unwilling or unable to move, unsure whether he's still close enough to see her. Then she waits some more.

Too scared to move. Too miserable not to. She eases up just enough to crawl.

Crawling.

Through the cypress swamp. Out of the wetlands. Wondering all the while what her hands are going to come down on—rattlesnake, cotton mouth, snapping turtle, wasps, brown recluse? There are plenty of things out in these swamps worse than a psychopath with a gun, experiences as brutal and as deadly.

The experience so far has been plenty unpleasant enough. I'm gonna try to keep anything else from happening.

Try all you want to, you probably won't make it through the night.

—Yes you will, the soft male voice says. I'm gonna help you. We're going to get through this together.

Goddamn it. I can't take much more of this, she thinks, and starts to cry again.

Beth Ann Costin stops by the Dollar Store not because she wants to, but because it's the only option at this hour—and it closes in ten minutes.

Out of certain necessities like Diet Coke, toothpaste, and coffee filters, she plans to zip in, grab what she needs, and zip out. Not only because she's so tired, but because the way the creepy stock boy tends to stare at her and follow her around the store.

But she never gets what she's here for.

Not three steps in, and she hears the large lady with enormous black bags beneath her eyes buying Puppy Chow and candy bars telling the short, yellow-shirted clerk with the dated haircut how Shelby Summers is missing.

In a moment of horror, she thinks about how happy she had been that Grayson missed his appointment, how perfectly Shelby matches the girls he describes in his demented fantasies, and how he mentioned her in one of their sessions when bragging about having original Taylor Sean paintings and having been invited to her home to purchase them.

Turning and running out, she bumps into an elderly man easing into the store behind her.

Damp.

Muggy.

Sticky.

Loud.

Walking along a pine tree-dotted ridgeline on the east side of a dried up slough, Shelby misses her mom and Marc and Julian so much the emotional pangs produce physical pain.

She's never felt so alone in her entire life—not even following Savannah's disappearance.

She feels feverish and her moist skin itches. Every cell aches. Every stumbling step is difficult and painful.

Drone.

Buzz.

Hum.

Chirp.

Croak.

Crickets and frogs and mosquitoes and gators and every kind of noisy incessant insect create an aural assault louder than the busiest city streets of the biggest busiest cities in the world.

Oh God, if I die, please, please don't let Mom find my journal.

She thinks about how much it'd hurt her mom, how much of it's not true—even if it was in the middle of the moment when she wrote it.

If I wanted to hurt her, to have her hear my raging rants, I'd've said them to her.

Mom can be a pain, but I wouldn't hurt her for the world. She's had enough of that. Far more than her fair share.

Given that, her mom's pretty cool. Overprotective as a mofo and a little volatile, but otherwise cool. Hell of a lot better than her parents were to her. And she could be fun and funny. She was the most creative person Shelby knew—making her and Savannah's childhoods magical.

How much better things would've been if Savannah hadn't been taken.

And now me. Fuck. Maybe Mom wasn't overprotective enough.

I've got to get through this and get back to her.

What's the best way? Think.

I can't. I'm just . . . Nothing makes any . . . I'm just so . . .

Stop! Take a breath. Think.

Where the fuck am I?

Follow the ridgeline to the river.

What if I'm heading inland? I can't tell. Some environmentalist I turn out to be. I'm lost as fuck. It'd break Mother Earth's heart to see how inept I am. What would she do? What would Kerry?

Kerry.

Thinking of him makes her sad too. Such a decent man. Been so good to her, so kind. Treats her like an adult. Same way

Marc does.

Marc.

So good to her mom. Sees past her trauma and scars to the wounded little orphan. Doesn't just see the artist, but the woman. So so so glad he's there for her. Especially now. God, I hope she doesn't drive him away. Hope he doesn't let her.

Memories of Mother Earth remind her of her animals, the little wild things rehab she has in her backyard. She was going to call her mom after she was married and tell her what to do with them, how to care for them, who to give them to, but . . .

This is what you're thinking of? Come on. Focus. Quit trying to distract yourself, and figure a way out of here. Hurry. Or die.

—You're going to be okay.

This time the voice is unmistakably outside of her—so much so that she whips her head around toward where it had come from.

No one is there.

—Who is it? she asks.

—A friend. Here to help.

—An imaginary friend?

—Martin Chalmers thinks he saw someone on his property last night staring at Lithonia Lodge through binoculars, Keith says.

He, Will, and Sam are in his office, each having returned from tracking down leads.

Weary. A little worn. But not without resolve.

—I'll get a team over there, Will says.

—I've got a guy who'd be perfect for the job, Sam says. Get one chance not to fuck up footprints and other evidence.

—Call him, Will says.

—Will do, she says. I talked to the contractor and the corps general. Nothing there. Gonna talk to Taylor's parents in the morning. And we need to get someone over to the Planned Parenthood Shelby was talking to in Tallahassee.

The fluorescents of Keith's office are overly bright in the dim building, and it's odd for them to be on this late at night. There's a harshness in their illumination that seems unkind, even judgmental—a thought Sam realizes says far more about her level of fatigue than the quality of light in the room.

—Beth Ann Costin believes she's got a client capable of taking Shelby, Keith says.

—Yeah? Sam says.

—Says he's mentioned her by name.

—Yeah?

—But she can't tell us who because it'd violate confidentiality.

—What? Will says. So why tell you that much?

—She's torn. She wanted me to tell her what to do. She really wants to tell, but it'll probably cost her her license.

—What'd you tell her? Will asks.

—Something unethical.

—Oh yeah? Will says, his eyebrows arching.

—That you, me, and Sam are the only ones who'll ever know.

—If it turns out her client really does have her, Sam asks, what we gonna say led us to him?

—I'm working on it.

—You saying you're gonna lie? Sam says. Fabricate—

—Not evidence. Just how we got to him.

—Fuck, Sam says.

—It gets worse. He's rich and powerful and in public office.

—Motherfuck, Will says with a smile.

—Exactly.

—Y'all in? Keith asks.

Sam smiles.

—You had me at 'client capable of taking Shelby,' she says.

The two men laugh.

Then the three of them fall quiet a moment, fatigue seeming to finally overtake them all.

—I know I'm wasting words, Keith says, but you two should really think about shuttin' it down for the night and getting some rest for tomorrow. First light, we'll have the full team here and will hit the ground running. You'll be better for Shelby if you're at least a little rested.

—But how much time do we really have? Sam asks. What time is landfall predicted?

—About three tomorrow afternoon, Will says.

—Which means we'll have outer bands by morning.

—Yes, ma'am.

—So, she says, I say fuck sleep.

—She's got a point, Will says.

Keith smiles.

—Does, doesn't she?

189

Will bangs on Davis Allen Grayson's door.

A solid, ornate door befitting the exclusive condominium complex situated in the shadow of the state capitol.

—Mr. Grayson? Police. Open up, sir.

There's no answer, no indication inside that anyone is home.

He bangs again and, noticing a doorbell button for the first time, presses it.

Again, nothing.

In the distance, lit from below, the capitol tower rises in the darkness, phallic and overbearing, but beneath it, the old, original, restored capitol is stately, classic, seemingly permanent. Elaborate. Intricate. Artistic. Red-and-white striped awnings. Chiseled seal over tall entry columns. Glass dome. Flagpole piercing the night sky. Red, white, and blue. Red, white, and yellow. Black and white. Three flags slowly waving in the breeze. American. Floridian. MIA/POW.

Pulling out his cell, he thumbs in Grayson's number and waits. After four rings, the call is answered.

—Hello.

Out of breath. Annoyed.

—Mr. Grayson?

—Yes. Who is this?

—Detective Will Jeffers. River County Sheriff's Department.

—What can I do for you, Detective?

—I've got a few questions for you. Where are you?

—Home.

—Good. I'm at the front door. Come let me in so we

can—

—Oh, my. That's a bit awkward.

—What is?

—Well, Detective, I'm afraid you've caught me in a bit of a little white lie.

—How's that?

—I'm not actually at home yet.

—Where are you?

—I can be home a little later. Give me your number and I'll call you.

—Sir, this isn't a social call. Where are you?

—How's that? I'm losing you. Not much signal here.

—Where's that?

—Detective? Can you hear me? Are you there? Detective?

—I can hear you just fine.

—Hello. Hello. Are you there? Detective?

Then nothing—save Will's palpable anger sending out plenty of signal of its own into the ether.

—You asleep? Sam asks.

—No, ma'am, Daniel says.

She can hear the smile in his voice.

—What're you doin'?

—Still trying to solve your case. Anything new on your end?

—Nothing worth sharing.

They are quiet a moment.

—So, Sam says, I was thinking.

—Yeah?

—Instead of waiting 'til morning, why don't we wake Ron and Rebecca up tonight?

—Like the way you think, Special Agent, he says.

Which is why an hour later they're racing toward Citrus together on a dark, empty, fog-shrouded highway beneath a half-full milky moon.

—This is nice, Sam says. Romantic.

Daniel is driving, his profile outlined by the bluish glow of the dashboard. She is slightly reclined in the passenger seat, turned toward him a bit, admiring how handsome, how tall, how calm.

—'Tis, he says, reaching over, pulling back her skirt, and rubbing her leg, adding, Makes me amorous.

—Name one thing that doesn't.

He starts to say something, then stops.

She laughs.

—I'm sure there's something.

She shakes her head.

—Not that I've found. Not even chasing down leads in a child murder-abduction case. You think the two cases are related?

—Don't see how they couldn't be, but nothing to suggest it so far, is there?

—No.

—You'd think an abductor would take a child or a teen, not both? he says.

—If they're not connected, it'd be like someone getting

struck by lightning twice.

—True, he says. Good analogy there, slim.

They are quiet a moment, the yellow dashes and reflector dots of the rural highway rising out of the fog, the silent slash pines lining the road visible in the periphery spill and brume bounce of headlights.

—I find the drama involving the Youngs, Taylor, Trevor, and Dr. David as fascinating as anything in the file, he says.

—It is, isn't it? It's just unbelievable parents would be willing to let both children die rather than save one.

He nods.

—Religion, man, she says, shaking her head.

He continues to nod, but a small smile creeps across his face.

She smiles back. As a religion professor and a person with a deep, profound faith, he's religious in a way that makes him as far away from people like the Youngs as he possibly can be and still be considered religious, but she never misses an opportunity to fuck with him about religion.

—I know, he says. We're all fuckin' nuts.

—You're not. You're like the coolest cat I know, all Zen and shit, but you'll have to explain these people to me.

—In a word, he says, fear. They've been taught to believe in a God of wrath who makes up arbitrary laws and punishes those who don't follow them to the letter. They're afraid.

—So they'd kill their kid?

—Sure. Think of Abraham.

—Who?

He tells her. As he does, she leans forward and looks up through the windshield at the moon and the silhouettes of tree tops lit by it. Pale light. Blue sky. Black trees.

193

—And he's the hero? she asks.

—Yeah. Every culture, every time, every religion has fear-based elements that think sacrifice is necessary to appease the gods—or the equivalent. And the god they serve is so authoritative, they don't dare question anything they're taught. No matter how bizarre.

—Thanks for being the way you are, she says.

—Would you love me if I were like them?

—I'd have to. I don't have a choice, but I'm glad you're not.

They are quiet another moment, and she reaches over and touches the side of his face with the back of her hand.

—We're so lucky to have found each other, she says.

—Yes we are. Yes we are.

—And we know it.

—Yes we do, he says. Yes we do.

Think.

I am.

No. Of something nice. Quit with all the negativity. Things are bad enough. You're making them worse with all your hopeless thoughts. It's gonna be a long night. But even if it's not, even if you're about to die, make sure your final thoughts are thoughts worth having.

She thinks about the first time she and Julian made love, how sweet and sincere he had been, how tender. He was the first guy to ever be inside her—the first and only, whether she makes it out of the swamp or not.

She loves him in a way only love songs and fairytales can convey—and none of them come close. They are passionate and playful and perfect for one another, the incarnation of their devastating love growing inside her right now.

His mom works so much that her trailer had become their love nest. Because of the way her own mom is they didn't get nearly as much time alone in it as they would've liked, but she didn't know of any other couple their age who had a place like it all to themselves.

She smiles.

Doesn't know of any other couple their age having a baby either.

They're just getting started on their journey through life together, have much to learn and experience, but they're already so good together, so crazy, so committed. She likes that he's the only guy she's slept with—and likes it that he's not much more experienced than she.

Of all the love-inspired artistic expressions she's encountered, none have so fully and completely and accurately captured the feelings and textures and tastes of her experience as much as a short story Marc had written she had virtually memorized attempting to emulate.

Continuing to comfort herself and occupy her mind to keep from freakin' the fuck out, she tries to rewrite from memory the story Marc titled simply "First Love."

Reliving the innocence and intense intimacy of the story's couple, she thinks she and Julian love each other like that. Just like that.

Had Marc loved a girl like that when he was her age? Had to.

Does he love Mom like that now? Must. Good for you, Mom. It's about time.

So warmed and comforted by the story and her thoughts of Julian, she thinks she might actually be able to sleep now.

Searching around, she finds a cypress tree with a hollow base, slips inside, and lies down. Soon, she is leaving the world of swamps and dangerous abductors behind, drifting down into unconsciousness. Down. Down. Down.

Of all the things Marc finds in Shelby's eclectic journal entries, nothing touches him more than, moves him as much as finding his story "First Love." He recalls her saying how much she liked it a while back, but had no idea just how much until he sees her comments about it, how she's so inspired by it she wants to write a similar story of her own, and by the fact that she pasted the entire story into her journal. Unable to resist, he reads the beginning of the story again.

It's been a while since he's read the story, and he finds that it moves him—especially in the light of it speaking to Shelby. He'd like to finish it, but can't. He's indulged in it long enough. Probably too long. This isn't about connecting with, but finding Shelby.

—What is it? What's wrong? Taylor asks.

He realizes a few tears are trickling down his cheeks.

—Are you okay? she asks. What's going on?

He tells her.

—Oh, Marc, she says, obviously touched.

She comes over to him, removes the journal pages from his hands and places them on the coffee table, then pulls him up into an embrace.

Tenderly, she kisses the tear streaks on his face.

—Thank you, she says. And not just for speaking to my Shelby with your amazing work, but for loving her and me and all you're doing now.

He doesn't say anything, just nods.

—Come over here, she says, leading him over to the couch. Lie down with me.

—I can't. I've got to keep reading.

—Five minutes, she says. Let me hold you for five minutes.

—No. I've got to keep—

—I know. And I want you to, but— What is it? Why're you so upset?

He realizes he's showing more emotion than he realized.

—Sorry.

—Tell me, she says.

—I can't believe I fell back asleep this morning, he says. If I hadn't, maybe she wouldn't be missing. At least the search would've started sooner.

—Lie down, she says. Now.

He does.

—It wasn't your fault. It was the middle of the night for you. I should've been the one calling and waiting. You were sweet to let me paint, but you shouldn't have been put in that position. It's my fault. Slide over.

He shifts toward the back of the sofa, and she lies on her side next to him.

Slipping her left arm behind his neck, she begins to caress him with her right, tenderly touching his face, gently tracing the outline of his arm, abdomen, and chest.

—You're the best man I know, she says. That I've ever known. I'm so blessed to have you in my life. So's Shelby.

Her words are wispy whispers at his ear, ticklish and touching.

He feels comforted and cared for, his mind a montage of all the times just like this one when post-traumatic Taylor was put away and his twin returns to him, times of affection and connection, intensity and intimacy, secrets and solace.

—Sorry I'm such a mess sometimes, she's saying. I'm trying to be better—you make me better. Please don't leave me.

—I won't.

—Please don't stop loving me.

—I never will.

—Next to Savannah and Shelby, you're the best thing to ever happen to me.

They are quiet a moment, her continuing her ministrations, and he can feel himself starting to slip away, succumb to sleep.

—I've got to get up, he says. Get some coffee, get back to reading.

He feels her nod next to his head.

—Yes, she says. Me too. I'm gonna help. Just two more minutes.

Long, low roofline.

One story.

Small.

Simple.

Stucco.

Asymmetrical.

Ron and Rebecca's ranch-stye house is plain and rustic and fits what Daniel knows of them and their religion.

The exterior of the aging domicile is clean and neat and well-maintained, but generic, colorless, soulless. The lawn is mowed, but not manicured. No flowers. No shrubs. Not a single tree for shelter on the lot.

Daniel is bothered by the lack of trees and what he thinks it says about the Youngs' worldview and religious beliefs. He could be wrong of course, but disrespect for and disregard of nature is so typical of arrogant, ignorant, apocalyptic people convinced of both their superiority to all other living things and the ridiculous doctrine that God is going to destroy the earth soon anyway.

Ron Young answers the door fully dressed, though, from the condition of his eyes and hair and the time it takes for him to open, it's obvious he's been sleeping.

As Daniel had expected, the man's attire is modest and lacking in modernity.

After opening the old wooden door, he just stands there awkwardly, waiting, a not unpleasant expression on his peculiar pale face.

—Mr. Young? Sam says.

—Yes?

—I'm Samantha Michaels and this is Daniel Davis. We're with the Florida Department of Law Enforcement. We need to ask you and your wife a few questions.

—Now? he asks with a slightly bemused look on his face.

—Right now, sir. Yes.

—Rebecca's asleep.

—Wake her. We'll wait.

He leads them into the living room then disappears down the hallway.

Like the exterior of the house, the interior is without passion or personality. No family photos. No mementos or memorabilia. No collectables. No color.

The only decorations adorning the walls or displayed on tabletops are religious icons of the Catholic variety, but even these are of the most modest, desaturated, and stripped down design—not the iconography associated with the excesses of cathedrals, but the asceticism of monasteries.

Ceramic crosses. Pewter crucifixes. Well-worn wooden rosaries.

When Ron returns with his wife, everyone sits, and Sam explains what's happened and the purpose of the late-night intrusion.

—Oh, the poor child, Rebecca says.

Like her husband, she is fully dressed. Plain. Pale. Uptight. Upright. Rigid.

Not particularly unattractive, but unappealing in every way.

—Why wouldn't she call and tell us a thing like that? Ron says. What's wrong with her?

—How often do you speak? Sam asks.

He nods.

—Well, yeah. You're right. She doesn't talk to us. But something like this…

—When's the last time you spoke to her?

—Her sixteenth birthday. Not long before she ran away.

—Like the Bible says, Rebecca adds, How sharper than a serpent's tooth it is to have a thankless child.

Daniel smiles. The quote is Shakespeare, not the Bible, but he doesn't mention it.

—You haven't had any contact with her since then?

—Not for . . . sixteen years, Ron says. Doesn't seem possible. We've tried, of course—especially when the girls were born. We keep hoping she'll . . .

Separation Anxiety

—She's been out of our lives longer than she was in it, Rebecca says.

—Why do you think? Daniel asks.

Neither respond, and their gazes drift over to each other.

—You said she was thankless. What do you—

—We love our daughters very much, Ron says. Pray for their souls every day. Every day. But Taylor is lost. And has been for a very long time. She hasn't been the same since she and her sister were taken away from us.

—It's what happens when man trespasses on the providence of God, Rebecca says.

—What is?

—Abominations.

—Taylor is an abomination? Daniel asks.

Ron clears his throat and Rebecca stops talking.

—What Becca is trying to say is our poor little girls were snatched from the hands of a loving God and cut on and killed by a prideful man disdainful of God's laws. They're both in limbo.

Daniel nods as he begins to understand their twisted, inhumane point of view.

—So you really don't think Taylor should still be alive, he says.

—Not in her current state. No, sir, I don't. God created Taylor and Trevor together, to be together, to remind us all of the joining, the oneness we're all capable of—with God, with others. We can't know his will.

Of course your God is masculine and dictatorial.

—Their lives and deaths were in his hands. Our job is to submit to God's will, not fight against it, not keep it from happening. Our precious little angels are in limbo, their souls stuck. They—

—Daniels eyes widen.

—You think Taylor doesn't have a soul?

—No. Of course she does.

—But it's in limbo?

—With Trevor's. Like it's supposed to be. They're linked. Connected. Always have been. Always will be.

—So Taylor is alive, but shouldn't be and her soul is in limbo?

Not for the first time, Daniel marvels at the crazy things people do with religion, and wonders at the intelligence of Ron and Rebecca Young. He knows smart people are capable of believing some absolute absurdities, but thinks every case of prolonged, militant ignorance demonstrates an absence of a certain type of intelligence. Something somewhere is missing, which makes him smile—Ron is saying the same thing about his daughter.

—You find me amusing? Ron asks.

—No, sir. Sorry. I was thinking of something else.

—What about your granddaughters? Sam asks.

—What about them?

—How much contact do you have with them?

—Them? Ma'am, Savannah's dead. Only Shelby is left.

—Of course. How often do you talk to Shelby?

—We have no contact, Ron says.

—Really? None?

—Taylor has turned her against us.

What do you expect from a woman without a soul? Daniel thinks.

—You're saying you never talk to her?

—Never have.

—Sir, doesn't the ten commandments say something about not bearing false witness to a law enforcement officer?

Daniel laughs.

—You will not mock the Lord our God in this house, Ron says. I assure you of that.

—I assure you I wasn't.

—I think it's best if you go now, he says, starting to stand.

—I have Shelby's phone records.

—And?

—You've been calling her.

—I most certainly have not, he says.

As he sits back down, he hesitates a moment and looks over at Rebecca.

—Rebecca?

—I'm so sorry, Ron, she says, a tremor in her voice. I know I disobeyed you, but I'm weak. I want my granddaughter in my life. I want to know her. I lost both my girls. I just want . . .

As she talks, she continues to sit upright, the posture of her rigid body so erect it provides a confusing juxtaposition to the contrition and brokenness of her words.

Her body is a barrier, holding back her humanity, Daniel thinks. Repression. Control. Denial. Carefully holding it all in. He wonders if there's a real person inside there any longer— and wonders if wondering that makes him more like Ron, who doubts his daughter has a soul, than he'd like to admit.

—Am I the head of this household or not? Ron says.

—You are. I'm so sorry. I never got through. She never returned any of my messages. I still haven't talked to her.

—You're saying you've had no contact with her?

—Yes. None.

—Neither of you have spoken to or seen Shelby? Ever?

They both nod.

—We've seen pictures, Ron says.

—How? Sam asks.

—And how'd you get her number? Daniel adds.

Rebecca looks at Ron, who holds Sam's gaze.

—You'll never believe it, she says.

—Try me, Sam says.

—His secretary.

—Whose? Sam asks.

—The doctor who plays God.

—D. Kelly David?

Red Maple.

Tupelo.

Buttress-bottomed cypresses.

Alligator lilies.

Cypress knees.

Adjacent to the thick cypress bottom, in a small clearing, the largest, tallest cypress knees she's ever seen rise out of the ground like the giant stakes of a medieval fortress. Jagged. Phallic. Spirals.

Cypress knees grow up from deep roots that are deprived of oxygen for long periods of time by floods.

Wandering among them in wonder, she cranes to see the

pointy tops some ten to twelve feet in the air.

Typically, the tops of the knees reach the high-water mark for an area, which means the flood through here must be enormous.

Bathed in moonlight, the clearing seems a magical place.

Letting her fingers follow the contours of aging wood, she's filled with a nearly irresistible urge to hug them.

She smiles at this. Am I offering love and comfort or trying to get it?

Ancient.

Alluvial.

Sacred.

What she feels right now is the closest she comes to magic, what she's experiencing, the closest to transcendence.

The swamp is alive, its soul surrounding her. She feels it.

What's wrong with us? We're so fuckin' ridiculous—starving this holy place because of goddamn greedy development and for rich boy toys' water recreation.

It frustrates her more people haven't joined the fight to save the river and swamps, but being out here like this shows her just how artificial an existence she is still living, how far removed from nature, how isolated by structures and cars and pavement and concrete and steel and air-conditioning—though she's missing the fuck out of some air-conditioning right about now. Being out here, so deep, so cut off from everyone but the swamp itself, reminds her just how vital to its survival, to everyone's survival, the work she and Kerry and others are doing really is.

I've been doing less since I started seeing Julian. Fuck. It's so hard to stay balanced, not to get lost in love, not to let happiness blind you. Got to do better. Got to get out of here first. Before you can do anything else. You've got to survive this night. Right now.

She hears the old man's voice again. Hey, neighbor. Hears the loud explosions of the gunfire breaking the serene silence of the early morning on the river.

Get out of here. Got to find a way. How? I'm just wandering around, lost as fuck. How can I get back to the river? Is that even the thing to do?

—It is, the kind male voice she's been hearing says.

—Huh?

—The thing to do, he says.

No longer a disembodied voice, this time there's a body to go with it, and though she never met the man, and though it's entirely impossible, she knows with a certainty with which she knows very few things that the man is Remington James.

—How . . . she begins.

—I don't know.

—But . . . you're . . .

—I know.

—I'm not crazy, she says. And I'm not just imagining you.

—Not just, no.

—Why didn't I see you earlier?

—Not sure. I was there just like I am now.

—You're so real.

—I think so, he says with a wry smile.

Just then—

—Freeze.

Her abductor's voice reaches her at the same moment the beam of his flashlight does.

Separation Anxiety

Remington is gone. Was he ever there?

—Don't move, her abductor says. I mean it. I'll shoot you and leave you here.

She hears what sounds like a handgun being cocked.

I'm gonna die. Right here. Right now. Alone in the woods. Where is Remington? Where'd you go? They'll never find my body. Never know what happened to me or who this son of a bitch is.

Like the light, the voice is coming from behind her. She has no idea where he is, how far away. Closing her eyes, she tries to judge the distance his words are traveling, but the crickets and frogs and other noisemaking animals and insects make it impossible.

I don't want to die—not now, not here, not like this. But what if what's waiting for me is worse?

—You're not alone, Remington says. You're not gonna die out here. Take a breath. Listen to me. Do what I tell you.

She's back to being able to hear but not see him.

—Pretty impressive, her abductor is saying. Took a lot longer to find you than I thought it would.

—Whatta you want? she says. Why're you doin' this?

He doesn't respond.

—I just wanna go home. Please.

Nothing.

—Please.

Still no response.

—They'll pay you, she says. A lot.

—RUN! Remington yells.

His voice screams inside her as much as outside.

And she listens to it.

207

Ducking, she darts behind the nearest cypress knee for cover, pauses a fraction of a second, then runs toward the cypress and tupelo trees to her right.

—Good, Remington says. You're doing good.

Thwack. Thwack.

Rounds hit the cypress knee behind her.

The handgun's explosion shatters all other sounds, and the swamp goes silent.

Eerie. Dissonant. Desolate. Disquieting.

No wind. No hums. No chirps. No croaks. No noise.

Nothing.

The soundless swamp is creepy and disturbing.

In the aural void she can hear her own blood pumping through her body, rushing past her ears as she runs.

At first she tries to clinch her toes, attempting to keep her sandals on as she runs, but soon abandons that effort in favor of speed and quickness.

Running.

Stumbling.

Tripping.

Pinging like a pinball, she careens off the swollen bases of cypresses, bumped from one to another by the force of her weight and movement.

More shots.

More scrapes.

More silence.

Please don't let me die. Please.

—Don't look back, Remington says. Just run.

She wants to look over her shoulder, see how close her

pursuer is, but knows it will only slow her down, make her run into a tree or trip over a limb. Besides, how will knowing how close he is help? Just run.

The bottoms of her feet are cut and bleeding, every footfall painful. New scratches, cuts, and tears on her face and hands and arms and legs. Heart and lungs exploding. Side stabbing. Still she runs.

She wants to stop, to fall down and cry and cry and cry. But she keeps moving.

Marc wakes to the sound of Taylor screaming.

Still lying on the couch together, they must have fallen asleep.

He pushes up and turns toward her.

—What is it?

At first he can't tell whether she's still asleep or not.

—Taylor. Taylor. Are you okay? Are you awake? Wake up.

—Shelby, she says, jumping up and beginning to pace.

—I know, he says sitting up. We're gonna get her—

—She's being chased. Someone's after her. He's got a gun. Oh God. She's in so much pain. Her feet. Her face. She's all cut up. Bruised and bleeding. Oh God. My baby.

—It's okay, he says. It was just a dream.

—No. It's happening right now.

—We fell asleep. It was just a dream. You were dreaming.

—It's not a dream. It's . . . I can't explain it exactly, but it's real—a connection to her. It's not a dream.

—Where is she? Who's after her?

—I don't know. I can't see it. Only feel it. Feel her. Oh God. Shelby. My little girl.

—So no one's had her this whole time? Someone's after her now?

—I don't know. I'm not . . . I can't . . . I'm just not sure. Stop asking me stupid questions and just find her. We've got to find her. Now.

Will calls Grayson's number again—and again and again and again.

Each time, he gets the man's voicemail.

—Mr. Grayson, this is Detective Will Jeffers. River County Sheriff's Department. It's extremely urgent you call me back. I'm investigating the disappearance of a teenage girl from my county. Your name has come up during the course of our investigation. I need to talk to you as soon as possible. I can't stress enough how important it is. If I have to, I'll put out a BOLO and have every law enforcement officer in the area searching for you. Do yourself a favor and don't let it come to that. Call me right back. I'll be waiting.

When he ends the call, he presses in Keith's number and tells him what's going on.

—No doubt he could hear you? Keith asks.

—None.

—Okay. Let's give him ten minutes or so to call you back. If he doesn't, let's track his ass down.

—Roger that. I'll let you know. Where are you?

—Heading back down to Lanier Landing. Somebody reported seeing someone around Shelby's car.

—It hasn't been towed yet?

—Zeke's trucks were busy with a wreck this evening. I figured it could wait since the car's been processed and didn't turn up anything.

—Think it could be our guy?

—It's possible.

—Want backup?

—You know what the Rangers say? One riot, one Keith.

—You wanna wake an old lady up, don't you? Sam asks.

—You don't? Daniel says.

She smiles.

They are back in the car, roaring down the empty rural highway, moonlight bathing blacktop and slash pines and the wispy edges of the vanishing fog.

—We're a lot more alike than we appear, she says.

—We are, he says, but not when it comes to . . .

—To what?

—This.

—Waking up old ladies?

—The relentless, single-minded pursuit of a lead.

—Good try there, slim, but you're just as dogged.

—You kidding? Dogs aren't as dogged as you.

—So you're okay if we don't wake up the old lady?

—Don't get carried away. I didn't say that. In fact, I'm jonesing to wake up the good doctor too.

She smiles.

—See?

—Proves nothing. No matter how bad I want to talk to the doctor and his secretary, you want to worse. Way worse. You're about leads the way I am about . . .

—Sex, she says.

—You think I'm as doggedly obsessed with sex as you are investigating?

—No. It's not even close.

—Thank you.

—You're way, way more obsessed with pussy than I am cases.

He laughs.

—I can prove it, she says.

—Really? How's that?

—Would you rather pull over on a side road and fuck or to talk to the old lady?

—Can't we do both? I'll be quick.

Can't run another step.

—Not even if it'll save your life? Remington asks.

I can't.

Crying now, the sadness of the world entire atop her.

Her little heart is punching her chest like it's trying to burst out and breaking in two at the same time.

For a while, as she banged into buttresses and tripped over fallen trees, she knew he was behind her because of the occasional play of the beam on the bark and bushes and the random round buzzing by, but it's been a while and she wonders if she's lost him.

Or is that just what he wants me to think?

Separation Anxiety

Out of the cypress swamp, she climbed a low-running ridge, following it for several minutes before jumping down and tromping through several bogs and mud holes—both of which felt so soothing on her feet she was almost able to forget about moccasins.

Now, she finds herself crying her way through a wiregrass longleaf pine flat, the trees sparse, the ground smudged with rosebud orchids, pawpaw, and even the occasional Chapman's rhododendron.

Hearing a rattler not far away, she whips her head around and sees—

Bobbing.

Cackling.

Leaping.

Yellow eyes, white dots on brown feathers.

—It's just an owl, Remington says.

Nearby, a burrowing owl, which is capable of leaping and hovering twenty feet above the ground and making some thirteen different calls, one of which mimics a rattlesnake, bobs about, the white spots on its small body looking like a fresh dusting of snow in the glow of the moon.

—Damn, man, she says. You scared the fuck out of me.

She's so distracted by the bird that it's a few moments before she realizes she's stopped and hasn't been shot.

Did I lose him?

—You did, Remington says.

She doubts it, but is too tired and weak to do much more than find a place to hide. At the far edge of the flats is a titi swamp. She can walk that far, find a place to snuggle in, have herself a good cry, and stay put 'til morning.

—She's out of danger? Marc asks.

—NO, Taylor says, her voice rising. It's just not so immediate. I think. I'm dealing with impressions. And she has . . . some kind of help . . . some kind of protector presence. Savannah maybe. I don't know. Can't tell exactly.

He nods.

She's still pacing around the living room. He's standing now too, hovering over the chair he had been sitting in earlier.

—You don't believe me, do you? she asks.

—Huh?

He's glancing down at the printed pages of Shelby's journal and doesn't quite catch the question.

—I don't blame you. I just . . . I want a partner who doesn't think I'm mental because I'm linked to people.

—People?

—Certain people more than others. I feel it with you.

—Because we're twins, he says.

—If we truly are, you'll know what I'm saying is true.

—Just because I ask questions or at first thought you were having a dream doesn't mean—

—So you do? she says. You believe I'm . . . connected.

—I know we are, he says. Why would I question it for others? 'There are more things in heaven and earth, Horatio, than are dreamt of in your philosophy.'

She nods.

—Exactly. I'm gonna put on some coffee. Want some?

—Sure, he says, and follows her into the kitchen. Who else? he asks.

—Am I connected to? Savannah and Shelby, of course.

Separation Anxiety

Not my parents at all. I've often wondered if Trevor and I were adopted. I'm sure it would've come out during the trial or something, and who adopts conjoined twins, but . . . I just have a hard time believing we came from them. We. I. I've always felt like a we more than an I. Always. I've never told anyone this, but . . . I've never lost my connection with her.

As she talks, she removes a canister of coffee from one cabinet, a bag of sugar from another, and a box of filters from a third, and he wonders again why they aren't all kept together.

—With who? he asks.

—Trevor. I still feel her. Always have. It's the reason I believe in the afterlife. How can I not? What do you think about that, Horatio?

She pauses, filter in hand, for him to answer the question.

—I think for some the veil between the seen and unseen worlds parts more easily, he says. And I knew you were one of those people from your paintings long before I ever met you.

The kitchen is overly bright for the middle of the night, its surfaces cold, spotless.

—You don't think I'm crazy?

—Have you read my novels?

Her eyes widen and she has the look of someone who's realized something they think should have been obvious to them already.

—Guess I just thought it was fiction.

—It is.

—That you didn't necessarily subscribe to the more Southern Gothic elements.

—That's smart. Most readers make the opposite assumption. Think none of it's fiction. But I'd think knowing me the way you do . . .

215

—You're right. I guess I just . . . Well, you're just so levelheaded.

—Just compared to you.

She smiles.

—Maybe that really is it. You're so much less volatile than me.

—So are the residents of most psyche wards.

—True.

As she fills a plastic container with tap water, he notices the small gift Shelby made her as a little girl propped up on the window sill, and he has to blink back tears.

Colored pipe cleaner flower on small fence of Popsicle sticks, fading felt tip pen letters. If mothers were flowers, I'd pick you.

—I spend my life in make-believe land, he says, hoping she didn't see his reaction to the aging dust-covered grammar school gift, and you're calling me all left brain and shit.

—You're right. Sorry.

She glances from his gaze to the craft project over the sink.

—So sweet, she says, her voice cracking beneath a sniffle. The girls made that for me for Mother's Day when they were seven. Year before Savannah was taken. One Mother's Day I have two girls and by the next only one. Will I still have at least one next Mother's Day?

—Yes. Any idea where she is? he asks. Did you sense anything that might help us find her?

She frowns.

—Only that it's isolated. But it's not a bad place. Not a . . . . It's a dangerous place, but safe too. Like . . . It's got to be the woods or some natural place, I think.

When Will's phone rings, he answers it without looking at the screen, expecting it to be Grayson, anxious to talk to him.

—Detective Jeffers?

It's not Grayson, but the voice is vaguely familiar.

—Yes.

—It's Beth Ann Costin.

—Hey. And call me Will. Please.

—Sorry to call so late, but the sheriff said you were up and it'd be okay.

—Sure.

—I'm just so scared and I keep hearing things and I thought if I spoke to you I'd be able to get a little sleep tonight.

—No problem. How can I help?

—Have you spoken with Mr. Grayson yet?

—Not really. Why?

—Well, it's . . . I just wanted to make sure when you do you don't say anything to him that'd let him know I'm the one who contacted y'all about him.

—No, ma'am. I wouldn't.

—He scares me so much. And he's said . . . He reminds me of my obligation to confidentiality all the time—and he does it in a threatening way.

—I understand. Men like him count on your fear. Men like him are a big part of the reason I became a cop. One way or another we're gonna put an end to you having to live in fear.

—Thank you so much. But I just don't want him to hurt anyone. And I don't want to lose my job if I can help it. Though I'm not sure that's going to—

217

—Beth Ann?

—Someone's in the house.

Is it Grayson? Had something he said set him off and sent him in search of Beth Ann?

Fuck! He's too far away. Can't get to her in time.

—Listen to me. Stay on the line. I'm radioing dispatch right now. I'll have a deputy over there in just a moment.

No response.

—Okay?

Nothing.

—Beth Ann? Beth Ann?

Keith cuts his lights as he nears the scene.

The landing is quiet. Empty.

Piecey patches of fog hover just above the surface of the water. Pale. Phosphorescent. Picturesque.

Beyond the river, the tall tips of trees are rimmed by the partial moon's pallid glow.

From a distance, he can see the shadowed shape of a figure inside Shelby's car, backlit by a security lamp behind the neighbors' trailer.

He's about to pull up and get in position when he gets a call.

—Sheriff McFarland.

—Sheriff, Malcolm, the young African-American deputy says. We just got a BOLO from a probation officer in Bay County. Raymond Wayne Hennessey didn't report to Potter Correctional Institution to be locked up during the storm and can't be found.

—Damn it.

—He's the child molester who stalked Taylor Sean, Malcolm says. You think he was really stalking Shelby?

—I have no idea, but it'd make more sense. Send it out. Let everyone know.

After ending the call, Keith sits for a moment, idling, thinking, then parking about thirty feet away, gets out quietly, pulling his pistol as he approaches the vehicle.

Standing back, he taps on the driver's window, orders the man out, then assumes a shooter's stance and waits.

Slowly, awkwardly, Julian crawls out of the car.

Keith can tell the boy's been crying.

—Julian? he says, holstering his gun. What are you doin'?

—I miss her so much. Just wanted to smell her, be near her—something of hers.

—So you trespassed on a crime scene and broke into her car.

—Didn't break in. I have a key.

—Anyone else have one? Keith says.

Julian shrugs.

They are quiet a moment, the wet movement of the river and the distant dissonance of insects the only sounds.

The river smells of fish and must and brine. Fresh, yet slightly fetid.

—I thought she changed her mind. Stood me up. Killed our kid. I've spent all day fuckin' hatin' her.

The irony is not lost on Keith. The betrayed became the betrayer—except he was never the betrayed. How easily lovers hurt each other. Smash what they have. Trample the other's trust—and not just young lovers.

—Y'all couldda been lookin' for her 'stead of talking to me.

—We were doing both.

—If somebody hurts her, you're gonna have to shoot me, 'cause I'll kill 'em.

—Won't come to that. We're gonna find her. She's gonna be all right. I'll deal with whoever took her. Don't you worry.

Breaking down, Julian begins to cry again.

—I love her so much.

—I know you do. Come on, I'll drive you home.

Titi swamp.

Tree hollow.

Curled up.

Uncomfortable.

Exhausted.

Fitful sleep.

Perchance to dream.

In the peaceful early morning, the light in the swamp is incandescent, resting tenderly on the oak leaves and Spanish moss, the pine needles and palmetto fronds, the maple and tupelo and cypresses.

Clearing.

The small field is lush and meadow-like, the soft ground a bouquet of brown-eyed Susans—ovate leaves, stems tapering down into stalks.

The fragrant scent is both fresh and delicate. Subtle. Nature's perfume.

Separation Anxiety

She is wearing a beautiful lace-edged white dress, impossibly bright in the brilliant glow of daybreak.

Birdsong.

The music of morning, the earth fresh and new as the first day.

Before her, in an altered version of the same dress, her mom is regal, radiant, her twin sister, Trevor, still connected, still conjoined, a smaller, weaker, sicker copy of her mom.

Taylor and Trevor. Together. Again.

She's about to say something to her mom, when she realizes her own sister is present—and not just, but conjoined like they never were in life.

—Look, Mom, we're like you.

—Like us, Trevor corrects.

There's something wounded in the woman's words, and it hurts Shelby—for the woman and the small discarded child she had been. Savannah feels it too, and Shelby feels her feeling it.

Shelby cranes her neck to see Savannah.

—I'm so happy to see you, she says. I've missed you so much.

—I feel complete again, Savannah says.

Savannah is no longer a child the way Shelby herself was the last time she saw her, but older and yet somehow timeless, and she realizes that she herself is no longer sixteen, but ageless in a way that makes all four women, mother and daughters, aunt and nieces, sets of sisters, the same ageless age.

—Mom? Shelby asks.

—Yes, sweetie?

—Are we gonna die?

—Of course.

221

—Soon? Rejoin our sisters?

—Would that be so bad?

—No, ma'am, I guess it wouldn't, but what about Marc and Julian?

—You want me to get him to kill them too?

—Who? Who is he?

—He's an it.

—Ma'am?

—An it. A thing. Not human. You'll see soon enough.

Savannah begins to cry.

Shelby feels her enormous pain and sadness.

—Don't cry, Vannah.

—Don't tell me what to do, she says.

—What's wrong? Why are you so sad?

—Wouldn't you be? You will. So much pain, so much loneliness, so much longing.

—Mom, Shelby says, turning toward her, why are Savannah and I joined the way you and Trevor are?

—You don't have to be. None of us do.

Taylor steps back while shoving Trevor, snapping bones, splitting organs, splattering their torn white dress crimson.

Trevor screams as she falls to the ground, her abdomen ripped open, her viscera hanging out, then begins to cry.

Taylor stands over her smiling, her teeth smeared with blood.

—A grateful sister appreciates your sacrifice, she says.

—MOM, Shelby shouts. NO.

—You do it too, honey. It's fun.

—I can't.

222

Separation Anxiety

Suddenly, Taylor is there, a hand on each girl.

—Do I have to do everything? she asks.

Prying the girls apart. Tearing them asunder. Easy as rending a garment.

Shelby screams in horrific pain and tries to wake herself up, but can't, can't climb out of the deep dark well of her subconscious to the safety of her hollow tree trunk in the titi swamp.

—Talk to me, Will says when the deputy at Beth Ann's house radios.

I-10. Racing back toward Tupelo. Lights flashing. No siren. No traffic.

—There's no one here.

—What?

—Not a soul.

—Goddamn it, Will exclaims.

How the fuck could I be so stupid?

—No sign of a break-in, the deputy says. No sign of violence.

—You're sure? You've looked everywhere?

—Looking again now to double check, but I'm tellin' you, she ain't here.

—Look for her, but I'm gonna call the lab too, so don't trample the place.

—Yes, sir.

—Find her. Find something for me. Call me when you do.

Switching to his phone, he calls Keith, saying just four

words to him when he answers his phone.

—I fucked up. Again.

—Think you can handle the old lady on your own? Sam asks.

She has just gotten off the phone with Keith.

—Maybe I'm overestimating my abilities, but I think I can, Daniel says. What's up?

They are winding around 98, the Gulf to their left, thick woods to their right, nearing the spot where they met and left his car on their way to interview the Youngs.

—Just got a BOLO for a sex offender who harassed Taylor, and another girl's missing. I've got to get over to Lithonia Lodge.

—What? Who?

—Which one?

—The girl. I assume the sex offender is Hennessy.

—I say girl. She's actually mid-twenties. An intern at a counseling center. Suspected a client of abducting Shelby. Will contacted him and now she's been taken.

—Fuck.

—I know, she says.

—Wonder if he took her to cover his tracks, or because he needed a new girl?

—Which would mean Shelby's already . . .

—If it's even related, he says. May not be.

Sam pulls the car off the highway onto the shoulder next to Daniel's car, a plume of white dust from sand and oyster shells rising around it.

Separation Anxiety

—You got dimes? he asks.

She checks the battery life on her phone.

—Yeah.

He leans in and kisses her.

—I love you, he says. Like I've never loved anyone. Take care of yourself.

—You watch yourself with the old lady there, mister.

He starts to get out, but she pulls him back for more kissing.

—Wasn't finished. You just told me you loved me like no one ever.

They kiss for a few more minutes, their attraction and arousal palpable.

—If you don't get out now, I'm not gonna let you. I'm gonna force you to rip all my clothes off and fuck me 'til morning and forget my job and young girls could die.

—Erection killer, he says, pulling back and opening the door.

—I've yet to find anything that can kill your erection, superman.

—That's a much better note to end on, he says.

As she drives away, he stands for a moment staring out at the Gulf.

Inhaling the briny breeze, he realizes it's not unlike the way his eyes are breathing in the beauty—the shadowed undulating waves rhythmically rolling in and out, the shimmering path of moonlight emanating from the wan and waning orb.

Everything is night quiet. Still. Peaceful. Just the gentle, relentless tide touching the shore as if caressing a lover's cheek.

Alone.

He's filled with longing like the bittersweet pang and pleasure of nostalgia, and he realizes it's not just for Sam.

This is his religion. Sand and sea, sky and silence. But so, too, is helping track down abducted sixteen- and twenty-year-olds and the sociopaths who take them.

She feels like she's deep in the Gulf, swimming toward the surface, but no matter how hard or long she swims, she can't make it to the top.

Why can't I surface? What's wrong? It's like I'll never make it up. Like it's not possible.

Wake the fuck up!

Heart about to explode.

Lungs about to fill with water.

Drowning.

Death.

Come on. Now! Right now. Wake the fuck up!

Kicking her feet. Pulling with her hands. Reaching. Grabbing. Flailing.

Surfacing.

She regains consciousness with the horrific images of her ripped and torn family still haunting her head.

Does he have Mom too? Are we both going to die? Is that what it meant?

I want my mama. Please. God. Oh God. Please. Don't let me die out here like this. Please protect Mom too. Bring us back together. You've got to. Please. I'm a good person. I don't deserve this. Please help me find the river. Help me get back home.

She looks around in search of Remington, but sees no sign of him.

I'm so scared. So tired. So fuckin' alone. So fried. Can't think. Can't feel anything—but fear.

Whatta I do? Whatta I do? Whatta I do?

Come on. Come on. Come on.

You know what to do. Just do it.

It's still a little while before dawn, but it's fast approaching, and she can feel the shift in atmosphere. Changes in the air. Barometric pressure falling.

The storm is closer now. A lot closer.

I've got to get back to the river. Get help. Find Mom.

See. You know what to do. Just do it.

Where am I? Have I been running straight inland this whole time?

Racing down the rural road toward Lithonia Lodge, Sam receives a call from a number she doesn't recognize.

—Hello.

—Agent Michaels?

—Yes.

—This is Porter Weston.

Porter Weston is one of the few African-American deputies in Keith's department. Young, bright, motivated, he hasn't even made detective yet, and has already told her he'd like to be an FDLE agent one day.

—Hey, Porter. What's up?

—Got something I want to run by you.

—Okay.

—You know how things are for us within law enforcement agencies.

—Us?

—Minorities.

—I certainly do, she says, wondering where he's going with this.

—Racism, sexism, homophobia. It's systemic. The culture, you know?

—I do.

Though not out, Porter had always seemed gay to her—something she feels far more justified believing now. Very few heteros would be sensitive enough to list homophobia next to racism and sexism.

—Well, sometimes my ideas aren't too well received, but I've got two I think need to be . . . Can I share 'em with you?

—Of course.

—The first one might be sort of out there, but . . . I don't know. I'm a . . . I like to read. Do you? Have you read Marc Hayden Faulk's books?

—I haven't. No.

—It's just . . . he's got a . . . One of them has a plot about a missing girl. Teenager. A little younger than Shelby, but . . . I'm not saying it means anything, but I think it could. It's kinda scary how similar it is to what's going on here.

—What happens in his book?

—The girl is raped and tortured repeatedly and murdered. Some pretty sick shit in the book. Nobody's mentioned it and I thought what if . . . I mean, we've got to look at everything, right?

—Absolutely right.

—I'm not even saying it's him. Just that what he wrote could be inspiring whoever's behind it. Or have something to do with it.

—No, yeah. I'm glad you mentioned it. I know how things are but I think you could've told this directly to the sheriff.

—Keith's a good guy. He is. But . . . I don't know.

—I understand. I like your idea. Only thing is . . . hard to believe this is connected to Savannah's disappearance. And Faulk was nowhere around back then.

—That we know of, he says, but yeah, like I said, just thought I should put it out there. The second thing is far more . . . I mean, she was around for Savannah.

—Who?

—Taylor Sean. Is anyone looking at her? I haven't really heard her mentioned as a suspect and . . . it's usually someone connected to the victim, isn't it? This Sean woman is out there. I mean, you hear stories, you know? Have you seen her paintings? You familiar with Munchausen syndrome by proxy? Why is she getting a pass?

Cages.

Critters.

Care.

Shelby's small wild animal hospital—wire cages at the back of the property not far from the river—is nearly full, and looking in on the patients not only gives Taylor something to do, but makes her feel even closer to Shelby's innate goodness.

As Marc continues pouring over the printed journal pages, she slips out into the dark, quiet night, padding over the dew-damp lawn down to the restless creatures roaming their

229

pens.

—Hey, she says, her voice soft and high. It's okay. Settle down little buddies. Shelby'll be back soon.

It's amazing how palpable her presence is here, how aware her menagerie is she is gone, something is wrong.

—Sensitive little buggers, aren't you?

She wonders how much of their agitation is the approach of the storm and how much is missing their little earth mama.

She's about to give them even more comfort food—perhaps far more for her than them—when Raymond Wayne Hennessey steps out of the shadows of the river-rimming cypress trees and grabs her from behind.

Massive mitt over her mouth. Python arm wrapped around her, squeezing her to his behemoth board-hard body.

Stifling screams.

Held fast. Unable to move.

Whiskers rubbing her cheek and neck.

Foul breath.

Mumbling mouth at her ear. Gibberish.

Dragging her toward the rim of darkness around the brightly lit backyard.

Helpless.

Hopeless.

Rape? Imprisonment? Death?

Does he have Shelby? Will I see her? Will I die without ever knowing what happened to her?

Wrinkled face. Sagging, hooded eye. Short, gray hair.

Separation Anxiety

All that is visible in the narrow gap of the opened but chained apartment door.

—Ms. Helpner?

—Yes?

Her voice is old and weak, but doesn't sound groggy, which with how quickly she answered the door makes Daniel think she hadn't been sleeping.

—I'm Daniel Davis with the Florida Department of Law Enforcement. Sorry to disturb you so late—or early—but Shelby Summers has disappeared and—

—Oh, the poor dear.

—Yes, ma'am.

—Hasn't she been through enough? How can she possibly—

—Oh, you mean Taylor.

—She was the sweetest child. I know the Bible says God won't put more of a load on us than we can bear, but . . . she's been through so much. Too much.

—May I come in and ask you a few questions?

—Who'd you say you were again?

He hands her one of the cards Sam had made up for him. It reads: Daniel Davis, PhD, Special Consultant, Florida Department of Law Enforcement, and has the gold embossed logo on it.

She takes it through the small opening, lifts her glasses, and brings the card to within a couple of inches of her squinting right eye.

—Doctor? What kind?

—Philosophy and religion.

—Interesting.

231

She closes the door, removes the chain, and opens it to let him in.

The dim apartment smells of must and mothballs and the slightest hint of urine, and looks to be the habitat of a housebound person.

Every surface of the cluttered and overly furnished space is covered—mostly with stacks and stacks and stacks of newspapers, magazines, and journals.

She leads him into the den and eases back into an aging cloth recliner with towels draped over the back and tucked into the seat.

Ruth Helpner is old and frail, her long, lean body failing.

Across from the recliner, a muted TV on a too-small table that looks about to collapse is tuned to a cable channel airing the old black-and-white film *Dark Mirror*.

When she sees him glancing around for a place to sit down, she nods toward the dining table in the adjoining room.

—Grab one of those.

—Sorry to wake you, he says.

—You didn't. I don't sleep much anymore.

He steps into the other room and finds that beneath the piled-high dining table, every chair is also being used for storage and stackage. Removing the magazines from the closest chair, he places them on the floor, and returns to the den with it.

—You think somebody got Shelby? she asks. Just like Savannah.

—What we're trying to find out.

She shakes her head very slowly.

—I can't imagine how poor Taylor must be doing. Of all the children we worked with over the years, she was our favorite.

—Yours and Dr. David's?

She nods.

—You were his . . .

She shrugs.

—Not sure exactly. Different things at different times.
A little bit of everything all the time. Assistant. Secretary. Wife.
Confidant. Friend.

—You two were married?

—No. I just meant . . .

—I see.

She tilts her head up, pushing her glasses up on her nose,
and looks off into the distance.

—Taylor and Trevor were just so precious. It was so
heartbreaking they had to be separated. Put the poor parents
through hell. It was hard on all of us, but Taylor suffered the
most. No comparison.

—You've kept in touch with her over the years?

—Somewhat. Not as much since . . .

—Since?

—I got so old and . . . worn out.

He gets the sense that's not what she was going to say at
all.

—Did something happen?

—Huh?

She's staring at the TV now, feigning distraction.

—Did you guys have a falling out?

—No. Nothing like that. All the kids were like my own.
But none more than Shelby and Savannah.

—Shelby and Savannah?

—Is that what I said? No. Taylor and Trevor. Though I just loved Shelby and Savannah to pieces too.

—How often do you talk to them?

—Who?

—Taylor and Shelby?

—Not much anymore. Send them a birthday card. Christmas.

—Ron and Rebecca said they got Shelby's number from you.

—Did they? I don't recall. I suppose I have it around here somewhere.

—Shelby's cell phone number?

She shrugs and waves her bony, arthritic hand dismissively.

—I was surprised. I understand staying in touch with Taylor, but her parents? Weren't they your adversaries? What does Dr. David say?

—I always felt bad for them. Never saw them as my enemies. I haven't spoken to Dr. David . . . in a while.

—Were you with him when he lost his license?

He recalls reading the brief newspaper article Sam had clipped and placed in the file:

A doctor with a residence in Leon County was stripped of his license to practice medicine in Florida today over misconduct and patient abuse, state officials said.

Dr. D. Kelly David was decertified by the Medical Board of Florida this week. He resides in Tallahassee, according to medical board documents.

According to a Florida Department of Justice complaint, "The respondent engaged in multiple extreme departures from the standard of practice in the care and treatment of patients."

Separation Anxiety

David's license was temporarily suspended and then reinstated with restrictions. The medical board ordered that he undergo "proctoring" by another surgeon and complete a series of courses on ethics, undergo psychological counseling, and attend a professional boundaries program.

The doctor failed to comply, according to state officials, and his license was revoked.

Ruth Helpner shakes her head.

—So sad, she says. Did so much good—and that's what he's remembered for.

—What happened to him?

—I don't know the specifics. I had been gone a while by then.

—Why'd you leave again?

—It was just time. Too old. Really, Dr. David was too. He was such a good man. So dedicated. So tireless.

From somewhere behind the piles of papers, a light gray Maine Coon cat with black streaks and white chest and paws slinks out, stretches, then bounds into Ruth's lap.

—Well, good morning, Miss Missy, she says, beginning to rub the animal's head. How are you?

—From what I read, Daniel says, attempting to keep her focused, it seemed very personal to him.

—Dr. David? It was. He was a conjoined twin. His brother Karl was killed to save him. I think everything he ever did was because of that. He's so driven. So brilliant.

—Came across as obsessed.

—Certainly. What genius with a mission isn't?

—Couldn't've been easy to work for.

—But he did so much good. Helped so many twins and their families.

So you keep saying, he thinks. Why? What's on the other

scale that you're trying to counterbalance for?

—As obsessive and driven as he was, he seemed to be even more so with Taylor and Trevor.

—It's what he's most known for. He fought so hard for them. They became like his own children. He had a daughter near Taylor's age who died of leukemia. She became a surrogate, I think. Taylor I mean.

—Are they still in touch?

—I don't think so. You should ask him—you should talk to him about all of this. I'm just a feebleminded old lady.

As she talks, she continues to rub Miss Missy absently.

—You had a falling out with him, right? Why? What aren't you telling me?

—What do you want from me?

—For you to stop holding back. Shelby Summers is missing. Help me find her. Taylor's been through enough, right? Help me get Shelby back to her safely. Dr. David lost his license, lost you and Taylor. Why? What happened?

—He just . . . he just . . . he was so obsessed, so possessive. He just went crazy. That's all. It's tragic, but we all lose everything eventually. Is it more tragic for a genius to lose his mind? Maybe. I don't know. None of us want to lose anything.

—Where is he now?

—I haven't kept up with him.

Appearing bored and disinterested, Miss Missy eases out of Ruth's lap and out of the room.

—You don't know where he lives?

—After it closed, he was still living in his hospital.

—The River Park Inn Center for the Twin?

—Yeah. Even when it was open, he had quarters on the

top floor. He used to have another place too, but I never went to it. Have no idea where it is.

—Okay, Daniel says, standing. I have to be honest, Ms. Helpner, I don't think you've told me everything. I just hope it doesn't cost Shelby Summers her life.

She doesn't say anything, and he returns the chair to the dining room. When he turns from stacking the magazines back onto the seat, she is standing there and it startles him.

He waits but she doesn't say anything.

—Ma'am?

—Huh?

—Did you want to—

—Got to lock the door behind you.

She begins walking toward the door and he follows her. At the door, he pauses a moment.

—My number's on the card I gave you. Please call me if you think of anything else that might help us locate Shelby.

She nods.

—Dr. Davis is a senile old man now, she says, but he was a great physician who helped a lot of people. Whatever else he may have done, no matter what he may have become, try not to forget that. And be careful out there. Storm'll be here soon.

Violent, whirling, spiraling cyclone.

Large-scale, warm-core, low-pressure storm.

Christine.

Nearing now.

Intense. Imminent. Inevitable.

Massive man stepping from the darkness, seizing Taylor, pulling her into the blackness.

At first, Marc can't process what he's just seen. Doesn't believe it.

As he searches for a weapon of some kind, he calls 9-1-1.

—This is Marc Faulk. I'm at Lithonia Lodge. Someone just snatched Taylor Sean. At the back of the property. Down by the river. Send police now. Hurry. He's huge. Think it's Raymond Wayne Hennessey.

Without waiting for a response, he disconnects the call, drops the phone, and rushes out into the night, an aluminum baseball bat his only weapon.

Running, calling, searching.

What if I hadn't glanced up when I did?

But you did.

What am I gonna do? I'm no match for—

He reaches the edge of the yard where the light ends, steps into the darkness, momentarily blinded, and waits for his eyes to adjust.

To the right. What? Something. He senses something from sound and smell before he sees anything.

Eyes adjusting.

Taylor on the ground. Enormous man on top of her.

Running.

Bringing back bat.

Swinging.

Last moment. Hennessey hearing, turning, standing.

Blocking the blow of the bat with his huge hands, Hennessey actually grabs it and yanks it from Marc. Quickly flipping it around, he lifts it above his head, holding it like an ax, and prepares to strike.

Flashlight beam.

Gunshot.

—FREEZE, Sam yells.

The area is suddenly, shockingly quiet from the round she just fired into the air.

No crickets.

No frogs.

Nothing but rapid, jagged breaths.

—I will shoot you. No hesitation. No—

Lowering the bat, Hennessey bends to place it on the ground, then lunges toward Sam, closing the fifteen feet between them faster than he looks capable of.

She fires another round, this time at Hennessey. Then another.

Two rounds. One in each leg. And he's still coming toward her.

Two more. One shatters a kneecap and he crashes hard to the ground. Then he's crying and mumbling to himself incoherently.

—I keep fuckin' up like this, Will says, I'm turning in my badge.

—You haven't done anything any of the rest of us wouldn't've done, Keith says.

—Plus you busted a grower tonight, Sam says. You're way ahead of the rest of us.

—Shit, Will says. You brought in Raymond Wayne

Hennessey.

The three of them are in Keith's SUV, Sam having just joined them in their attempt to drop a net over the area around Beth Ann Costin's house before Grayson can get away with her.

—But, Will continues, if anything happens to Beth Ann because I said the wrong thing to Grayson . . .

—It won't. We're gonna get her back and bury Grayson, Keith says. Promise you that.

Lights flashing in the declining dark of the waning night, siren silent, they roam the mostly empty streets, back roads, and highways of Tupelo looking for Beth Ann.

—What does Grayson drive again? Sam asks.

—Late-model Lincoln, Will says. Black.

—You guys sure the roadblocks are back far enough? she asks.

—No way to be certain, Keith says, but we got 'em set up pretty damn fast.

—Only three ways out of town, Will says. We got him hemmed in. He's gotta be hidin' somewhere.

—Three ways by car, Sam says. Four if you count boat. You got somebody set up on the river?

—Got somebody at the landing, but there's a lot of places to put a boat in.

—I'm assuming he didn't come to town pulling a boat with his Lincoln, so he'll have to steal one if he tries to leave that way.

—True, Keith says. Tell me again why you aimed for Hennessey's legs. Why not splatter his brainpan all over a cypress tree?

—Thought he might have Shelby. Wanted to be able to ask him. He needed what little brain he has for that to happen.

—And you don't think he has her?

—I can't say for certain, but I'm pretty damn sure. Got an FDLE buddy of mine talking to him now. Hennessey has anything to give, he'll get it out of him. Then he'll get him to the hospital . . . eventually.

—Like your style there, slim, Keith says with genuine appreciation.

Sam smiles and nods.

—Look at that, Will says. It's like you can see the air changing. Won't be long 'til the storm's here.

Beyond the blinking caution light they're speeding toward, the tops of slash pines lining the lonely highway are swaying; behind them, the first of false dawn is only gloom.

—As if this shit ain't hard enough in good weather, Keith says. Got every deputy I have working. No one else to call in. We need to be helping more with evacuations and shelters. Now we gotta find fuckin' Grayson.

—Taylor. Taylor. Wake up.

—Huh?

After coming back inside from their encounter with Raymond Wayne Hennessy, she had taken something and had more wine and had quickly fallen back asleep on the couch. As she slept, Marc had continued to read through Shelby's journal.

—You're having a bad dream, he says. You're okay.

She jerks out of his grip and sits up.

—You're safe. It was just a dream.

—Oh my God. That was so . . . It's like Shelby, Savannah, Trevor, and I were all having the same dream.

—You're okay. It's over.

241

—We were all together in a clearing in a swamp. All four of us. It was so beautiful and peaceful. Shelby and Savannah were conjoined like me and Trevor. We were wearing the prettiest white dresses, then we were ripped apart. It was awful. So painful. So bloody. I can't believe I fell back asleep. I want to help you.

—It's fine. You've been through so much. I'm just reading and you obviously need the sleep.

—Found out anything else?

—Just what an extraordinary young woman she is. Truly. You've done an amazing job with her, Taylor.

She's gazing into the distance, and he can tell she's not listening to him.

—I think it's possible Shelby and I were having the same dream.

—Really?

—You think I'm crazy?

—What do you think it means?

—Don't know, but it gives me an idea.

—What's that?

—I think I can connect to her—even more so—but if I'm all the way asleep, I have no control over it, and I can't remember enough of it. But what if I'm hypnotized? Go under enough to reach her, but be aware enough to bring what I learn out.

She pauses, but he doesn't say anything.

—You think I've lost it, don't you? she asks.

—Not at all.

—Good, 'cause I want you to put me under.

Pulling up to the secluded nineteenth-century inn D. Kelly David converted into a hospital and center for twins, Daniel is filled with a sense of foreboding, as if the gloomy old place is as haunted as it looks.

Broken windows.

Leaning beams.

Overgrown grass and weeds. Spreading vines.

In the play of partial, pale moonlight and deep shadow, the faded white boards look like bleached bones, the crumbling and dilapidated structure, neglected, forgotten, forsaken.

During the latter part of the nineteenth century, the development of the steamboat and railroad produced a growing tourist business. People streamed out of hot and dirty cities in Alabama and Georgia to find healthful air, water, and tranquility along the banks of the Chipola and Apalachicola rivers. River Park Inn, located on the banks of the Apalachicola near the end of the train tracks—where at various times cotton, lumber, citrus, and turpentine were delivered to waiting boats—was an old antebellum mansion turned into a hotel and spa by a visionary business man named Fred George Gaskin.

Eventually, as the river became less and less a highway, the inn closed, and was ultimately abandoned—until decades later when D. Kelly David bought and restored it for his twins hospital, orphanage, and research center.

Now, after three incarnations—antebellum mansion, river hotel and spa, hospital and research center—the eerie old wooden monstrosity lies, like the House of Usher, in ruin once again.

Set on the edge of the swamp, the secluded, empty hospital is some twenty miles from the nearest town. Daniel doubts he has cell coverage, but he doesn't want to go in without telling Sam where he is.

Withdrawing his phone, he checks it—and watches as one bar of signal goes to half to none, then back to one again. While there's signal again, he touches Sam's name on the screen—a simple action that makes him miss and long for her even more.

The call fails.

He tries again, and again it fails.

Two more tries, and then he gets her voicemail. Quickly he tells her where he is and what he's doing.

—I think he might be involved—even behind it all. From all accounts, he's really gone crazy. He's always been obsessed with Taylor. She was like a surrogate daughter, replacing his daughter who died of leukemia. Maybe he did the same with Savannah and now Shelby. Ruth Helpner knows far more than she's saying. You should probably interview her. It's gonna take more skills than I have. I'll let you know what I find. Call me back. I love you.

Stepping out of his car, the moist heat clinging to him like he's at a health club taking steam, he pauses a moment to try to slow his racing heart and fill his mind with something other than fear.

Sam's forever trying to get him to carry a gun, and in moments like these, he wishes he did. He does find a flashlight in the trunk, which is some comfort, and he leaves his car running with the lights on.

Three stories.

Two wings.

Columns.

He bangs on the enormous front door beneath the shard remnants of a giant chandelier. And waits.

Nothing.

He can't imagine anyone living here, but if so, it'd be

nearly impossible to hear a knock on the door from anywhere in the hospital but very near the door itself. He searches for a doorbell or buzzer, but finds neither, and decides to walk around back.

Stepping carefully through the tall grass and weeds, he alternates the beam of his light between just ahead of his feet and the short distance before him.

Nearly all of the tall arched window frames are boarded up behind broken glass and everything about the place is collapsing, crumbling, but he can see in the rotting remains how magnificent it must once have been.

It takes a while, but eventually he makes his way around to the back of the building, the sounds of the unseen river growing louder.

To his surprise, he can see a light on in the last room on the left on the third floor.

Seeing a buzzer by the door of a delivery dock, he climbs up and rings it.

From inside, he hears the buzz, but nothing after it, save the sounds of decay and the return to silence.

As he presses the button again, he notices that the cargo door is open a small distance—enough for him to slide through.

When after the second and third buzzes he gets no response, he pushes on the door, but it doesn't budge. Placing the flashlight on the ground, he moves to the other side and pulls the sliding door with both hands. Inch by inch, bit by bit, he gets it open enough to squeeze through, which he does.

Storage area.

Damp, dank hallways.

Overturned wheelchair. Upended gurney.

Desultory dripping.

Weak, narrow beam surrounded by utter darkness.

245

Observation window reflecting back the beam.

Nursery—creepy empty cribs.

OR.

Smell of deterioration, mortification, mildew, atrophy, abandonment.

Stairs.

Slowly ascending the steps. Deeper in. Darker.

Hallway. Rooms. Hotel/hospital.

Long, dark corridor.

Presence. Not alone. Shit. Someone here. Stupid.

As fear begins to constrict his heart, he realizes just how long it has been since he has had an anxiety attack.

Strip of light. Last door on the left.

Turn back or keep going? Have to keep going. Can't not know what's in there, who's here. Can't be married to Sam and be the kind of man who'd turn back.

Then start carrying a gun, dumbass.

Note to self: Get one of Sam's many guns and keep it in the car.

He eases down the hallway, dragging his feet along the tile floor, turning occasionally to shine the beam behind him to see if anyone is coming up in back of him.

—Florida Department of Law Enforcement, he says, feeling, as he always does when he says it, like a fraud. Identify yourself.

There's no response and no sound—so why does he feel like he's not alone?

—Dr. David?

Waits.

—Is anyone there?

Separation Anxiety

Vividly remembering the last anxiety attack he had in a long hallway, he begins to relive it—realizing how perfect his current circumstances are for one to occur right now.

He had been in a hotel hallway, stationed outside of Sam's room while she was inside trying to get some sleep.

They were newly in each other's lives. Not a couple. Not even dating. It had been a while, so much had happened since, yet he remembers it as if it had been the night before.

He had been reading a book on psychopathology. Sam had just been attacked by the arson serial killer known as the Phoenix, and sitting there watching over her, guarding her door, he had realized how ridiculous he was being.

You are no match for those who would hurt Sam. What would you do if a killer showed up, throw a book at him?

You are weak, impotent, powerless. Who're you kidding? Sam can defend herself better than you can.

And then it had begun.

It pounced on him like an overpowering predator. All at once. Palpitations. Severe chest pains. Can't catch his breath.

Awash with adrenaline, trembling, shaky, sweating profusely. Body temp spikes.

He's gonna die. Right now. Death is here, has come for him, and there's nothing he can do.

Jumping up, trying to run, he experiences extreme vertigo. He reaches for the wall to steady himself, but loses control of his legs and falls to the floor. Suddenly, he's being crushed by an unbearable weight as the whole world collapses down onto him.

Paralysis sets in and he can't move so much as his mouth. Can't scream. Can't yell for help. Can't do anything but stare up into the demon-like face of the killer.

He's come for me. I'm dead. Then he'll break down the

247

door and burn Sam in her bed.

You're out of your mind. No one's here. Look. Do you see anyone? No one's here.

Eventually, the attack ends, his mind and body righting themselves, returning to their previous settings, but he remains on the floor for a long time, disheartened, disgusted, depressed.

Now, here in the long, dark corridor of River Park Inn, echoes of previous attacks reverberate through him, but he's not having one, not yet.

Am I cured? If I don't have one now, I'd say I'm well on my way.

Pulling the phone out of his pocket, he checks for signal again. None.

Replacing it, he continues toward the door and the small splash of light on the floor coming from beneath it.

—Daniel Davis, Florida Department of Law Enforcement. Identify yourself and come out with your hands up.

Edging closer.

—Is anyone there? Dr. David? Are you in there?

He reaches the door and finds that it's not quite closed all the way.

With his back to the wall just left of the jam, he pushes the door open with his foot, pauses a moment, then looks inside.

Desk.

Chairs.

Bookshelves.

Couch.

Stacks.

Folders.

Files.

Papers.

Documents.

Empty.

Unless someone is hiding under the desk or inside the closet, the office is empty. Slowly moving inside, he checks those two places first. No one.

Switching off his flashlight and placing it on the desk, he begins to look around, flipping through the file folders and stacks of papers.

The documents and journals confirm what the pictures on the wall and desk suggest—this is Dr. David's office, and from what Daniel can tell, it appears to have most of his research, notes, and writings from over the years.

This paragraph, written early in his career, seems to most embody the empathy David feels for himself and people who drink from his cup.

The separated twin, particularly if sole surviving, spends his or her life with the very real sense that something is missing. He or she has a heightened awareness, agonizing in its acuteness, of loss, of aloneness, but most of all of separation. This feeling, not uncommon to all humans, of disconnect and isolation, the very hallmarks of what it means to be human, is experienced exponentially by a conjoined twin who has been separated from his or her sibling.

Faster now.

He scans the documents, combs the journals for insights into the man, and searches for any mention of Taylor and Trevor, Shelby and Savannah.

The more he reads, the more the picture comes into focus, the more disturbed he becomes.

—Oh God. No, he says, his words the only sounds in the vacuous silence.

The portrait painted by the papers of Dr. D. Kelly David is that of a decent man descending into madness, a crusader becoming increasingly obsessive and demented and ultimately dangerous.

During the Holocaust, Dr. Josef Mengele subjected some three thousand twins to cruel and horrific medical experiments. Only one hundred and sixty survived. Dr. D. Kelly David had very different motives, and would no doubt violently reject any comparisons to the Auschwitz Angel of Death, but the similarities are sickening—particularly in the way he desecrated the bodies of the conjoined twins sacrificed so their brother or sister could survive.

Perhaps the comparison is unfair. Mengele was a monster running a butcher shop, exercising his power and control, performing torture more than serious medical research—attaching one twin's eyes to the back of the other's head, amputating limbs, chemically changing eye color, even sewing the bodies of two twins together to create his own conjoined twins. David has done nothing like that, but he's on the same self-serving and sadistic spectrum.

Reaching for his phone to call Sam, he sees he still has no service. He moves over to the window in an attempt to find signal, holding the device up, trying different positions. Just as he sees a slight flicker as if he might have actually found some, the light in the office goes out and everything drops to black save the small, dim backlit screen of his phone.

I could be walking further inland. I could be walking straight toward him. Hell, I could be walking in circles.

Why can't I get out? Goddamn it! What am I doing

wrong? Where the fuck am I? Where am I headed? I should be able to figure this out. I can do this.

No you can't.

I can. I can do this. Just need to figure out . . .

I can't do this. I told you. My head's gonna explode just like the old man in the boat.

Hey neighbor.

I'm going crazy. Can't think. Can't do . . . anything.

She starts to cry again. Stop it! Now! Concentrate on what you're doing.

She's easing down a slope in a lush, leafed-out hardwood forest, feeling her way between beech, live and laurel oak, loblolly and spruce pines, maple, elm, ash, myrtle, and sweetgum, attempting to move quickly and quietly, her bare feet hurting so badly every gentle step is painful.

Dark magnolia leaves and reddish fruit join puffballs and witches' butter fungus on the forest floor. Above, mixed in among the tall magnolia, beech trees with light green leaves spread horizontally to catch the sun, giving the canopy a layered look.

Should I just curl back up and go to sleep? Wait for him to trip over me or the storm to drop a tree on top of me?

Where the hell is the river?

Pause. Take a deep breath. Think. Make your mind slow down and just go through it. Just like Kerry would.

She does.

When I was at Dad's camp, the river was east of me, but without knowing if he carried me upriver or down, there's no way to know which direction it is now. When I got out of the boat, it was on the left side. If we were headed downriver, then I've been heading east and the river is behind me to the west. But if we were heading upriver, then I've been heading west and the river is behind me to the east.

Think.

If we were heading upriver and I got out to the west, I would've run into signs of civilization by now—a dirt road or logging trails at least. Instead, I've gone deeper and deeper into the swamps. So wait for sunrise. See which way is east. Go the opposite. Piece of cake.

Should I hide 'til sunrise? Is that smart or just what I want to do?

She thinks of Julian, of their baby inside her, and she wants nothing so much in the world as to see him again, to be held by him, to make love with him again. And again. And again.

—I know how hard this is, Remington says, suddenly standing before her again. Believe me I know. But you're doing great. Don't be so hard on yourself.

—Where'd you go? she asks.

—Nowhere. I haven't left you. I've been right here the entire time.

—This is so . . . Whether I'm completely crazy or this is really happening, I wonder why I only see you some of the time.

He shrugs.

—I've got a few ideas, he says, but doesn't really matter, does it?

—Guess not. I just like seeing you, talking to you. I feel so alone the other times.

He nods. He's so understanding, so nice.

—Did you talk to anyone when you were lost out here? she asks.

He smiles and nods.

—Myself, my dad, my mom, my girl.

—Heather, she says. I met her at the opening they had for your exhibit *Last Night in the Woods*.

—I know, he says, nodding.

—How?

—I was there.

—How?

—'Cause I had to be.

—I love the message you left for her. It's written in the book. I've read it so many times I've memorized it. 'Dear sweet Heather, I'm so sorry for everything. You were right. I was wrong—about virtually everything, but especially how I had gotten off my path. See my message to Mom about that. If I get through the night, it will be because of you. I can't stop thinking of you. I love you so much. Everything about you. Everything. You've been with me tonight in ways you can't imagine. I'm reliving our all-too-brief time together. I took some extraordinary shots tonight, but my favorite photographs will always be the ones I took of you, my lovely, sweet, good, beautiful girl. I'm sorry I wasn't a better husband. You deserved me to be. Don't mourn for me long. Find someone who will be as good to you as you deserve. I finally love you like you should be, and I'm afraid I won't be able to tell you in person. Just know my final thoughts will be of you.'

When she finishes, he is crying.

—She didn't, you know, Shelby says.

—Sorry? he says, wiping his eyes.

—You told her to find someone who would be as good to her as she deserves.

—Yes, I did. And I meant it.

—She didn't. She hasn't found anyone. I don't think she's looking.

—Can't say that makes me sad, he says with a small

smile.

—I can't hypnotize you, Marc says.

—I can hypnotize myself, Taylor says. Do it all the time, but I'm a little fried so I need some help. Also need you to guide me. Ask me the right questions.

—Okay. Whatta you need?

—Quiet place. Comfortable chair.

—Got plenty of that.

He follows her over to the couch, where she sits down on the center cushion.

—With no interruptions. You take both phones and turn them to vibrate. Try not to let anything disturb me for at least half an hour. I'm so sleepy, it should be even easier to go into a trance. Before going under, I'm gonna ask myself over and over where's Shelby. Where's Shelby? But when I'm under, I need you to keep asking me. Make sure I focus on connecting to her and finding out where she is.

He nods.

—I've got to relax. Let all stress out of my body. Breathe in peace, breathe out anxiety. Go down deep and find Shelby. Breathe in relaxation, breathe out any blockage. I'm descending a flight of stairs. Going down to find Shelby. There are ten stairs. When I reach the fifth, I'll be entering clear, cool, clean water. It'll be very refreshing and I'll go all the way under. Deep, deep down. Then I won't feel anything. Just be floating. I'm gonna picture each number in my mind. Descend slowly. You walk me through it.

—Okay, he says. You're on the tenth step. Are you relaxed? Do you—

—Just tell me I'm relaxed. You lead me. I'll follow. Just

like the bedroom. Be my top. I'll be your highly suggestible bottom.

—You're on the tenth step and you're very, very relaxed, he says. You feel good. You're excited about seeing Shelby, about finding her. Okay. Take a step down. You're on the ninth rung and you're even more relaxed.

He takes her slowly down the steps, into the water and a heightened state of focused concentration.

—Shelby's out there. She wants you to know where she is, to find her. Be open to her. Listen to her. She's calling to you. Reaching out. Where is Shelby? Where is she?

Watching her, he's overcome by how surreal this is, how absurd, and he has a difficult time not laughing. Maybe she really is as under as she seems, but she looks no different than an actor pretending to be hypnotized.

—So tired, she says. Poor baby. Her feet are all cut up.

Her eyes are moving rapidly behind her closed lids, and her face shows the pain and distress of what she's feeling.

—She's not running anymore. Trees. Lots of trees. Lots of different kinds. Her poor little body. She only has a thin shirt and shorts. Lost her shoes. She's so lonely, so scared, so sad.

She raises her head up, then moves it all around as if looking, though her eyes remain closed.

—Where is this baby? Where are we?

Her face falls again, her brow furrowing.

—She doesn't know. She's lost. She can't tell me.

—Where is she? he asks. Where is Shelby?

—She doesn't know. Somewhere . . . in the river swamps.

That doesn't narrow it down much, but if she's right it gives them a place to start.

Arrival.

Christine announces her imminent landfall with a burst of hot, humid air—thick and acrid—like the hopelessness and decay of a dying old man's last breath.

Outer bands.

Rain.

Wind.

Gusts.

The tip of the storm touches Tupelo and the surrounding area with spits of rain, howls of wind, and another balmy drop in barometric pressure.

Daniel drops to the floor, sliding away from the window as the first raindrops begin to pelt it, then backs toward the desk, using his phone for light.

Adrenaline spike.

Hyperawareness. Alertness.

Is it the deranged doctor? Is he armed?

—My name is Daniel Davis. I'm with the Florida Department of Law Enforcement, he yells. Backup is on the way. Identify yourself and turn the light back on. Dr. David?

He reaches up and feels around the desk for his flashlight.

Finding it, he grabs it, rolls to his right, stands with his back to the corner and turns it on.

Fuck!

So scared.

Breathe!

He shines the light all around the room. No one is there.

Did the light just go out on its own? Lose electricity? Bulb burn out?

His heart is pounding so forcefully, the blood rushing through his ears sounds like a train thundering down tracks inside a tunnel.

Slow your breathing. Get it together.

He's about to slide over, check the other side of the desk, try to turn on the light, and close and lock the door, when he hears a loud cranking sound.

Like a record being played at the wrong speed, he hears a slow-growing whir and whine as lights fade up and tinny, poorly produced piped-in instrumental music begins to come from built-in speakers all over the hospital, echoing down the hallways.

The dim lights and distorted, dissonant music make the old mansion/inn/hospital feel like a haunted asylum from a midnight movie at an ancient drive-in theater.

He checks his phone again. No signal.

With his back to the bookcase-covered wall behind him, he edges around the desk, then, finding no one there, over to the door.

Holding the flashlight like a club, he quickly glances through the door, down the hallway.

It looks even more disturbing in the sickly illumination of the few flickering fluorescents. There's more trash and equipment than he was able to see with just the small beam of his flashlight, but no one is present among the mess.

Closing and locking the door, he slides a chair over and jams it beneath the knob, then scours the office for anything he can use as a weapon, holding his phone up and trying to call Sam as he does.

—I got 'im. I got 'im. In pursuit.

The deputy's excited voice pierces the silence in a lull in conversation between Keith, Will, and Sam.

Exhausted, talked out, they've just finished searching the landing and the camps near it, and are about to return to town when the voice comes over the radio, joining the relentless sound of the rain and wind and windshield wipers.

—Cleve, Keith says into the radio, his voice calm, commanding. This is the sheriff. Where are you?

—River Road.

Will frowns and shakes his head.

Of all the new deputies, Cleve would be Will's last choice to be involved in a chase. And it's not just his youth and inexperience, but his awkwardness and excitability.

—Heading which way?

—Eastbound. Toward the river.

—Okay. We're at the river. Near the landing. I'm gonna head back your way. Just go slow. Stay calm. There's nowhere for him to go. No need to rush him.

There's no response.

Keith guns the SUV, racing down the twisting River Road in the slanting rain. The twists and turns are sharp, the blacktop slick, the vehicle sliding a bit.

Will thinks about the number of lives this particular rural road has claimed—most drunk drivers, many kids, driving straight when the highway turns, smashing into a tree, crashing into the river.

—Cleve? Keith says.

—Sir?

—Do you understand? You need to calm down. Take a deep breath. Let it out very slowly.

—I'm good. I've got him. He's right in front of me.

On either side of the winding highway, swamp gives way to slash pine forest, interrupted only occasionally by a fish camp or dirt road.

—How fast are you going?

No response.

—Goddamn it, Will says.

—What? Sam asks.

—Cleve's just a little above retarded. He's gung-ho as hell. Spastic as shit.

—Cleve? Keith says again, his voice even lower and calmer. How fast are you going?

—We're almost to the dam, he says.

—We are too, Keith says. We'll pick him up from here. You pull back and block the road.

No response.

—Cleve. Discontinue your pursuit. Copy? Pull back and block the road. Cleve? Cleve?

They round the corner, and through the smear and streak of raindrops and windshield wipers, see the bridge over the dam beneath streetlamps, Grayson's Lincoln racing toward it, Cleve's patrol car, lights flashing, right behind it.

—Stupid son of a bitch, Will says.

—Cleve, Keith yells into the radio. Back off. Now.

The Lincoln fishtails, bouncing onto the bridge, its back end swerving on the wet pavement, then it starts to slide and spin. The rear of the car smacks into the guardrail, careening back into the center of the bridge, then flips and begins rolling down the road.

—Oh my God, Sam says softly into the stunned silence.

Eventually, the car comes to a stop about three-quarters of the way toward their end of the bridge, upside down, its roof completely flattened, its tires continuing to turn, flinging falling raindrops out into the deteriorating darkness.

Keith parks the SUV not far from where Grayson's car sits and the three of them climb out and rush over to it, but it's merely academic at this point. No one inside the car could survive what just happened.

Bending down. On the ground. They search for openings or access points, but the car is so compressed there's nothing visible but crushed metal and broken glass.

Hisses.

Creaks.

Ticks.

Lights flashing.

Smoke rising into the night sky.

And three helpless people standing on a bridge in the rain.

—I'm going, Taylor says. With or without you.

She has come out of her trance frustrated, agitated, angry, convinced if she goes downriver, gets near the swamp, she'll be able to pick up on where Shelby is.

—How? Marc asks.

—Julian will take me. He knows his way around.

—The storm's almost here.

—Then I have to hurry.

—This is insane.

Separation Anxiety

—I can find her. I know it.

—But—

—Goddamn it, Marc. My baby's out there. I've got to try. She's gonna be in the storm. You sayin' we can't be? I need your help. I shouldn't have to beg.

—Okay, but let me tell Keith what we're doing.

—Fine.

Thump.

Thump.

Thump.

Wake up. Time to die.

She wakes to the feel of raindrops falling on her face.

Gonna die today, she thinks.

Why do I think that? What did I dream? I mean, I've thought that all along, but it seems so certain now, so . . . inevitable. What movie is that line from? Wake up. Time to die. Two men. Rooftop in the rain.

Blinking.

Yawning.

Stretching.

So exhausted.

So sore.

So sad.

Doesn't want to move.

Get up. Now. Go.

She pushes her aching body up from the cool, damp ground. Stands. Scans the area.

261

False dawn.

Rain.

In the distance, the rain in the spaces between the pine trees looks like lingering fog. Trapped willowy wisps. Beautiful.

It's still too early and hazy to decipher which way is east, but she slowly spins around, searching the horizon for the brightest glow. She determines the spot and begins to stumble toward it, wondering why she's so certain this is the day of her death, and what line the movie is from. 'Wake up. Time to die.' Rooftop in the rain. Come on. What is it? Where's Remington? Wonder if he knows.

Rage.

Visceral.

Volatile.

Violent.

As Cleve walks up from the other side of the bridge, nearing Grayson's upturned car, Will lunges toward him.

Right hook.

Chin.

Connect.

Crumbling.

One lunging punch and Cleve is on the ground, Will on top of him. Pummeling the young deputy in the pouring rain.

Broken nose.

Blood-smeared teeth.

Yelling.

—You stupid son of a bitch. Why the fuck didn't you slow down? You killed her.

Keith. There. Pulling him off.

Sam. Stepping between Will and the barely conscious Cleve.

—She's dead. We killed her.

Gun.

Loaded.

Finding the weapon in the top left hand desk drawer fills Daniel with more dread than relief. What's a loaded .38 doing in a hospital?

Should I be more afraid than what I am? Is that possible?

The arc of D. Kelly David's personality portrayed in the files and journals from advocate and twin crusader to obsessed, knife-happy surgeon and reckless experimenter to demented, deteriorating demon-god doctor explains the gun's presence, but does he have it for aggression or protection? Is he out there in the echoing corridors of this arcane asylum, or is what he's afraid of, what motivates him to have a gun what's out there?

Checking his phone again, and again finding he has no signal, he takes the gun and flashlight and ventures out in search of cell coverage, wondering what awaits him on the other side of the door.

Nothing.

As before, no one is directly on the other side of the door.

He slowly shuffles down the hallway, aware each door holds a potential threat, looking over his shoulder often, pressing his back to the wall.

In some ways, it resembles a hotel more than a hospital—there is no nurses' station, at least on this level—

but in others, the tile floor and equipment, it's far more like a hospital.

He makes it to the stairwell, breathes a bit easier, and starts down.

Near the bottom, he gets enough signal. Calls Sam. Voicemail. Tells her where he is.

—I'm gonna look around some more. You probably won't be able to call back. Signal is for shit. But get somebody out here as soon as you can to help search. And a Crime Scene crew to process this place. David is far more disturbed than we thought. He started out decent enough, but wound up in Josef Mengele territory. Operating under the radar. Doing all kind of experiments. Immoral, unethical stuff. He's obsessed with conjoined twins—especially the one who doesn't survive. It's like he's trying to save his brother, Karl, over and over again. And he's most obsessed with Taylor and Trevor. I honestly believe he could have Shelby. He may even have taken Savannah. I hear something.

The River Styx.

Tributary.

Overgrown.

Surrounded.

Swollen bases.

Enormous cypress trees rising out of the water.

Exposed root systems.

Black water.

Gloom.

Mist.

Smattering of raindrops.

Julian maneuvers the boat around the mammoth water cypresses as best he can, the hull banging and scraping often, Marc and Taylor bracing themselves on the center seat.

—Just a little further, Julian says. We'll get past all these. Be on the big river.

—Once we're on the river, Taylor says, help me go under again.

Marc nods.

Daniel moves to the door on the first floor, following the squeaking noises. Opening it with one hand while holding the gun up with the other, he steps out of the stairwell and looks up and down the hallway.

To his right, there is only old abandoned medical equipment—piled, stacked, overturned. Everything is covered in cobwebs and dust.

To his left, near the opposite end of the corridor, is the source of the sound.

Ancient. Antique. High back. Wicker. Wheelchair.

Slowly rolling toward him.

Squeak.

Squeak.

Squeak.

Startling. Surreal. Horrific.

A deformed, diminutive young man, partially leaning over the side, struggling to inch it down the hall.

Beneath the dim, flickering fluorescents, and with the creepy, canned music echoing, the eerie scene is discordant, disquieting, disturbing.

One of D. Kelly David's experiments?

He glances all around, but sees no one else.

Squeak.

Squeak.

Squeak.

—Hey, the man says when he sees Daniel. Hey, mister. Who are you?

—Who are you? Daniel says, beginning to ease toward him. What are you doing here?

—My name is Carter T. Lee. I live here. Is that a gun?

Despite the macabre backdrop and the young man's shuddersome appearance, he has an innocent, childlike, upbeat manner, his voice sounding as if it's perpetually trapped in puberty.

—You live here? With who?

—Whom.

Daniel smiles.

—Not many here anymore, he continues. He left me again.

—Who left you? Where'd he go?

—Power keeps going out. Don't like being by myself. I really don't. But you better go. Don't want to be here when he gets back. No, sir, you don't. That's a fact. He's a bad one. I see you have a gun and all, but won't do you no good. Not against a god. No, sir, it won't. Could you push me to the kitchen before you go?

—How long you lived here?

—Whole life. Known no other. That's a fact. Where're you from?

—Kansas, I guess.

266

—What's it like there?

—Different. Where's Dr. David?

—You better go now. I don't like to be by myself, but I don't like seeing nobody get hurt or killed neither. No, sir, I don't.

—Just ended my career, didn't I? Will says.

Sam shrugs, but Keith shakes his head.

The three are back in the SUV, out of the rain.

—No way he won't press assault charges.

—There's a way, Keith says, nodding. To avoid reckless endangerment charges and losing his job.

—I'm sorry again, Will says. I'm the one that got her killed. Not Cleve.

Keith starts to say something, but all three of their phones begin to receive calls.

Sam and Will ignore theirs as Keith's comes in over the speakers in the vehicle.

—Sheriff, the night dispatcher says in her soft, slightly sleepy voice, we got a call from a Victor Wilson. He's got a camp on the river and he came to board it up before the storm.

—Yeah?

—His camp is only a few down from where the Summers girl's car was found. There's an old van parked on his property. He called 'cause he didn't recognize it. Doesn't know anything about it.

—Okay. Thanks.

—I ran the plates he gave me, she says.

—And?

—It's registered to River Park Inn Center and D. Kelly
David.

West.

Toward the river.

False dawn glow behind, storm darkness before.

Rain.

Running.

Limping.

Hurting.

Crying.

Shelby tries to move silently through the gloom—and
though she's not crying or breathing too loudly, her movement
alone through the dense woods is noisy. Alerting. Attracting
attention.

Slight slope.

Soggy, spongy ground.

Surface aquifer.

Reaching a seepage slope, she slows just a bit, the water
on the ground soothing to her feet.

The gradual incline allows water from just beneath
adjacent, higher land to seep onto the surface of the ground and
run across the slope. The gradually changing moisture across
the expanse of the wetland mosaic leads to the flourishing of an
enormous diversity of species.

She moves from upland pine—longleaf, pond, and
slash—to an herb bog, through a shrub bog, and into a cypress
and tupelo swamp, passing through myrtle dahoon, laurel
greenbrier, wiregrass, butterwort, orchids, and pausing to

breathe in the big, beautiful bog bouquet of whitetop pitcher plants emerging from the surrounding cutthroat grass and sedge.

Dawn. Bright glow behind her.

Raindrops making the plants dance. Sway. Tilt. Lean.

God, it's gorgeous. I want Julian to see it, want to bring him back and make love on the wet ground of this field of flowers.

Silly girl. You're gonna die today. Maybe they'll scatter your ashes out here.

Fuck you. I'm gettin' to the river, gettin' back to him. We will make love in this very spot one day. I swear it.

Even in her head her words sound hollow. Weak. Insecure. Empty bravado.

Just keep moving. What else can you do?

Is he really a wolf? Sometimes he wonders.

He wants to be. Wants to be for her. But is he?

And is that what she wants? Sometimes he scares her. He can tell. Sees it in her eyes, in her soul. But how can she be scared of him? How can a wolf be scared of a wolf? How can she not know? How can she not want what he wants? He wants what she wants? Wants to make her happy, wants to give her all of himself and all that she ever desires. How can that not be enough?

The wolf wonders if he's a wolf. But how can this be? Can the wolf really doubt? Is the wolf capable of an identity crisis?

Who am I?

You are the wolf.

Who is the wolf?

You are.

I am the wolf.

The wolf exists. The wolf is. The wolf is incapable of existential angst, of questioning and wondering, of doubting and second guessing.

The wolf is pitiless. Without remorse. Without regret. Then who else is in the wolf's head?

Storm rising.

Cloud-shrouded sun.

Daybreak. Nonevent.

Christine is all.

Over northern Gulf waters. Warm. Feeding. Fueling. Increasing.

Thwack.

Thwack.

Thwack.

Wind bangs old shudders and loose boards against the ancient inn, howling.

Pushing Carter toward the kitchen.

—Is anyone else here? Daniel asks.

—Lupa never leaves.

—Lupa?

—She can't leave anymore. Like me. Not able.

—Anyone else?

He shrugs.

—Who's usually here? Who lives here?

—Just me, Doc D, Lupa, and Rom. I sure am hungry. Can you push a little faster?

The lights blink out, the music grinding down, then back up again as the power comes back on.

—Lupa and Rom? Daniel asks.

—What he makes us call them.

—Who?

—Lupa and Rom.

—No, who makes you call them that?

—Him. Said he'd cut me if I ever called 'em any different.

—Rom as in Romulus?

—Yeah.

—Which rooms are theirs?

—Second floor. Upstairs. Where I can't go. She doesn't want to leave me down here alone, but he makes her. Where're you goin'?

—Can you make it from here? I'm gonna go talk to Lupa.

—Don't do that. No. No. No. You gotta go. Now. Please, mister. Before he gets back. Please.

Landfall.

Christine arrives with a vengeance. Pounding the Panhandle with sustained winds of 127 miles per hour. Tossing trees and telephone poles, snapping power lines, toppling cell phone towers, ripping off roofs, scattering shingles, leveling buildings, and sweeping away mobile homes like a child's toys.

Transformers popping, blue arcs like the body of a candle flame shooting into the air.

No electricity.

No phones.

No communication with the world outside Tupelo.

Keith's call gets dropped right in the middle of an evacuation update.

—That's that, he says. She's here.

They are on the small side road that turns off from the landing and runs parallel to the river, not far from Shelby's car, pulling up behind the van registered to D. Kelly David.

—Not that much can be done now anyway, he adds, but it's just us now. Everyone else is working shelters, flooded roads, and looters.

—We're flyin' blind too, Will says. No phones, no radios, no electricity. No nothing.

Sam looks at her phone.

—I've got a shit-ton of messages but I can't retrieve them, she says. Hope Daniel is somewhere safe and dry.

—I'm sure he is, Keith says.

—How long before we know if Shelby was in the car? Will asks.

—A few hours. They won't even try to go in until the storm passes through. We'll have to head back over to find out. Can't call or radio.

—Way I see it, Will says, either he had her and all three of them are dead in the car, or she's not in the car 'cause he had her somewhere else—dead or alive, tied up in a basement or buried in a shallow grave, or he never had her and whatever he was doing with Beth Ann is unrelated.

Sheets of rain.

Windswept water.

Waves.

Boat tossed about.

—We've got to get off the water, Julian yells. Find shelter.

—Just a little further, Taylor yells. Please. We're close. I can feel her.

Julian looks at Marc and shakes his head.

—We're gonna turn over, he says. Can't help Shelby if we all drown.

Stinging.

Burning.

Piercing.

Pelting rain like bullets.

Curtains of them like constant machine gun bursts.

Blind.

Wind and water assault her eyes and she's unable to see.

Blinking.

Blurry.

Buffeted.

Debris batted about.

Wind whipping limbs and branches around. Sheering off the tops of pines, upturning oak and cypresses, snapping birch and magnolias.

Leaning.

Pressing.

Pushing.

So loud.

Jet engine throttling up for take-off.

She pushes against the wind, but it pushes back, actually lifting her occasionally. For all her fighting and struggling, all the energy and effort she's expending, she's making very, very little progress.

—Don't stop, Remington says.

—Have to.

—No. Keep going.

—Where have you been?

—Right here. Come on. I know it's bad, but just a little further. Almost there. I'm not going to let you die. Not today. Not here. Not like this.

Darkness.

He's taken two steps down the second-story corridor when the power goes off and stays off.

Pitch-black blind.

He can see nothing.

But he feels something—a presence, a force—something in this darkness that is far more than the absence of light.

Back against the wall. Frozen in fear. Heart pounding. Heading toward hyperventilation.

As bad as it is, he can't help but think it's worth it just to have the music grind down to a halt.

Snapping on the flashlight.

Scanning the area.

Slow your breathing or you're gonna pass out.

Gun in his right, light in his left, he begins to make his way toward the opposite end of the hall.

Slowly.

Carefully.

Methodically.

He inches down the hospital corridor, holding his light just above his gun, turning to look behind him every few feet, sweeping beam and barrel through the blackness.

All the while, the howl of wind, the thwack of shudders, the tata tata tata tatta tat of torrents of rain sounding like roofing tacks being hammered in overhead.

Eventually, he makes it to the other end of the hall and opens the first of the three closed doors.

More blackness. The only illumination that of the small flashlight.

The room is not what he expects.

Spartan.

The small beam glides around the room, revealing isolated objects out of context.

Single twin mattress on the floor.

Modest, maimed chest of drawers.

Upturned wooden crate bedside table. Lamp. Small stack of books. Sketch pad. Empty glass.

Weapons.

Propped in corners, lying on the floor.

Shotguns.

Rifles.

Swords.

Bows.

Knives.

And then he sees it.

Fully one-fourth of the room.

Black paint on white wall.

The she-wolf, Lupa, standing, as if caught in midstride, tail tucked, ears up, head turned looking warily in Daniel's direction. Eight prominent tits, nipples protruding, hanging straight down under her body. Two human male infants, one sitting, the other on his knees, necks craned, heads up, suckling, receiving sustenance from their she-wolf mother.

Carter said he calls himself Romulus.

Twin sons of Mars, god of war, Romulus and Remus were rescued as infants from the Tiber River by the god Tiberinus and raised by the she-wolf, Lupa. The famous, feral children grew up to be the founders of Rome. While arguing over who would name and rule the city, Romulus killed Remus with a shovel.

Is the occupant of this room, the one who calls himself Romulus, a surviving twin? Did D. Kelly David play the role of Tiberinus, symbolically pulling him from the river behind the hospital? Does he identify with Romulus because by living he killed his brother? Who is Lupa?

Romulas, the wolf, is not a wolf at all, but the son of one—a lone twin, a solitary, sole-survivor, thanks to his adopted she-wolf mother Lupa. And yet surely he is part wolf now. At least wolfish. He had been transformed by his time at her tit. Part man. Part wolf. Half a human twin. Half the wolf son of

Lupa.

The wolf, Romulas, ignores the wind and the rain, the snapping trees and falling limbs. The hunt is all. Finding his prey, finishing his mission all that matters.

He's overcome with the urge to howl. Howl like the wolf he is. Howl like the wind swirling about him.

So he does.

He is the wolf. He does what he wants. And that, with impunity.

He howls again. His howl indistinguishable from that of an actual wolf. His transformation is complete.

The wolf's howl is immediately sucked up, torn from his mouth as if by a tornado. It joins the great howl of the wind and it is as if the world entire is a wolf howling—at the universe, howling at god himself, howling at hell, howling from a pain too intense, too deep, too brutal, too goddamn raw to simply speak.

Flashing lights of a deputy's cruiser. Pulling up beside Keith's SUV. Deputy, drenched from the few steps, climbs into the backseat beside Will.

—They went ahead and got the car open before it got so bad, he says.

He is pale and roundish with wet wisps of thinning whitish-blond hair.

—And?

—Grayson and Costin, he says. No one else. Summers girl was not in the vehicle.

—Okay, Keith says. Thanks.

—Sorry, boss, he says, then climbs back out into the downdraft-like downpour, into his car, and drives away.

—If Grayson didn't have Shelby, Will says, you think the doctor who separated her mom does?

Sam shrugs.

—His van is here, she says. Be a big-ass coincidence, don't you think?

The old paneled van is faded and dilapidated, and bares no markings save those of time. It rocks back and forth a bit in the gale-force winds, and it looks to be parked at the bottom of a waterfall.

—So . . . what . . . he . . .

—We know he's unstable, Sam says. Troubled. Lost his license. His daughter died. Taylor became a kind of surrogate. Say he's been obsessed with Taylor, with his daughter. Maybe he took Savannah and now he's taken Shelby. I should've looked at him closer back when Savannah went missing. So stupid.

—He's an old-ass man, isn't he? Will says.

—Mid- to late-sixties, I'd say. Not too old to abduct a sixteen-year-old girl. Or try to.

Keith looks at the van, then at the driving rain, the tilting trees, and the trash and debris flying around.

—Not like it's gonna lighten up, he says. Ready?

—As I'll ever be, Sam says. Let's do it.

—If we've been running around like crazy looking for that little girl everywhere, Will says, and she's been in the back of this van the whole time . . .

They jump out into the slanting rain of the storm.

Immediately, they're soaked through.

Deaf.

It's like they're standing behind a jet engine at full throttle.

Walking the few feet to the van is far more difficult than

278

any of them could've imagined.

Keith's hat blows away.

A trash can flying by hits Will's right side and knocks him down.

—You okay? Keith yells.

Will nods and Keith helps pull him to his feet.

—Where's Sam? Keith asks.

Will points to the front of the van where she's trying the door.

—How the hell she get up there so fast?

—Christine knows not to fuck with her, Will says with a smile.

Sam stops yanking on the driver's door and, holding onto the van's hood, makes her way around to the other side and tries the passenger's. Both are locked.

Keith tries the handle on the back doors, but they are also locked.

Breaking the glass of the back left door with the butt of his .45 automatic, he taps away the shards, reaches in, unlocks it, and opens it to reveal the crumpled-up dead body.

—I can feel her, Taylor yells. We're close. I swear. It's just a little further.

The boat is being tossed to and fro, the bow actually pointing in the wrong direction much of the time.

The wind and rain so loud, they can barely hear each other, even yelling as loud as they can.

The rain continues to pock their faces and hands, and even, through their clothes, their arms and legs and backs and chests.

Along the banks, all the trees are leaning north, their tops shaking like the weaves of black Pentecostal women under the influence of the Holy Ghost.

Julian continues to run the motor at full throttle, but it's no match for Christine.

—Marc, I swear, she says. I wouldn't say if I weren't sure. We're almost there. We've got to continue.

—We've come as far as we can, Julian says.

Marc nods, wondering if they've not come too far already. The thought makes him shudder, and he feels as if death has somehow just joined them in the small boat.

—It's just around the next bend. A hidden camp set back in the woods.

Does she really know that? he wonders. Or is she just trying to get us to keep going?

—Which side?

—What?

—Which side? he yells even louder.

—There, she says, pointing to the left side.

—Let's pull the boat over to the bank and go the rest of the way on foot.

—What?

Before he can repeat himself, a downed tree hits the right side of the hull, spins the boat around, and flips it over. Rain and wind and water, and then nothing.

Shelter.

Shelby breaks out a back window and climbs in, cutting

herself but not caring. Never so happy to see walls and a roof before in her entire life.

Collapsing.

She falls prostrate on a musty old rug and doesn't move.

—I'm so proud of you, Remington says. You made it. You're almost—

In shock.

Drained.

Spent.

Exhausted.

But, for the moment at least, protected from the hard rain and savage wind.

Dark water.

Zero visibility.

Capsized craft. Driving down, down, down.

Taylor surfaces, gasping, coughing, takes a big breath, then swims for shore beneath the beating rain.

Glancing back. Julian and Marc heading in too.

Slipping.

Pulling.

Climbing.

Falling.

Clawing.

The clay of the bank is as slick as ice, and it takes a while, and the help of exposed pine and cypress roots, to make it up to the soft, soggy ground.

For a few moments, she can't do anything but lie there in

the soaked soil and let the wind and water assail her, but soon she is sensing Shelby again, and pushes herself up and begins to run in the direction of the source.

Unable to move fast, she's sure Marc and Julian will catch up to her soon, but whether they do or not, she can't stop moving toward her sweet girl.

Nothing Daniel has seen so far has prepared him for what he finds in the next room.

He's grateful it's shrouded in darkness, that he only sees it in snapshot-like flashes as the narrow beam flits around the room.

Twin beds pushed together—one a hospital bed surrounded by medical equipment.

On one side—the regular twin side: Desk. Piles of paper. Stacks of folders. Heaps of books. Computer.

On the other: Mounted, boxy old TV. More medical equipment. Posters and reprints of Taylor Sean's art. Shock. Reeling.

How?

Framed photographs—some fifty or more—standing on a long shelf, a table, the windowsill, hanging on the wall.

A life in pictures.

Half a life at least.

Aging images.

D. Kelly David. Arc—middle-aged to old man.

Young girl. Years. Growing family resemblance. Weak. Infirmed.

Later. Another young girl. Frankenstein family. Smiling man. Unhappy young woman. Unhappier young girl.

He kept her alive.

The resemblance to Taylor is stunning—especially as she grew. The child bride growing into young woman and mother of a stolen child is a pale, sickly shadow of Taylor.

Trevor Young is alive—or was. Savannah Summers is alive—or was. Prisoners of the demented doctor.

At a loss. Mystified. Confounded. Stunned.

David had somehow saved Trevor after separating her from Taylor and had kept her in a sort of half-alive state, and then at some point had kidnapped Savannah to create his own little sick, twisted version of a family.

Running out of the room, he rushes to the third closed door, finding it locked. Padlocked on the outside. Prison.

Three kicks and he has the door open. Little girl's room. Savannah's prison cell.

Shaking his head, growing even more disturbed and nauseated, he makes his way back into David and Trevor's room and begins to go through the documents on the desk and near the bed.

D. Kelly David is far more monstrous than he could've ever imagined.

Because Taylor and Trevor shared many of their abdominal organs, Trevor has suffered with liver and bowel problems her entire pain-filled life. Unable to absorb food properly. Bowel obstructions. Liver failure. She's undergone numerous surgeries, suffered through one life-threatening infection after another. It's unfathomable what David has subjected her to over the years just to keep her something resembling alive.

Though he doesn't overtly say so, it's clear from his notes and journal entries he kidnapped Savannah in an attempt to make Trevor happy and create a family for her.

At some point in the not too distant past, Savannah died in what David refers to as an accident—something he's suspiciously vague about.

Was she trying to escape? Is that it? Did you kill her because she stopped submitting?

Daniel stops reading. Checks behind him again. Rubs his eyes and tries to process what he's just uncovered.

If David is Tiberinus and Trevor is Lupa, who is Romulus? And where is he? Somewhere in this dark asylum? Coiled? Readying to strike?

When Taylor opens the cabin door and sees her sister lying on the hospital bed in the center of the room, she is surprised and, somehow, surprisingly, not.

Eyes wide.

Catch of breath.

Speechless.

No wonder I never stopped sensing her. She never died. All this time . . . and . . . my twin . . . my sister . . . my other half.

I thought I was sensing Shelby. And I was, but somehow—guess when I got so close to her—I started picking up on Trevor instead.

She eases over to the bed and looks down at her dying doppelganger. Though the face is stress-lined and pain-aged, it's her face.

Lifting the covers, she pulls back the bunched and gathered gown to see a scar that matches her own—plus many others, that unlike Taylor's artistic scarification, represent unimaginable invasion and intrusion.

Slowly, blinkingly, Trevor opens her eyes and squints up

284

at Taylor.

Her small, sad mouth forms an O accompanied by an ooohhh and drifts into an aaahhh.

—Trevor?

She nods and smiles.

—Is it really you? How . . . What . . . I don't . . .

Her body is largely childlike. Diminutive. Underdeveloped. Though her face is identical save for the effects of suffering, there's what appears to be a simplicity and innocence in her eyes.

—I'm Taylor. Your sister.

Another nod.

—What are you doing here? Where is Shelby?

—He's got her. You've got to find her. Fast.

—Guess we can eliminate the doc, Will yells.

—Fuck! Sam yells.

—The fuck is goin' on? Keith says.

The three of them are standing in the storm looking at the dead body of D. Kelly David inside the rusting old van. The old doctor's body is a bloody mess, the result of a particularly violent assault with a sharp and serrated blade.

—Think Shelby could've . . .

—Look at the violence and brutality, Sam says. No way she could stab with that kind of force and repetition.

—Then who? Will says. Grayson? Julian? Marc? He killed Shelby? One of them killed him?

—Let's talk about this in the truck, Keith says. No need to be out here. We've seen enough.

—Goddamn it, Sam yells.

—What is it?

—Daniel, she says. He went to interview him.

—Who?

—David, she says, nodding toward the dead doctor. What if he runs into whoever killed him? No way to call him. We've got to go.

—Okay, Keith says. Load up.

—Y'all go ahead, Will says. I'm gonna stay here.

—What for?

—You don't want to know.

—No, Keith says, but tell me anyway.

—Everything comes back to here, to the landing, to the river.

—Yeah?

—She's out there. I'm going after her.

—In this?

—Told you. I'm gonna take the search and rescue boat. It's built for—

—It ain't built for this, Keith says. Nothing is.

—It'll be fine.

—I'm going with you, Keith says. Sam, you take my truck.

Daniel finds Carter in the candlelit kitchen where he left him.

—Sorry I was gone so long.

—Not a problem, no, sir. Just havin' a little candlelight

dinner. Yes, sir, I am.

He notices the file folder in Daniel's hand.

—Whatta you got there?

—Is Romulus Ethan?

—How's that?

—Is Romulus's real name Ethan?

—Don't call him that. Just Romulus. Better yet, be gone and don't call him anything at all.

According to the file, Ethan Kerr is a conjoined twin who supposedly died to save his brother, but like Trevor, David kept him secretly alive. Perhaps brain damaged from lack of oxygen or just early childhood trauma, Ethan has continually displayed anti-social behaviors—something all David's experimenting on him hasn't helped.

Like Trevor, he's undergone numerous surgeries, but unlike her, he's shown a nearly superhuman resiliency.

Over the years, Ethan has nursed a growing grudge against David and an identification with Trevor as a wronged and wounded mother figure—an Oedipal complex with his surrogate family, which, Daniel suspects, included a kind of sibling rivalry with Savannah that ultimately led to her death.

Demented. Deadly. Delusional. And he's now the leading candidate to have abducted Shelby.

As Shelby lies unconscious on its floor, the houseboat she's in becomes unmoored in the rising river, blows loose from the bank, and begins to be pushed downstream.

—Who's got her? Taylor asks.

—Ethan, Trevor says. He's gone crazy. Calls himself Romulus. Very dangerous. He just snapped. He's been through so much. Always been troubled, but I thought he was . . . I thought I had saved him, been a good mother to him, but . . .

—Where is he?

—He plans to bring her here. You should go get help.

—They're on the way. Are there any weapons here?

—You can't shoot him. Please.

—I won't, she says. Unless I have to—to save Shelby.

—Kelly has a gun cabinet in the bedroom.

—Kelly? she asks, rushing over to the bedroom. This is his cabin? How are you alive? Why didn't he ever tell anyone?

She does.

Her voice is soft and weak, and especially difficult to hear with the wind and rain slamming the small cypress cabin.

Taylor notices that in addition to Trevor's obvious physical infirmities, she suffers certain mental or emotional ones as well, but she can't tell if it's just that she's juvenile and underdeveloped or if it's something more systemic.

—You've been his prisoner all these years? Taylor says.

She's holding a loaded 12-gauge shotgun now, its barrel pointed at the floor.

—No, he's taken care of me. I wouldn't be alive if it weren't for him. Our parents wanted me dead.

—No. They wanted us—

—Yes, they did. He's been so good to me. I owe him . . . well, everything.

Taylor realizes David has told Trevor a certain version of the events over the years—one in which he is no doubt heroic and godlike.

288

—He took my Savannah, she says.

—For me, yes, Trevor says. I'm so sorry. I wouldn't've had him do it. I swear, but I was the best mama I could be to her. You've got to believe me. I tried to get him to give her back. I did. If I could have even contacted you, I would have.

Taylor's not sure she believes her—this person who was once the half that made her whole.

—Why?

—Huh?

—Why'd he take her?

—For me. For us. So I could have what everybody else had. He was so good to me.

—Why wait until she was eight?

—I think because of how sick I was. All the operations. To see if I was gonna live.

—Where is he now?

—Ethan has him. Kelly started to suspect that he killed her.

—This Ethan killed my Savannah?

—He said she drowned in the river, but Kelly didn't think so.

—This wasn't that long ago, was it? Taylor says.

—No.

—I knew she was alive. Sensed it. Felt it when she died.

—Ethan told Kelly he planned to go get Shelby for me—he's so devoted, so . . . he says I saved him. I guess he thought he'd replace Savannah. Kelly tried to stop him. Ethan took him hostage. Brought me here. Went to get Shelby. Gonna bring her here.

—What is this place?

—Our little getaway. Kelly built it for us. We really couldn't go anywhere else. If anyone ever saw me, they'd try to take me away from—

She winces and tries to shift her frail little body in the bed.

—You okay?

—Rom—Ethan didn't bring any of my medications or anything.

The door slings open, wind and rain rushing in, and Taylor comes up with the shotgun.

—Don't shoot, Julian yells above the wind, lifting his hands.

Taylor lowers the gun as Julian steps in and pushes the door closed. Once he has the door secured, he turns to say something to Taylor, but Trevor catches his attention and he looks back and forth between them.

He's soaked through, his dark hair plastered to his head.

—Where's Marc? Taylor says. I need you two to go get help. Ethan, the man that has Shelby, is bringing her here.

—I've been yelling for you, he says. Why'd you leave?

—What? Y'all knew where I was going. Figured you'd catch up to me before I got here. Why? What is it?

—I've been trying to save him. Don't really know CPR, but I did the best I could.

—*What?*

—He wasn't breathing. He hit his head on something. The boat or motor. The tree.

—No. I saw you two swimming to shore.

—I was pulling him.

—What are you saying? *No.*

290

Separation Anxiety

Something at Taylor's center completely caves in, just falls way into absolute nothingness. Implosion. Desolation. Despair.

Julian begins to cry.

—It's raining so hard. The wind . . . I did the best I could. He . . . Why'd you leave? I've been yelling and yelling.

Ethan Kerr was born. Then he died. Sacrificed for his conjoined twin, separated for his brother.

Dead, but not buried.

Reborn.

Romulus.

Carried by the river to his she-wolf mother.

Born of Lupa.

Transformation.

Reborn again. Re-reborn.

Wolf milk from wolf mother.

A wolf is born.

Now *the* wolf.

And the Wolf won't stop coming. He has no range. He has no limit. He has nothing now, *there is* nothing now but the hunt.

Storm surge.

Flashfloods.

Tides. Mean water levels. Slope of continental shelf.

Push of storm winds.

Inundated.

Mangled marinas.

Destroyed docks.

Landscapes leveled.

Waterfront homes floating away.

Christine's fury forces some fifteen feet of Gulf water to join the already high tide, drowning the area with a wall-like wave of warm, salty sea. At just ten feet above sea level, Tupelo is susceptible to flooding, and soon all low-lying areas are under water.

—Time to get up sweet girl, Remington says.

—Huh? Shelby says. Time for school?

He smiles.

Such warmth, she thinks. Such . . . she's so glad he's here with her. How would she have gotten this far if he hadn't been?

—School of a kind, I guess, he says.

—What does that—

—Shelby, he says, louder this time. Wake up. Now. Right now. You've got to get up and get off the—

She wakes on the floor of the houseboat and looks around.

He was just here. Where'd he—

She can feel the boat moving, rocking back and forth as it rides the rough river toward the bay.

How long before it crashes into something? Or blows apart?

Like so many makeshift houseboats along the river, there's not much to this one. A wooden utility shed atop a base of two-by-fours enclosing blocks of Styrofoam, the unit was not built to be on the river, let alone in a Cat 3 hurricane.

She jumps up, disbelieving how loud the wind is.

Whirring. Whistling. Whipping.

The small floating structure is racing downriver far faster than she would've imagined possible, rocking and spinning as it does.

She tries to open the door leading to the little porch, but is unable to, the wind pushing against it just too strong, but then the boat turns, the wind shifts, and she is able to force it open.

Hard slanting rain hits her like buckshot fired at close range, and she holds up her hands defensively in front of her face.

Should I jump in and risk getting hit by debris and drowning, or ride the river until the house blows down?

A sheet of plywood pulls loose from the roof of the porch, lifts away and disappears into the storm.

Then another.

And another.

She pulls the door closed and steps back.

Think.

I'm gonna die. Where the hell is Remington? Where'd he go? I need—

Breathe. Relax. Make a good decision.

The back of the houseboat catches a counter current and spins around, crashing into a stand of cypress trees in the water near the bank.

Boards cracking, splintering, snapping, Styrofoam blocks breaking free and floating away.

Careening off the swollen buttresses, the boat is slung back into the center of the river, gaining speed again.

Back end lower than the front now. Taking on water. Trailing lumber, trash, bits of debris behind it in the riotous river.

More boards blowing off.

Wind and rain so loud. Can't think. Driving me crazy.

Fuck! What do I do?

But before she can decide, the decision is made for her.

As the entire right side of the small structure is ripped off and what remains of it crumbles into the water, a falling beam catches her on the back of the head, knocking her unconscious as she collapses with the craft into the dark, angry waters.

Wide.

Heavy.

Powerful.

The search and rescue boat rockets down the river, its wake lost in the broiling, storm-churned waters. Keith and Will in rain gear racing through the blizzard bead-curtain of rain would have long since been yanked out and blown away were it not for being strapped in.

Will is driving, Keith standing next to him shining the searchlight along the banks and in the water.

—The hell is that? Keith yells.

Will looks over in the same direction and sees a blue bateau caught in a thick pine root system at a forty-five-degree angle, rocking up and down in the storm surge. He slows the boat, the bow dropping, and swings over to take a closer look.

Keith unstraps himself and comes around to the other side of the boat. Inside the blue river craft, the body of an old man, his legs wedged under one of the benches, half his face missing, dangles with the drift.

—Gunshot wound, Will yells.

—Sure as hell is.

—Think it means we're gettin' close?

—Depends on how far the storm knocked the boat around before setting it up in those roots.

—Keep going? Will asks.

—Yeah.

—Hold on.

Will guns the boat back into the center of the river, heading downstream, as Keith grabs the spotlight with one hand and the support bar with the other.

Visibility is so limited, it's as if they're flying a private plane at night without instruments, the searchlight mostly illuminating driving rain, the windswept surface of the river, and storm-bent trees.

They haven't gone far when the first rounds begin to ring out.

Whizzing by.

Thwack.

Thump.

Twing.

The first few rounds hit the boat, but then one catches Will as another takes out the light.

Collapsing, Will jerks the steering wheel, spinning the boat so hard around it nearly capsizes, and slinging Keith out into the river.

Water.

Darkness.

Boots filling. Hard to swim.

When Keith resurfaces, he takes in a deep breath, rain falling into his open mouth. As rounds begin to pierce the water around him, he submerges again and swims for the opposite bank as fast and hard as he can.

When Shelby opens her eyes, she tries to scream, but can't.

Mouth taped, wrists and ankles bound, she's lying on her back on the soggy ground, her upper body shielded from the storm some by the open hollow of a cypress tree.

Above her, firing a rifle at targets she can't see, her abductor looms in black paramilitary attire, seemingly unaware of the rain and wind and weather.

Even above the din, she can hear a boat bang into the bank not far from them, the motor continuing to run at what sounds like full throttle.

Her abductor looks down and points his gun at her.

—Be right back, he says, his voice flat and low, barely audible in the storm. Best be here.

He walks away, and she wiggles back and forth and sits up.

The man walks over to the boat, climbs on board, his rifle ready, and kills the motor.

As she begins to test her restraints, someone grabs her from behind and she screams into the tape covering her mouth.

—It's me.

Julian. She knows it instantly. Before she turns. Before she sees him. She knows. Warm relief washes over her and she's happier than she ever thought she'd be again.

Separation Anxiety

—Come on, he says, helping her up. Let's get out of here before he gets back.

Shock.

Collapsed.

Bleeding.

Immobile.

Hanging.

Will's strap holds him just above the floor of the boat. When it crashes into the trees and roots and mud of the bank, he slams into the gunwale, but doesn't break loose of the binding.

He tries to get up.

Can't.

Chest hurts like hell.

Blood seeping steadily.

Tries to cut the engines.

Can't reach the switch.

When the man steps onto the boat, he knows he going to die.

Goddamn it! Not like this.

He steps over cautiously, then sees Will is no threat.

Kills the motor.

Younger than he thought. A kid really.

Taken out by a fuckin' kid.

At least this'll be my last fuckup for today.

—You smiling? the man asks.

297

Will doesn't respond.

—I amuse you?

Don't respond, he tells himself. Don't give him the satisfaction.

—Go ahead and say it, the man says.

Will wonders what the fuck he's talking about, but doesn't ask.

—Go ahead and tell me I don't have to do this—in your case I'd agree. Just be a waste of a bullet. Your life is leaking out of you as we speak. I extend this conversation a bit and I can save the bullet for someone else.

Don't engage. Nothing you can do is gonna change anything.

—Ask me nicely, and I'll leave you to your fate, the man says.

Will doesn't say anything.

—You're probably right. Gonna die either way, but why not have a little more time? Why not ask me nicely for that?

Don't do it, Will says. Don't you do it.

—I don't understand, but okay. Have it your way.

He raises the rifle and sights down the barrel.

—Okay, Will says. Please. Please don't shoot me. Let me have a few more minutes. I'm begging.

He lowers the gun.

—I didn't think you were going to, he says. Thought you might prove me wrong, but no. Everyone's the same. Even the real religious. You religious? You'd think they'd be anxious to get to heaven, but everyone's the same.

He then raises the gun again.

—You sadistic son of a bitch, Will says.

Separation Anxiety

The man shoots him in the forehead, splattering brain and blood all over the bottom of the boat.

From across the river, Keith is powerless to prevent Will's execution.

He yells.

Fires his gun.

Screams.

Threatens.

Begs.

Drowned out by the bitch, Christine, he's not sure if the man heard anything but the shots, but he didn't even respond to them.

Powerless.

Helpless.

Impotent.

The chief law enforcement officer for River County can't keep his classmate and friend and investigator from being shot at pointblank range just a little over a football field away.

—You don't leave the swamp alive, he yells. You hear me? I'm gonna bury you out here. Today. Right now. I'm coming for you.

Not alone.

Shelby stumbles through the swamp, pulled along by Julian.

—He just killed someone else, she says.

—Who else has he killed?

She tells him about the old man in the boat.

—Well, he's not gonna get us. Come on.

They begin to walk faster.

—Who is he?

She shrugs.

—I was gonna ask you.

—Where're we gonna go?

—Cabin not too far from here, he says. Your mom's there. She's got a gun.

—What? she says, mystified. Mom's where? With a what?

He explains.

She starts to cry again, her tears indistinguishable from the raindrops running down her cheeks.

—I thought I'd never see you again, she says.

Keith, exhausted, leaden with wet shoes and garments, swims out into the river, having to stop often and tread to lift his head above the wakes and waves.

Tempted to take his boots off, he knows he'll be glad he didn't once he reaches the other side. If he reaches the other side.

River's hard enough to swim in good conditions. Add fatigue, boots, and a fuckin' hurricane and . . .

Doesn't matter. I'm gettin' across and then it's lights out motherfucker.

He swims and swims and swims. Makes little headway.

No matter how hard he tries to go directly across, he's

being carried rapidly downstream.

Goin' more aside than across.

Fighting.

Flailing.

Kicking.

Clawing.

Weary.

Weak.

Spent.

No sleep.

Stress.

Doesn't matter. Nothing does—'cept gettin' across and squaring things for Will.

Jesus, Will! How the hell'd I let this happen?

Nearing the cypress house.

—Almost there, Julian says. Just a little further. Get you dry. Get a gun and blow that bastard's head off.

—You couldn't really shoot him, could you?

—To save you? he asks. In a heartbeat.

Wondering if he really can, he leads her through the pitiless storm, hunched over her protectively, sheltering her with his raincoat, toward the sound of the generator and the small, dimly lit cabin.

—There's something I've got to tell you, he says.

—Yeah?

—I just don't want it to be a big shock to you.

—What is it?

—Your mom's sister. She's alive.

—What?

—She's in the cabin.

—She can't be. Are you sure?

—Yeah.

—How?

—I don't know.

—It's just not possible. Is Savannah?

—I only saw your aunt. And baby . . . she doesn't look very . . . She's . . . You can tell she's sick, that she's been sick a long time.

—Okay. Thanks for telling me.

They reach the cabin and step up onto the porch, even the partial covering making a huge difference.

Shelby pauses at the door and takes a deep breath.

—Sorry you don't have longer to prepare, he says, but we've got to get inside.

She nods.

—Ms. Sean? he yells through the door. It's Julian. I have Shelby. We're coming in. Don't shoot.

He eases open the door with a creak loud enough to be heard over the gale, and as they're stepping through, he's knocked down as the man who abducted Shelby grabs her with one hand and holds a pistol to her head with the other.

Taylor's relief at seeing Shelby is so momentary, so evanescent, it's as if she really didn't experience it.

As Ethan shoves Shelby forward and kicks the door closed, quieting the room somewhat from the storm, she raises the shotgun and points it at him.

Julian pushes himself up, then for a moment no one

moves or says anything, and there is only the furious force of the wind, the pummeling of the downpour.

I can't take any more, she thinks. It's all too much. Discovering Trevor's alive, losing Marc—oh God, no, please, Marc can't be dead—finding Shelby only to have him take her right back again. It's just too much.

—Ethan, no, Trevor eventually says.

Her voice is feeble, tentative, more pleading than demanding.

The poor thing, Taylor thinks. The horrors she's been through. No telling what kind of twisted, conflicted relationship she has with this sociopath.

—I told you what to call me, Mama.

He's just a boy, Taylor thinks. Not much older than Shelby.

Outside, the storm eviscerates the swamp, sheering off the tops of trees, upturning ancient timbers, beating down undergrowth, drowning wildlife, banging on the cypress house.

—Romulus, Trevor says, put the gun down, baby. Don't do this.

—I got her for you. So we could be a family again.

—Not like this, sweetie. You've got to stop.

—Listen to her, Taylor says.

—No, ma'am. You listen to me—unless you want to see what's on your daughter's mind, put that shotgun on the floor.

Taylor doesn't move.

At first, he seems too surprised by her noncompliance to respond, then his eyes widen and his expression turns incredulous.

—You don't think I'm serious? he asks.

The generator stalls and sputters and the lights dim and

brighten, fade and flicker, then go back to full strength.

—You didn't kidnap my daughter just to kill her.

—You people. You're all alike. Why can't you just leave us alone? Do you have any idea what we've been through? What's been done to us? What? We don't count? We can't be happy like everyone else?

—We can, Trevor says. But not like this. Where's Kelly? He'll tell you.

—He's part of the problem. The biggest part.

—He saved us.

—He enslaved us, he says.

—We wouldn't be alive if it weren't for him. Where is he?

Shingles and cypress boards begin to fly off the cabin, the roof and walls shaking, pictures falling off hooks, glass shattering on the floor.

Marc's dead, she thinks. No. He can't be. But he is. The sweet, gentle man is gone. So many dangerous things in the swamp today and he hits his head and drowns. You can't even think about that right now. Must save Shelby. Make his death mean more. Save her.

Ethan pauses to consider the structure, then turns his attention back to Taylor.

—Last chance. Drop the gun. 'Course we'll probably all be dead soon anyway.

He won't do it, will he? Of course he will. He's a . . . You can't predict what he'll do.

Julian shifts his weight.

Ethan looks at him like he'd forgotten he was there. Then shoots him.

Shelby screams.

The sound is deafening, the acrid odor of gunpowder filling the room.

Shock.

Stillness.

Silence.

For a moment, time seems to unspool like a film reel in an unmanned projection booth. No one moves, no one speaks. There is only the storm.

—Okay. Okay.

If you put down the gun he's gonna kill you and make Shelby his slave. Eventually, he'll kill her just like he did Savannah.

More boards blow off.

—NO, Trevor yells. Ethan, no. Don't do this.

—Don't call me that. Don't call me Rom either. I'm the wolf now. Call me the wolf.

—Where's Kelly? Let's talk to him.

—All he's done to you and you want him?

—I need him.

—All I've done for you and you want him?

—Where is he?

—Gone. Won't hurt us anymore.

—No. No. No.

Trevor begins to cry.

The lights dim again, making the creepy old cabin in the woods seem even more like what it is. A haunted place of confinement, an isolated death house.

—Tell me you didn't kill him you . . . sick . . . animal.

—What? the wolf says, anger drawing in his face. What'd

305

you say? What'd you call me?

—Why? Why'd you—

—All I've done for you. The way I worship you, Lupa. And you turn on me? Over him? Over that sick—

—Don't you dare talk about him like that. He was the greatest man to ever live—the only reason you're even alive, and you killed him.

—You better watch how you talk to me.

—Why? 'Cause you'll kill me too? Go ahead. I don't want to live without Kelly.

Pulling the pistol away from Shelby's head slightly, he begins moving toward Trevor.

More shingles peeling off.

More boards ripping away.

So loud. So hard to hear.

The force, the sheer power of the thing outside trying to get in . . . is . . . inevitable. The other wolf, the one outside, will blow the house down.

—I mean it, he says. Stop.

—You thought, what, you were gonna take his place? That'd it be you and me and my niece? You silly, stupid boy.

Is she doing what I think she is? Taylor wonders. Get ready. Just be ready.

His grip on Shelby loosens, and as he steps over to the bed, Shelby shrugs herself away from him, jumps on the floor, and scrambles toward Julian.

Taylor has a perfect shot now. Close. Can't miss. Brace for the kick. Squeeze the trigger.

She does.

And nothing.

Separation Anxiety

What's wrong? Why isn't it firing?

He turns toward her, a wolfish grin on his face, swings the gun over in her direction.

As he squeezes the trigger, his hand explodes, the pistol clattering to the floor. Then his chest blooms with blood and he crumples as Keith walks in from the back of the house, gun still trained on the mortally wounded wolf.

Crawling around Trevor's hospital bed, Taylor rushes over to hold Shelby, her ears ringing, eyes watering.

Evening.

Sunset.

Storm passed.

Peaceful.

Raindrops still falling from trees and leaves in the woods. Tick. Tick. Tick.

The air is clean and fresh as if untouched, unspoiled, undiscovered.

Blue sky above. Bright pink glow igniting the western horizon.

Sam and Daniel in a borrowed boat taking Taylor, Trevor, Shelby, Julian, and Keith back to the landing, back to what their lives will now be, as FDLE techs process the various crime scenes.

Sam is driving, Daniel standing beside her, the others, in shock, sit silently around Trevor's stretcher in the back of the boat.

Boat of bodies.

Marc and Will, their upper bodies covered with blood-stained white sheets, wet from river spray, rainwater, and their

307

own blood, lie in the bottom of the boat like fallen soldiers being carried home by their unit. Taylor sits on the floor beside Marc, her hand on his hard, unmoving chest, Shelby not far away, her small hand on her mother's back. Across from them, Keith crouches near Will, the wind blowing the occasional teardrop out of his resigned eyes onto the sun-squint skin at the crinkled outer corners of his white-creased crow's feet.

—You sorry you missed all the action? Daniel whispers to Sam.

She smiles.

—Thank you for coming to make sure I was okay, he adds.

—I'd do it again and again, she says. And again and again.

Night.

Late.

Lithonia Lodge.

Candlelight.

No power. No water. But safe.

Julian and Shelby in her bed, on their sides in the middle of the bed, inches apart, a cast on his leg from where Ethan's round broke the bone.

—I'm so sorry, Julian says.

—You kidding? For what?

—The things I thought. Way I acted.

—Whatta you—

—I thought you'd bailed.

—I never would.

—I know. That's what I'm saying. I lost faith. Put you in more danger 'cause I's so fuckin' pissed. I'm retarded.

She smiles.

—You are kind of, she says.

He laughs.

—Forgive me?

—Before you asked.

—Can you love a retard?

—More than anything, she says, and closes the distance between them.

Down the hall.

Alone.

So very alone.

In bed.

Tears.

Can't sleep.

Should get up and go to the hospital. She could not sleep just as easily in Trevor's room.

When Taylor rolls over, Marc is lying there.

She starts smiling and crying. Instantly. Simultaneously.

Both on their sides. Middle of the bed. Intimate. Whispering. Inches and worlds apart.

—I miss you so much, she says.

—I'm right here.

—I'm so sorry. I should've never . . .

—What?

—Let you love me.

He smiles that warm, sweet, strong smile of his.

—You didn't have a choice in the matter.

She laughs, and it causes her to cry harder.

—I'm so sorry I didn't stay and save you.

—It wouldn't've made a difference.

—I didn't know you were hurt.

—I know.

They are quiet a long moment, breathing one another's breaths, looking into one another's truths.

—Say it for me, he says, as he has so many times before. Say I am so loved. Say it out loud.

—I . . . I can't.

—Yes you can.

—But you're gone.

—I'm right here. Always.

—No one's ever loved me like you did.

He nods.

—Like I do. And they never will, he says.

—No one can even tolerate me.

—Say it, he says. Say, I am so loved.

—I . . . am . . . so . . . loved, she says, sobbing now.

He looks at her even more intensely.

—You made me believe that, she says. You're the only person who ever— Do you wish we'd've never met?

—Of course not.

—I was awful to you and got you killed.

—There is that, he says with a smile.

Separation Anxiety

—See?

—You did neither, he says. And I have no regrets.

—Really? Truly?

—It's funny . . . I always thought dying in the middle of writing a novel would just be the worst kind of . . . I don't know, unfinished life. That I'd have such a sense of incompleteness, but I don't. It was so important before and now . . .

Alone in her room—her real room—Shelby studies the framed photographs from *Last Night in the Woods* by Remington James, the book open on the desk in front of her.

Touching the wood and glass of the frame as she gazes at the pictures they hold, she traces the images, makes a tactile connection to them, to Remington.

Incandescent.

Luminous.

Radiant rain.

Arcing sparks.

Falling drops of fire.

Field of fireflies.

—I only made it because of you, she says, her words soft, barely audible in the silent space. I know that as surely as I know you were really there with me.

She continues to touch both the book and the pictures as she speaks.

—I know you were there then because of how not here you are now.

She pauses a moment, hoping to hear his voice.

—Please say something, she says.

He has. Remember.

She reaches over and removes from the wall the only image in the series not taken by Remington or one of his traps.

Reverently pulling it to her as if a relic of her new religion instead of just a snapshot taken by Remington's grieving but grateful mother.

—You saved her too, she says.

Just before being rescued by a passing fisherman, Remington's mom had grabbed his camera and snapped a picture of his final communication.

The image is that of a cypress tree trunk on the bank of the Apalachicola River, the letters MM carved into its bark.

A monument.

A memorial.

A remembrance.

Memento Mori.

Remember you're mortal. Remember you're going to die.

For Shelby, a grateful girl with a new lease on life and a new life growing inside her, a reminder to live—truly live—every moment of the rest of her life. Something she intends to do, a remembrance and memorial of her own she will make with every single breath.

CPSIA information can be obtained at www.ICGtesting.com
Printed in the USA
LVOW12*1710161113

361591LV00018B/157/P